THE LADIES OF CREMORNE

I was ambling towards the hockey fields when I heard a familiar female voice sigh, 'Oh don't do that here, Terry! Can't you wait until tonight?'

I poked my head around the corner and saw none other than our English teacher, Miss Rosamund Dunaway, standing against the wall in the passionate embrace of a handsome young man.

Rosamund Dunaway was by far the youngest and prettiest teacher at Dame Chasuble's. She was quite a stunner with long, liquorice-black hair and a perfect hour-glass figure that was the envy of the school. Obviously she and the young man were well acquainted for she made no protest when he broke off their embrace to unbutton his trousers . . .

The Ladies of Cremorne

Anonymous

Introduced and Edited by Merida Hawksworth

HEADLINE
DELTA

First published in 1996
by HEADLINE BOOK PUBLISHING

A HEADLINE DELTA paperback

10 9 8 7 6 5 4 3 2 1

ISBN 0 7472 5128 2

Typeset at The Spartan Press Ltd,
Lymington, Hants

Printed and bound in Great Britain by
Cox & Wyman Ltd, Reading, Berks

HEADLINE BOOK PUBLISHING
A division of Hodder Headline PLC
338 Euston Road
London NW1 3BH

This is for Teddy Godfrey of Hendon
and Minnie Harper of Oxford

Introduction

This fifth selection from *The Cremorne Chronicles* un-
doubtedly contains one of the raunchiest stories that ever
appeared in an underground 'horn book' of the Edwardian
era. An explicit and unexpurgated memoir of a feisty young
teenage girl, the manuscript is open and unashamed in its
vivid descriptions of many varieties of sexual delights. Like
other books in this series, it reveals a rich and bawdy seam
of sensuality that lurked behind the facade of iron-clad
respectability which characterised the rigid social structure
of our great-grandparents.

But unlike its predecessors – *Cremorne Gardens*, *The
Temptations of Cremorne*, *The Ecstacies of Cremorne* and
Cremorne Scandals – the saucy script of *The Ladies of
Cremorne* was not written by Max Dalmaine. The urbane
Anglo-French writer was the editor of the Cremornite
Club's scurrilously rude magazine, in whose pages the
Cremorne novels were first serialised. However, the link
with Dalmaine survives, for the book was written by his
mistress, the beautiful Sophie Starr whose favours he shared
with the Prince of Wales (soon to become King Edward
VII), Lord Roger Tagholm, Jeffrey Martin QC, and several
other distinguished gentlemen of the Cremornite fraternity.

The Cremorne Club was named after a notorious pleasure
gardens in Chelsea which was closed down in the 1870s.
Ostensibly, the club (which was formed in 1894) was set up
as a dining society by a group of young men-about-town.

However, the truth of the matter was that the raffish clientèle paid an annual membership fee of one hundred guineas (approximately equivalent to five thousand pounds a year today) for far more than just the splendid weekly luncheons at the Club's premises in Bayswater. A series of wild parties were the main attraction of this men-only club. They were held at the luxuriously appointed residences of such well-known London luminaries as the sophisticated Portuguese diplomat, the Marquis de Soveral; Colonel Alan Brooke of the Household Cavalry; the immensely wealthy merchant-banker and philanthropist, Sir Richard Segal; and the Oxfordshire landowner, Lord Montague Skinner.

Surprisingly, Sophie Starr does not attempt to hide either her own identity or that of her friends, perhaps because with so many important members the Cremornites believed themselves to be above the law. This would not have been an idle boast, for they constituted a loosely organised exclusive group of powerful Establishment figures from which the general public was rigorously excluded. The circulation of the monthly magazine was so controlled that the use of real names became a kind of curious private joke, a daring if indulgent game for the cognoscenti.

Sophie Starr came from humble beginnings, being born on 21 June, 1885 to Adele (née Wellsend) and Peter Starr who lived above the family's general store in the small Hertfordshire town of St Albans. Due to the secret generosity of her maternal grandmother (for Adele had enraged her father, a prominent prosperous local farmer, by marrying beneath her and he carried out his threat to cut her out of his will), Sophie was able to take up the place she won at a local grammar school.

As will be seen from the first chapters of Sophie's unexpurgated autobiography, she inherited her radical views from her English teacher, Miss Rosamund Dunaway, who also introduced Sophie, as she delicately writes: 'to the delights of *l'arte de faire l'amour*'. Then, leaving school for London with her bi-sexual friend, Alexandra Henderson, both girls became swept up in a series of passionate affairs as they pledged themselves to the cause of women's suffrage.

Readers will be interested to know that in the summer of 1910 she married Mr Arnold Bentleigh, a pharmacist from Streatham. Two years later the happy couple decamped to New Zealand (which had already granted women the vote some fifteen years before!). She settled down quickly, working with her husband in their chemist's shop in Auckland and within five years the Bentleighs owned three retail pharmacies in the city. By the time they returned to England for a short visit in 1922, the Bentleighs had produced a son and two daughters. This was to be their only trip back to Britain although it is pleasant to record that Sophie – as far as we know – lived happily in New Zealand until her death at the grand age of ninety in September, 1975.

From her book, it is plain that Sophie loved to shock the staid social climate of the time with her saucy stories. Clearly, she was quite happy to share her many erotic adventures with her readers. Her own personal philosophy would appear to be that expressed by the famous actress of the Edwardian era, Mrs Patrick Campbell, who roundly declared that consenting adults had the right to do whatever they wanted 'so long as they don't do it in the street and frighten the horses.'

Certainly Sophie was far from ashamed of her memoirs. In 1909 she wrote to Alexandra to say: 'I am sure that my erotic adventures will please every lover of gallant literature and those of a liberal disposition will agree with me that there is no sin in giving way to natural desires and enjoying to the utmost all those delicious sensations for which a beneficent Creator has so amply fitted both sexes.'

It may well be that Sophie's racy tales of amorous affairs, intimate intrigue and wild orgies were further enhanced both for herself and the eager subscribers to *The Cremorne* (the monthly journal of the Cremorne Club) by the spice of illicit publication. Certainly, the sales of the magazine were lifted by the serialisation of Sophie's salacious exploits. In March 1910 the louche but highly enterprising financial director of the Cremorne Club, Sir Richard Segal, engaged a French printer to bind up these erotic essays into book form. Three thousand copies of *The Ladies of Cremorne* were produced by François Jacoupy & Cie and later that year were clandestinely smuggled back into Britain.

Of course, neither the book nor *The Cremorne* magazine were ever on open sale and original copies of both publications are now extremely rare. Indeed, the text of this and other *Cremorne* novels recently republished by Headline Books has only been made possible by the discovery in 1988 of a complete set of *The Cremornite* dating from February 1904 to November 1909 during the refurbishment of an old mill house in the West Oxfordshire village of Standlake.

Thanks to the more enlightened social environment of the 1990s, the general reader is now able to enjoy Sophie Starr's scandalous narrative which will delight and amuse as well as providing the student with an unconventional insight into the manners and *mores* of a long-vanished world.

As the noted historian Dr Louis Lombert comments in *His Mighty Engine* [*Baum and Newman, University of Maryland Press, 1969*], a seminal study of Victorian and Edwardian erotic fiction: 'Sophie Starr offers a voluptuous assortment of endless arousals through explicit, uninhibited prose for which *The Cremorne* was justly famous. Ignored for too long, these entertaining erotic stories lay bare the secret preoccupations which lay behind the public face of turn-of-the-century respectability! No lover of gallant literature will be disappointed by Sophie's sparkling prose.'

MERIDA HAWKSWORTH
Birmingham
September 1996

The truth is rarely pure and never simple.
Modern life would be very tedious if it were either
and modern literature a complete impossibility!

Oscar Wilde

Foreword

*[An extract from a letter written by Sophie Starr
to George Bernard Shaw on April 2nd, 1910]*

I simply must tell you how thrilled I have been by the kind reception given to my volume of autobiography. Only this very morning I received a letter from the noted theatrical producer, Harley Granville-Barker, which reads:

> *My dearest Sophie*
> *Whilst reading your book I found myself travelling on an enchanted voyage of voluptuous delights enhanced by your stimulating prose. The lusty narrative has given me a great appetite for a taste of those forbidden fruits so eloquently plucked in these graphic tales of licking and lapping, fucking and sucking.*

In addition, many congratulatory messages have also arrived in the post during the past few days from such luminaries as Lady Ethel Phybbs-Woodrow, Lord Roger Tagholm and Doctor Jonathan Elstree as well as from several well-known people whose names can be found in the smart weekly magazines.

Frankly, I was slightly surprised that no-one has complained about what some readers might feel is the scandalous exposure of their roles in the more lurid of my experiences. Indeed, far from being reluctant to see their names in print, friends such as Babs Fawcett and Phil Colnbrook were happy to refresh my memory of the *recherché* events which took place shortly after my seventeenth birthday and thanks must go to them as well as to my other close chums who were kind enough to help in the preparation of my book.

On the other hand, from certain other sources I have heard that some disquiet has been expressed whether it is seemly for a girl to write such an explicit account of her life. Certainly, my book has been deemed highly unsuitable for reading by the lower orders. How strange it is that throughout our history the upper classes have taken it upon themselves to decide what is and what is not proper for the *hoi-polloi*!

However, whilst I would have no objection to any adult reading about my intimate adventures, it is highly doubtful if any persons from outside the charmed circle of the upper echelons of London Society will ever be able to read the book. And even if copies were made available to the general public, I doubt if it would hasten the day of the workers' revolution, for as poor Oscar Wilde commented: '*In England education produces no effect whatsoever. If it did, it would prove a serious danger to the upper classes and probably lead to acts of violence in Grosvenor Square.*'

Chapter One

'Come on everybody, look lively,' urged Miss Beatrice Blundred, the newly appointed games mistress at Dame Chasuble's Academy for Daughters of Gentlefolk, in a brisk tone of voice. She was speaking to a grumpy group of scholarship girls as she tried to enthuse them into starting a four-mile walk on an exceptionally hot afternoon.

'Oh really, Sophie Starr, surely there's no need to look so miserable,' she added.

'Well, I can think of better ways of celebrating my seventeenth birthday than tramping through the woods on such a muggy summer's day,' I replied defensively.

But Miss Blundred would have none of it and retorted: 'And I can think of many worse, my girl. Anyway, your birthday isn't till tomorrow and it isn't as if I'm asking any of you to take part in a race. Just stroll along the path in your own time to Hatching Green and then return to the school via Rowley Lane. Now, off you go, girls, remember that a good beginning makes a good ending.'

'As the actress said to the bishop,' I murmured to Alexandra Henderson, my best friend and one of the prettiest girls in the senior school. She was a truly lovely creature with rosy cheeks and large brown eyes and when her full red lips parted in a smile, two delicious dimples formed in her cheeks as two rows of pearl-white teeth were revealed. Slightly taller than me, Alex was also blessed with firm round breasts which were topped by the most luscious nut-brown nipples one could wish to see.

Alex giggled her appreciation. I think Miss Blundred probably heard my impertinent remark but she said nothing except to shoo off her reluctant charges into Gustard Woods and then, turning on her heel, she strode back along the narrow path to the school.

'I notice that Miss Blundred isn't practising what she preaches,' I observed as we began our two-mile trek to Hatching Green. 'Still, at least she trusts us to take our walk by ourselves. She doesn't feel it necessary to keep a gimlet eye upon us all the time like Miss Smeeth used to do.'

'Well, we all know the reason why Miss Smeeth had to leave so suddenly,' sighed Alex who, like most of us, had few opportunities to enjoy social intercourse with any members of the opposite sex except for fathers, uncles or brothers and consequently had channelled her sensual needs into erotic play with other girls. 'Mind you, she deserved to be sacked. I mean, neither you nor I minded her getting into bed with us and tickling our pussies, but she was quite wrong to seduce someone like Clarissa Candleford who is only just sixteen and almost a virgin.'

'Come now, Alex, that's almost like saying Clarissa is only a little bit pregnant,' I protested, although in fact I well understood the reasoning behind Alex's remark. It was doubtful if any girl at Dame Chasuble's was entirely *virgo intacta*.

'Oh, all right, I take it back. Nevertheless, you can be assured that Clarissa won't have to worry on that score,' shrugged Alex as we trudged along the path. 'She took to Miss Smeeth's tribadic attentions like a duck to water. Not that we didn't too, of course.'

'True enough, and I won't deny that I enjoyed being frigged by her dildo,' I concurred but then went on: 'On the other hand, wouldn't you agree that we really outgrew that pleasure once we found the opportunity of enjoying ourselves with boys?'

Alex mulled my words over for a moment or two and then replied thoughtfully: 'Yes, but I still like being brought off by a girl just as much as before we were fucked by young Terence Jackson. I'm not saying I didn't enjoy it but, quite candidly, I found more satisfaction in our own all-girl escapades.'

'Ah well, each to her own but for me it's more the other way round,' I said with a smile. I recalled the passion of that wonderful afternoon at the end of the Spring term which I spent with Terry in his bedroom at Jackson Lodge. Perhaps it was this sensuous memory that made me feel even warmer as we walked along in the bright sunshine. Be that as it may, when we came to a small clearing partially shaded by a clump of trees from the bright rays of the sun, I added: 'Phew, it's much too hot to walk! Let's sit on that mossy bank for a while. After all, Miss Blundred herself told us that we didn't have to race.'

'Sophie, that's the best idea you've had all day,' agreed Alex. She gave a yawn and then she added: 'I don't know about you but I rather fancy a nice little snooze.'

We took off our blazers and rolled them up to use as pillows and then, giving each other a friendly cuddle, we sank down in each other's arms. Alex yawned again and very soon she fell fast asleep with her pretty head resting in the crook of my shoulder. My eyes closed too as I thought about that marvellous night of passion with Squire Jackson's handsome youngest son. Terry had been home for the spring vacation from Edinburgh University where he was studying medicine. We first met each other not all that far from where Alex and I were now enjoying our rest . . .

My lips curled into a smile when I recalled how embarrassed Terry had been when I first clapped eyes upon him. For my readers to understand why this was so, I must explain the circumstances of our meeting. It all happened on a most pleasant April day some eight weeks before. During a free afternoon I decided to revise my French vocabulary out of doors rather than sitting cooped up in my study. Scholarship girls were allowed the privilege of studying in their own time and we could work where we liked so long as we stayed within the school grounds.

Anyhow, I was ambling down towards the hockey fields with my exercise book under my arm when I heard a male voice coming from behind the sports pavilion. Who could this be and what was he saying? My curiosity was further aroused when I quietly walked the side of the pavilion towards them and now heard a familiar female voice sigh: 'Oh don't do that here, Terry! Can't you wait till tonight? I'll leave my window open so you only have to climb up the drainpipe and then we can pleasure ourselves till dawn.'

'Yes, Rosie darling, and I can't tell you how much I'm looking forward to fucking you later on, but right now my cock is fairly bursting to slide into your delicious little snatch! It's been six long days since we made love and I haven't even frigged myself since!'

I poked my head around the corner to see none other than our English teacher, Miss Rosamund Dunaway standing against the wall with Terry Jackson. Their arms were entwined about each other in a most passionate embrace.

Now Terry Jackson was a fine figure of a man, broad-shouldered and almost six feet tall. I recognised him instantly because, although we had not actually been introduced, I had spoken briefly to him at the start of the spring term when I had attended a lecture he had given to the Geographical Society on his recent visit to Turkey.

As for Rosamund Dunaway, she was by far and away the youngest and prettiest teacher on the staff. She was only in her early twenties and quite stunning with long, liquorice-black hair and light blue eyes. Obviously Miss Dunaway and Terry had already consummated their relationship for she made no protest when he broke off their embrace to unbutton his trousers and pull out his huge stiff cock.

'Feel how hard it is, Rosie!' urged Terry as he pulled down his trousers. At once she clasped hold of his thick truncheon and fisted the pulsating shaft up and down in her hand. Miss Dunaway dropped to her knees and I had a clear view of Terry's massive chopper as she slipped her hand under the shaft and massaged his balls whilst her lips closed over his knob and she began to suck his cock.

I took a deep breath and pinched my nipples as I watched Terry stand with his back against the wall, his legs astride and his colossal tool arching out from his crotch. Miss Dunaway knelt before him as if she were worshipping his rock-hard prick, bobbing her head back and forth along his swollen shaft.

'M'mm, that's *wunderbar*, as your colleague Fraulein Gottlieb would say,' breathed Terry as he closed his eyes and Miss Dunaway gobbled on his twitching tool. I continued to watch with increasing fascination at the way she made herself comfortable by letting the side of her face rest against his thigh as she crammed more and more of Terry's cock inside her wet, willing mouth.

Her long fingers circled the base of his rigid rod as she lapped the sensitive underside of his shaft. Terry clamped his hands on the back of her head, pushing down on the mop of silky dark hair. Somehow Miss Dunaway managed to take every inch of his palpitating prick into her throat.

Using her free hand, she toyed with his wrinkled pink ballsack and naturally this sweet stimulation soon brought Terry to the boil and he called out through gritted teeth: 'Get ready, Rosie, I'm coming, I'm coming!' In response Miss Dunaway sucked even harder on her fleshy lollipop and squeezed him even closer to her until his balls were slapping against her chin.

With a sobbing cry, he shot his hot, frothy seed down her throat. She swallowed his entire emission, smacking her lips as she milked him of the last drops of jism. Terry's lean muscular frame quivered with convulsions of delight and he pulled her upwards until her face was next to his own. Then they wrapped their arms around each other and sealed their mutual joy with a fervent kiss.

She pulled away from him and, looking down at her watch, she exclaimed: 'Goodness me, is that the time? I must fly or I'll be late for this afternoon's rehearsal of the school play. We're doing *A Midsummer Night's Dream* and I'm producing it, for my sins.'

'Oh dear, aren't there any good actresses amongst the girls this year?' he grinned as he pulled up his drawers and trousers. The old proverb says that listeners never hear any good of themselves, although I could not prevent myself blushing when Miss Dunaway replied: 'That's not the problem. Girls like Lizzie Plymouth, Sophie Starr and Felicia Copeland-Thomson are very talented but they've been lazy and haven't always turned up for rehearsal on time to work on their lines. So I planned to read them the Riot Act this afternoon but I can't very well do that if I'm late for rehearsal myself!'

'Well, there's time for one last kiss,' I heard Terry insist. I clapped my hand over my mouth as I realised that I too had forgotten about the rehearsal. I hurried away as quickly as I could, looking over my shoulder every few yards to see if Miss Dunaway was behind me.

Fortunately, Terry Jackson kept her in his arms for a further few valuable minutes. I had time for a brief chat with the other members of the cast (I was playing Titania) before a slightly ruffled-looking Miss Dunaway came into the school hall and we began work.

After the rehearsal had finished, I wasn't entirely sur-prised when she asked me to stay behind for a few mo-ments. I believed I was going to get a wigging for not being completely word-perfect, but this was not the reason Miss Dunaway wanted to speak to me.

'Sophie, I'll come straight to the point,' she said briskly, gesturing for me to sit down next to her. 'I believe you took a stroll around the sports field this afternoon. Was there any particular reason for this?'

'Not really, Miss Dunaway,' I answered as coolly as possible, although I could already feel a warm blush work-ing its way into my cheeks. 'I had to revise some French and thought I might as well look at the book in the fresh air on such a nice day.'

'You didn't walk to the sports pavilion for another specific purpose?' she pressed and I shook my head and said truthfully: 'No, Miss Dunaway. In fact, I only de-cided at the last minute to go there because I saw some girls walking towards Trippett Meadow. I knew if I joined them I would start talking and not get enough work done.'

She gave me a long, suspicious look and I stared back with an affected wide-eyed innocence.

However, I have always believed in the maxim that attack is the best form of defence, or as my brother Daniel would say to his college team-mates before a hard game of rugger: 'Whatever else you do, chaps, make sure you get your retaliation in first!'

Not that I felt threatened by the situation – after all it was the randy teacher and not myself who had been suck-ing Terry Jackson's cock! I was simply a chance onlooker who happened to be passing by. Yet I was unhappy with the situation for I genuinely liked Miss Dunaway. I took no pleasure in seeing her squirm with anxiety, concerned that lurid stories about her antics with Terry Jackson might spread throughout the school.

Whatever the reason, I remarked boldly: 'Don't think I don't realise why you are asking me all these questions, Miss Dunaway. There's no need to worry, I shan't say a word to anyone about what I saw behind the pavilion. All I ask is that you take the same attitude if you ever catch me in such an embarrassing position. Unfortunately, there's precious little chance of that happening around here, more's the pity!'

Miss Dunaway smiled with relief and squeezed my arm as she replied: 'Quite so, Sophie, and that's why Terry and I were so foolish this afternoon. It's just so difficult to find any time to be alone together.

'My dear, I can't thank you enough for being so understanding,' she went on. 'You're a sweet girl and I won't forget this kindness. Do come up to my room and we'll open the box of fancy chocolates and the bottle of crème de menthe I received last week from my sister who is studying philosophy at the Sorbonne in Paris.'

This seemed much more fun than reading through my French vocabulary and I had no hesitation in accepting this invitation.

'Have you tasted crème de menthe before, Sophie?' enquired Miss Dunaway as she passed me a glass of the bright green peppermint liqueur.

'Oh yes, it's one of my favourite drinks,' I answered. As we were about to put the glasses to our lips there was a knock on Miss Dunaway's door. The young teacher rose to her feet and said: 'Damn! Who can that be? Well, whoever it is I'll get rid of her before you can say Jack Robinson.'

She walked to the door and opened it just enough for me to see that her visitor was one of the maidservants who was clearly passing on an important request from the headmistress, Miss Randall. I didn't catch what was being said but Miss Dunaway said heavily: 'Very well, I'll be there in five minutes.'

Then she turned to me and sighed: 'It appears that Miss Randall has received a written letter of complaint from Sir Norwood Foxhill about the behaviour of some girls when he was out riding with the local hunt. Goodness knows why, but Miss Randall wants to see me about it. Look, I shan't be long. Why don't you stay and help yourself to those delicious French chocolates until I come back?'

Miss Dunaway bustled out of the room. I went across to the table on which rested the decorated box of chocolates and whilst I decided whether to pick out a croquette, dragee or pellatine, my eye fell upon sheets of what was obviously a letter to Miss Dunaway from her sister, Alison, because the accompanying envelope bore a French postage stamp.

At this point let me state without reservation that what happened next was totally indefensible because it is disgraceful to read someone else's correspondence without prior permission. I cannot even attempt to justify the fact that curiosity got the better of me! All I can say in mitigation is that at first I thought I would read only the top page. Alison's letter was so interesting, however, that I read through the colourful epistle to the very last paragraph. Luckily, Alison and Rosie Dunaway are now amongst my close friends and they have given their consent for me to reproduce the letter in full. It ran as follows:

Darling Rosie,
Thank you for your lovely letter, I'm so glad that you and Terry Jackson have finally managed to find a time and a place to cement your friendship! Is he as ardent a lover as Pelham, that nice boy you met at Angela Sykes' birthday party?

Still, I'm very happy because yesterday I was fucked with great style by a handsome Yankee gentleman named Abner Harrison, the cultural attaché at the American

Embassy. *We met at a party given by a mutual friend and were immediately attracted to each other. Abner told me that the previous day he had been introduced to Dr Kishawe Vedgama, the famous Indian palmist, who had surprised him by giving a surprisingly accurate picture of himself just by studying the palms of his hands.*

'My, you surprise me, Mr Harrison,' I said to Abner. 'Do you really think that character can be judged by palmistry? Surely you cannot believe such superstitious nonsense!'

Abner was rather hurt by my brashness and answered: 'Well, there is often more than what you might imagine in these old customs. Palmistry is a very old science. Let me look at your left hand and see what your lines show.'

'But I'm right-handed,' I protested as he took my hand and turned it over to scan my palm.

'That doesn't matter,' he said promptly. 'With everybody, the left hand shows the natural characteristics and the right hand tells of talents and traits picked up since birth. May I have your permission to continue?'

Ah well, affecting an interest in palmistry (which I still believe is mere hocus-pocus like all forms of fortune-telling) was as good a way as any other to allow me to hold hands with a member of the opposite sex! For what it's worth, Abner informed me that my deeply curved heart line showed that I was a physical and passionate person and I could not resist bursting out into a fit of giggles and saying: 'Oh Abner, did it need the study of palmistry to flatter me in such a fashion?'

He had the grace to grin and said: 'No, Miss Dunaway, though I would use any means available to flatter the prettiest girl I have seen since I arrived in Paris two months ago. I must go now but I hope we can finish this conversation over dinner tonight.'

'I would love to,' I replied and we dined at Au Coin de

Feu, one of the smartest restaurants in Paris. As we climbed in the fiacre to take me back to my little room, Abner asked if I would care for a nightcap at his apartment on the Rue de la Paix. I know it was forward of me, but then I've always maintained that I can resist everything except temptation!

Ten minutes later we were sitting next to each other on a velvet-covered sofa in Abner's drawing-room. He poured two large cognacs but I had time only to take one tiny sip, for when I put my glass down on a side table, Abner turned his face towards me and kissed me hard on the lips. My lips opened to let his tongue slide inside my mouth and then after we had kicked off our shoes the broad-shouldered American scooped me up in his strong arms and carried me into his bedroom. Abner gently laid me down upon the fluffy eiderdown and soon we were entwined in a most sensuous embrace. He expertly eased off my dress, kissing me all over as his eager hands ran all over my trembling body until he ripped down my knickers and I lay there stark naked.

'My dear girl, you are simply exquisite,' Abner breathed as he shucked off his jacket and in a trice he had whipped off all his clothes except his drawers. His back was towards me as he tugged them down to reveal two tight bum cheeks and my pussey was already tingling when he turned round to show me his magnificent stiff shaft which rose sturdily upwards out of a mass of curly black hair, slightly curved but of such thickness!

I reached out and stroked his diamond-hard love truncheon which possessed such a quality of warm smoothness that it was sheer bliss to touch. Our mouths pressed together as I grasped hold of this exciting tool, rubbing it up and down to cap and uncap the fiery red-headed helmet, making it swell and bound in my hand.

Matters took their natural turn and Abner slipped a

pillow under my bottom to allow for greater penetration and he leaned over me and placed his huge mushroomed knob gently between my yielding pussey lips. Oh Rosie! What ecstasy coursed through my veins when Abner slowly slipped his thick prick into my juicy cunt. His cock seemed to swell even more inside my clingy cunney which received it so eagerly.

At first we lay motionless, billing and cooing like two turtle doves until I began a slow rolling motion with my buttocks to which Abner immediately responded by moving his chopper slowly at first, withdrawing all but the very tip before sliding back in to the hilt as I let out tiny little yelps of sheer delight.

'Alison, you have a deliciously tight quim, but I'm concerned that my cock might be stretching your sheath too much,' he murmured politely, but I put his mind at rest when I whispered, 'No! No! I adore having your big cock inside me. Fuck me, Abner, fuck me! Aaaah! Aaaah!'

He increased the tempo as he felt my excitement rising and with a sharp cry he slammed the entire length of his beefy shaft into my cunt. In no time at all I was bucking and writhing in sheer unadulterated lust. We drove onwards, enjoying each other's body to the full until he panted in my ear that he was fast approaching the point of no return.

'Can I spend inside you, darling?' he gasped and when I nodded my agreement he smiled broadly and with a hoarse cry he sprayed my love funnel. At the very moment wonderful waves of my own climax crashed through me in great concentric rings like the water in a still pond when a pebble is dropped into it from the banks.

Abner pulled out his shrunken todger from my cunt and I cradled his head in my arms as he rolled over on his back next to me, his chest heaving up and down as he sought to regain his composure. However, my blood was up and I grabbed hold of his limp cock and flogged my fist along the wet shaft in a vain attempt to coax it up again for another glorious poke.

'Sorry, Alison, I'm strictly a one-off guy,' said Abner sadly as he looked down at his crestfallen cock. 'Lie back, though, and I'll gladly bring you off by frenching your sweet little pussey.'

So I parted my legs and relaxed as he clambered up and knelt before me, kissing my breasts and my belly and then he buried his head between my thighs and began to lick and lap around the moist lips of my cunney.

Sister, I will readily admit that I was greatly disappointed when Abner informed me that his cock was hors de combat, but happily my passionate Yankee was an expert practitioner in the neglected art of cunnilingus. I lay back entranced as I basked in the heavenly sensation of his wicked tongue sliding up and down the length of my tingling crack. Oh, it felt as good as a real fuck and I pushed my mound up against his face to allow him to slide his tongue inside my yearning quim. How I purred with pleasure when the tip of his tongue began to play with my swollen clitty.

'Woooh! Woooh! Woooh!' I gasped when Abner prised open my love lips with his fingers and sank them into my juicy cunt. His tongue and his fingers were thrilling me and I felt myself climbing to the very highest pinnacle of sensual delights. Abner pushed his fingers deeper inside me and frigged me whilst he sucked my clitty into his mouth and nipped the sensitive bud with his teeth. I writhed wildly beneath him, holding his head firmly against my groin with one hand whilst I played with my erect titties with the other.

Then I arched my back and with a gigantic shudder I spent profusely, flooding Abner's face with cunt juice. He worked his tongue, though his jaw must have been aching, until again I shivered all over and achieved yet another tremendous climax. He gulped down my tangy spend and then sank back beside me. By this time, however, Abner's thick, meaty cock had recovered its lost strength and it now stood up as stiff as a poker and shaking with anticipation. I lovingly closed my fingers around his warm, wet shaft. Then I ran my thumb softly over the uncapped purple helmet and he closed his eyes and breathed roughly through his mouth as I lowered my face and licked all around the ridge of his knob.

I washed his cock with my tongue and gradually eased the fleshy blue-veined shaft into my mouth. Then I paused, took a deep breath and wrapped my lips tightly around his twitching tool and plunged him deep into the back of my throat, sucking slowly and meticulously as I cupped his balls in my hand. Abner groaned and grabbed at my head as I tightened my lips around his shaft and teasingly nipped his cock with my teeth.

Entwining his fingers through my hair, Abner began to pump hard into my mouth and I fluttered my wet tongue along the smooth underside as it glided to and fro. However, his pulsing prick was so big that I almost choked as I gobbled greedily on his knob. So when he began to thrust faster into my mouth, I slid a hand underneath him and jammed my forefinger up his bum.

'Hey, what the heck—' he groaned as I moved my finger in and out of his arse-hole, matching my movements to his until I felt his cock throb against my tongue and he jetted a fountain of tasty spunk down my throat. I gleefully gulped down his copious emission and there I thought would be the end of the affair, for Abner had already warned me that unfortunately he did not possess the abilities of the fabled Count Gewirtz who reputedly could spend three times before his prick lost its stiffness.

So I was pleasantly surprised when, after only a minute or two, Abner slipped his hand into my moist bush and I felt his fingers pulling open my pussey lips, although I felt the need to murmur: 'Abner, please don't warm up the engine unless you want to go for a drive.'

'Have no fear, we're off on a journey,' he assured me gaily. 'At least, you are if you would like a ride to fuckland on my cock.'

I did not have to be asked twice! Without further ado I climbed on top of him with my knees on either side of his lithe, masculine trunk. Next I lifted my hips and crouched over his thick prick and rubbed my pussey lips across his straining knob whilst I took hold of his thick rampant rod and positioned the tip so that it pressed directly on to my clitty. Rotating my hips, I edged slightly forward and allowed his quivering cock to slide into me. Ever so slowly I lifted and lowered my dripping cunt and each time more of Abner's prick was embedded inside my clingy cunney until I was fully spitted on his rampant rod and we melted away in sheer bliss.

'M'mm, that's simply divine,' Abner murmured as he felt my cunney muscles contract and relax. I rocked up and down on his sturdy shaft, moving backwards and forwards whilst he cupped my jiggling breasts in his hands, flicking the stalky red nipples between his fingers and rubbing them against the palms of his hands.

Faster and faster I thrust down to meet his frenetic upward jerks and I shook and ground my hips, leaning one way and then the other so that his cock was sliding in and falling out – though never completely!

He lifted his head to suck my titties which brought on my spend and just as the electric sparks crackled through my frame, Abner's proud prick spurted jet after jet of sticky jism up my love funnel, coating the walls with his copious emission which made my whole body glow with *lustful delight as I lifted myself off his glistening deflated shaft and rolled over next to him.*

By now I had surrendered myself to the powerful images of Alison riding Abner's thick hard cock which had formed in my mind. I put down the sheets of paper on the table and my hands trembled as I began to wonder what it would feel like to have a thick fleshy cock pistoning in and out of my own tingling pussey. I slumped down in a chair and, throwing up my skirt, I quickly pulled off my panties and stuffed them in the pocket of my dress. Then I let my fingers move lovingly across my curly bush and stray across the puffy lips of my already damp cunney. I rubbed around the rim of my juicy opening, wetting my fingers and then I slipped a finger inside my cunt and began to work myself off, pinching and squeezing my clitty which was demanding my full attention.

In no time at all I felt the familiar tremors of an oncoming spend rock through my lower body. I rubbed my tiny love button so hard that my arms and fingers were getting cramped, but my fingers continued to tease my clitty until the waves of the climax washed over me, sending blissful waves of sheer delight coursing through my veins.

'Oooooh!' I moaned as I heard footsteps in the corridor. I just had time to pull down my skirt before the door opened and Miss Dunaway came back with a gloomy expression on her face.

'Oh dear, is anything wrong?' I enquired and she groaned: 'I'll say there is! Miss Randall has called a staff meeting after supper to discuss Sir Norwood Foxhill's complaint.'

She went on to say that it would not now be possible for her to keep her assignation with Terry Jackson. 'I'm not only upset for myself but poor Terry will be so disappointed. Don't you remember how this afternoon he said he hadn't even frigged himself for a whole week in preparation for tonight? And there's no way I can get a message to him telling him not to come till midnight.'

'Surely your meeting will be over and done with long before then,' I observed but Miss Dunaway sighed: 'Oh yes, but I have some essays to mark which I must hand back tomorrow morning. I cannot see myself finishing this work much before then.'

Then she looked at me with a mischievous smile and said: 'Sophie, would you like to welcome Terry tonight? He'll be round at about eleven o'clock – I leave my window open and he shins up the drainpipe. I'll leave my bedroom door unlocked and you can wait there till I come back. Don't worry, he may be randy but Terry would never force his unwanted attentions onto even as pretty a girl as you.'

'That would be spiffing,' I answered with great enthusiasm. We sealed the arrangement by clinking our glasses together and downing our crème de menthe.

I could hardly wait till 'lights out' at ten o'clock and half an hour later I put on my dressing gown and slipped out to Miss Dunaway's room. Once inside, I turned on a small brass table lamp, slipped off my dressing gown and lay on the bed whilst I waited impatiently for Terry to arrive.

Terry was clearly keen to continue the game he had begun this afternoon, for just before eleven o'clock I heard the rustle of leaves as he climbed up the handily placed drainpipe and deftly swung himself through the open window and landed on his feet.

'Good evening, Mr Jackson,' I said lightly and the poor young man whirled round and gasped at the sound of a strange voice. He gasped: 'My God, it's you! The girl who was spying on Rosie and me this afternoon.'

'I was doing no such thing,' I replied indignantly and repeated the story I had told Miss Dunaway about how I had come across them by accident. 'In fact, Rosie was so grateful that she asked me to entertain you until she has ploughed through some marking which has to be finished by morning.

'I'm sorry, but the fact is that you're stuck with me till Rosie returns,' I finished. I noticed that Terry was gazing intently at me as I spoke. I blushed when I realised that my nightdress was made of such fine-spun cotton that it was almost transparent. He could see all my naked charms for the gown concealed nothing and even the silky bush of hair around my cunney was well revealed.

'Tush, there's no need to apologise,' he murmured as he drew out a bottle from the small bag he had brought with him. 'But if you really want to make amends, then you'll have to help me finish this bottle of Moet et Chandon. I took it out of the ice bucket half an hour ago and, as you know, champagne can only be drunk whilst it's cold. Such a pity we can't wait for Rosie!'

Terry didn't even wait for an answer. He pulled out two fluted glasses from his bag, expertly popped the cork and poured out the sparkling bubbly wine as he said: 'Now then, let us make a toast. As Rosie isn't able to be with us, here's to absent friends!'

'Absent friends,' I repeated as we clinked glasses together and then we toasted the school, Terry's college, and goodness knows what else. By now, Terry had removed his jacket, collar and tie, and we were sitting next to each other on Rosie's bed. Terry slipped his arm around my waist and said softly: 'Sophie, in my opinion we should seal our friendship with a kiss – don't you agree?'

'Oh yes,' I murmured. My heart began beating wildly when our lips pressed together and his mouth covered mine, prompting an exchange of twining tongues. We rolled back together on the bed and I thrilled at the way his calm, experienced fingers caressed my breasts, rolling my nipples into erection whilst I felt my tingling pussey becoming decidedly damp, moistening like a dew-drenched flower in eager anticipation of what was shortly to come.

As these lascivious thoughts formed in my mind, I lifted up my arms to let Terry pull my nightie over my head. He threw it down and, whilst we engaged in a further soul-stirring kiss, I felt Terry's hand creeping up my leg and I made no move to stop him. Indeed, my thighs fell apart and his searching fingers immediately took possession of my cunney! He broke off our embrace and with one bound he was down on his knees in front of me and pressing his face inside my curly bush. Then he looked up and said with great passion: 'Oh darling, you have the prettiest pussey I have ever seen! Now lay back whilst I pay homage to this delicious little treasure.

'I am sure your cunney juice tastes even better than vintage champagne,' Terry murmured as he placed a pillow under my bottom and then he burrowed his head again down between my thighs. I squealed with delight when he placed his lips over my pussey lips and sucked them into his mouth. The naughty boy found the magic button under the fold at the top of my cunney and he cleverly twirled his tongue all around it. The faster he vibrated the tip of his tongue, the more excited I became. I twisted and bucked from side to side as Terry's tongue slithered quickly along the grooves of my cunt, lapping up the emission of pungent pussey juice.

On each stroke I arched my body upwards and very soon I let out a high-pitched wail of delight as my cunney exploded, flooding his face with my spend whilst the delicious ripples of a truly exquisite climax spread out from my crotch throughout my body.

I was now so fired up that, as Terry rolled over to lie beside me, I reached down and grabbed hold of his hot thick shaft. Then, sliding down the bed until my lips were level with his cock, I extended my tongue and licked the purple knob of his magnificent cock. I swallowed hard and then took his twitching tool inch by inch into my mouth, snaking my mobile, salivating tongue around its girth, paying particular attention to the smooth-skinned helmet. I held it in a firm grip between my lips and rhythmically raised and lowered my tousled head, causing Terry to grunt and moan with pure, unalloyed delight.

'Stop, stop, Sophie!' he cried hoarsely. 'If you carry on like this I'll come in your mouth.'

With a petulant pout I released his throbbing tool and slowly rose to my knees. I cupped my breasts in my hands and tweaked the stiff rosy nipples as I giggled: 'I hope you like my titties, Terry, even though I'm sure they're not so big as Miss Dunaway's.'

'It's quality not quantity that counts,' he answered gallantly as he pushed me down on my back and swung across me, his hands gently pushing the two soft globes together as his tongue came out to circle around the little red soldiers. This sent lustful vibrations throughout my entire body. I bucked upwards against him with all my might as, mad with lust for each other, our lips joined and our tongues darted in each other's mouths.

My loins were now on fire and I opened my legs wider as, with my fingers, I parted my pussey lips, spreading the opening wide for his entrance. Then, in a voice cracking with emotion, I begged the dear boy to fuck me.

'Terry, I want your cock inside me. Please, I want it now!' I begged him as, writhing with anticipation, I grabbed hold of his pulsating prick and pressed the knob between the flushed lips of my cunt where it slipped in easily. I experienced no pain whatsoever from this first act of *l'arte de faire l'amour*.

At last I was being fucked! What gorgeous sensations swept out from my groin as Terry's thick cock slid in and out of my juicy crack, each inward thrust making his knob kiss the furthest reaches of my insatiable love funnel, every vigorous poke more enjoyable than the last. My pussey pulsated each time his throbbing shaft slid against the walls of my cunney and Terry whispered: 'Sophie, you have such a luscious little quim. How tightly it's holding on to my cock!'

'Yes! Yes! Yes! It's so huge, I feel so filled up,' I groaned as he slid his huge hard love truncheon in and out of my sopping sheath, making the bedsprings squeak as we fucked away at a frantic pace.

I raised my legs high to wrap them around his muscular torso, helping him to bury every inch of his cock inside my cunt. Wave after wave of sheer ecstatic bliss rolled through me as Terry's thrusting tool slid to and fro, moving faster now as my bottom arched up to meet it. He clasped my bum cheeks as we fucked like a couple possessed, his long thick shaft working backwards and forwards in my sopping snatch. I tightened my legs round his waist and squeezed as hard as I could to feel every ridge of his wonderful cock.

Terry's climax could no longer be delayed and after I had assured him he could come inside me, he cried out joyously: 'Work your hips, Sophie, that's the ticket! A-h-r-e! I'm there, brace yourself, here it comes!'

The sweet lad shuddered as jets of creamy spunk spurted out of his cock. He creamed the walls of my cunney with his deluge and my clenching cunney muscles now began to choke out my climax. I sobbed out my pleasure when my saturated clitty sent shudders of exquisite delight coursing through my veins as wave after wave of delicious pleasure washed over me.

Terry lay quietly over on top of me, careful to keep his still-swollen shaft inside my tingling cunney as we slowly calmed down. When he rolled off me, my hand stole down and squeezed his lovely cock which had afforded me such delectable gratification. I have always enjoyed toying with a prick and as Terry and I murmured sweet nothings into each other's ears, I continued to caress his cock which soon swelled to such an erection that I could scarcely span it with my fingers.

At this stage there was a gentle rap on the door. Terry said: 'Don't worry, Sophie, that's sure to be Rosie – no, don't move, Sophie, she isn't a jealous girl and won't mind at all that we've enjoyed some rumpy-pumpy whilst waiting for her.'

'I hope you're right,' I observed as Terry pulled back the bolt I had put into place when I had come in. It was he who was to be disconcerted, however, when our visitor stepped forward. It was not Miss Dunaway who entered the room but Alex, whose eyes widened as she exclaimed: 'Sophie! I wondered where you had got to! When I woke up and found your bed empty I remembered how worried you were about that essay on *Hamlet* that Miss Dunaway set us last Friday so I thought you might have come here to speak to her about it. But in my wildest dreams I never thought I would find you . . .'

Her voice trailed off as she gazed down at Terry's cock which, although it had now lost some of its stiffness, still hung thickly in a semi-erect state between his thighs. Then Alex smiled at me and went on: 'Perhaps you should introduce me to your friend.'

'By all means. Terry, this is my best friend Miss Alexandra Henderson; Alex, meet Mr Terry Jackson.' Then I broke out into a fit of giggling when Terry, stark naked and with his cock waggling like a piece of garden hose, took Alex's hand and kissed her fingers. 'A pleasure to meet you, Miss Henderson,' he said with a bow. 'May I offer you a glass of champagne? I'm afraid we've almost finished this bottle but there's enough left for you to wet your whistle.'

'Thank you, Mr Jackson, that would be very nice,' replied Alex. In no time at all formalities had been dispensed with and Alex took no offence whatsoever when I said: 'Now, Alex, it isn't right that you should be dressed whilst Terry and I are naked. Shall we put on some clothes or would you like to disrobe?'

Alex tilted her pretty blonde head to one side as she considered the question before she answered with a merry laugh: 'Well, it wouldn't be right for me to put you both to any trouble, especially as I'm only wearing a nightdress under this dressing gown.'

And to show us the veracity of her statement, she swiftly undid the cord of her robe and wriggled her arms out of the garment. Then she whipped off her nightie and stood in all her glorious nudity. She smoothed her hands over the creamy spheres of her large breasts and Terry stood open-mouthed and rooted to the spot whilst Alex pirouetted gaily around the room, flaunting her tightly rounded bum cheeks and the flaxen mop of blonde hair which sprouted in a thick triangle between her beautifully sculpted thighs.

Naturally, Terry's cock shot up to stand as stiff as a poker against his flat white belly. Knowing how desperately Alex longed to cross the Rubicon into womanhood, I cleared my throat and said: 'Look here, you two, I'm just going into the bathroom to wash my hands and face. Do feel free to carry on with whatever you have in mind.'

'Oh bless you, Sophie, you are a pal,' said Alex gratefully as I climbed off the bed and padded out into the bathroom. After I had washed and dried myself with Miss Dunaway's towel, I returned to find the lewd couple kneeling face to face on the bed engaged in a lascivious kiss. I watched Alex reach out and enclose his swollen stiff shaft in her fist, gently frigging his cock just below the uncapped helmet. Except for the rhythmic movement of her hand they were still, their bodies pressed together, their tongues and lips engaged in sensual exploration of each other's mouths whilst she continued to pull her hand up and down his thick, throbbing tool.

Moving back slightly, Terry snaked his hand around Alex's slender waist and grasped one of her beautiful bum cheeks whilst she responded by rotating her hips in slow, voluptuous circles, riding his intrusive grasp as they continued to kiss and cuddle. Now it was time for Terry to insert his twitching todger into Alex's juicy love funnel and he did not delay.

'H-a-r-r! H-a-r-r! H-a-r-r!' Alex cried out as she felt Terry's fleshy helmet slide into her welcoming cunt. Her hands slid round to clamp themselves on the taut cheeks of his bottom and his arms went under her shoulders as she lifted her hips to allow an easier passage for his thrusting cock which was squelching merrily in and out of her sopping slit. Terry increased the speed of his fucking and fairly bounced up and down as my trembling chum clawed at his jerking backside and heaved herself upwards at each stroke to draw his thick prick even further inside her excited quim.

'More! More! More!' she screamed, so loudly that none of us heard the door open. I was too engrossed in watching this erotic spectacle to notice that Miss Dunaway had finally arrived back in her room to find two of her pupils stark naked and one in the process of being threaded by her boyfriend!

I clapped my hand to my mouth when I looked up and saw her standing in the doorway. But even when he saw her, to his credit, Terry Jackson did not miss a single stroke. He continued to fuck Alex who was writhing and twisting uncontrollably as he ploughed on, his balls slip-slapping against her arse.

'Aaah! I'm there! Shoot your sperm, you randy rascal!

Y-e-s-s! Y-e-s-s!' yelled Alex in triumph as the force of her orgasm crackled through her body. Naturally enough, Alex was oblivious to everything except for the flood of frothy white seed which was inundating her lubricated cunney, driving them both to that blissful state of happiness only to be achieved through a copulatory conjunction.

'Wowee! What a wonderful fuck!' purred Alex as she threw her head back on the pillow. 'Did you enjoy being poked, Sophie?'

I looked at Miss Dunaway with a worried expression as I gulped: 'Oh yes, very much. I do believe that I should like to spend the rest of my life with a stiff cock up my cunt every night.'

'I quite agree with you, my dear,' broke in Miss Dunaway. She smiled when her interruption brought forth gasps of horror from Alex and Terry. Then she went on: 'Oh, don't fret, I'm not annoyed, I assumed that Terry would fuck Sophie. However, I'm surprised to see you here, Alex, and whilst I have no objection to Terry fucking your pretty blonde pussey, I do hope that he still has some spunk in his balls left for me.'

As she spoke she started to undress. My pussey began to tingle at the sight of her rounded white breasts. Despite his previous exertions, Terry's insatiable cock swelled up to a meaty semi-erect state when our English mistress divested herself of her knickers and exposed her luxuriant thatch of jet-black pussey hair in which nestled such a superbly chiselled crack with its pouting pink lips.

'M'm, let's see if Mr John Thomas is in a fit condition to continue,' she said thoughtfully, dropping to her knees in front of him. She cupped his balls in her hand and gulped his knob into her mouth, softly biting it and tickling it with the tip of her tongue. Then she thrust the whole of his beefy shaft between her lips and by her sensual sucking she soon managed to coax Terry's cock to its former majestic stiffness.

Then she eased his pulsing prick from her mouth and said to Alex: 'My dear, would you be so kind as to bring me my ladies' comforter – you'll find it in the drawer of the bedside table. And, Sophie, please may I play with your titties whilst I suck off Terry's gorgeous cock and Alex diddles my pussey with the dildo?'

Unfortunately, we weren't able to conclude this erotic evening in such a lascivious manner because only a minute or so later Miss Dunaway heard someone climbing the stairs. Terry, Alex and I dived into the bathroom as the footsteps became louder and we heard the sound of voices outside on the landing.

'Damn! I'll wager a pound to a penny that's Miss Walshaw and Miss Thomas,' whispered Terry crossly. 'Their rooms are on either side of this one and Miss Walshaw is such a light sleeper that Rosie and I can't do anything without her hearing us. We'll have to postpone our whoresome foursome for another time.'

Alex's face fell as she asked: 'Oh, must we really? I was so looking forward to bringing off Miss Dunaway with the dildo.'

'I'm sure you were,' he said with a heavy sigh. 'But we would all be for the high jump if we were caught by some nosey parker. Never mind though, girls, we'll only have to wait till later this week.'

This cheered her up no end and, when we judged it safe to come back inside the bedroom, Alex and I dressed ourselves and made our way quietly back to our dormitory.

These lewd recollections meandered through my mind that afternoon by the hockey field whilst I snuggled up closer to Alex. Despite the finger that was absently stroking my pussey, I fell fast asleep. However, I was soon awoken by a kiss on my already throbbing nipples. I opened my eyes to see Alex kneeling between my thighs with a wide grin on her pretty face. She had woken up and, seeing that I had dozed off, she had taken the opportunity to unbutton my blouse and pull down the straps of my chemise to bare my bosoms.

'Alexandra Henderson, you naughty girl!' I said sleepily as she bent down and lapped all around my nipples, her teeth tugging at the plump red titties. The twin peaks rose to her prodding until they stood engorged and quivering between the alternating nibbles and licks.

I felt quite light-headed as Alex began to take all the liberties she desired with me, kissing and sucking my curvaceous breasts. Almost before I knew it, she had yanked down my knickers and was brazenly handling the soft cheeks of my bottom, squeezing and pinching them as I writhed under her lascivious touch. When she eased a finger into my dampening slit, I sighed with joy and raised my backside to enjoy the delicious sensations to the utmost. Then her forefinger was joined by a second and then a third as she frigged me so expertly that I soon came off all over her hand.

Alex finished undressing me and then swiftly threw off all her clothes before she moved up over me. Still keeping her wicked fingers embedded in my cunt, she kissed me fervently on the mouth as we abandoned ourselves to the pleasures of our union. Her velvet tongue slithered between my lips to make contact with my own whilst her fingers plunged in and out of my juicy love funnel.

Then the raunchy minx replaced her fingers with her tongue and grasped the quivering cheeks of my bottom as she kissed my titties and belly button, swirling her tongue around the tiny whorl before dropping her face between my thighs and pressing her lips against the soft yielding pussey lips, probing the petals of my cunt as it opened like a flower.

'Ooooh! Ooooh! Ooooh!' I gasped when Alex began a slow and methodical suction of my tingling quim. From clitty to anus, the tip of her pointed tongue brushed the clingy wet cunney flesh, sending shivers of delight running through me. How I moaned at the exquisite sensations and threshed and writhed from side to side when Alex paid tribute to the puckered little rosette of my bum-hole. She reamed it with her tongue, scouring the outer edges of the muscles and flicking inside the opening before returning to my pussey, drilling her tongue against the sensitive membranes just within the lips of the dripping crack.

After I had spent a second time, Alex arranged me so that I lay partly on my left side. My left leg was stretched out almost straight, my right leg drawn up, the heel of this foot being hooked behind her neck. Her right cheek rested on my left thigh, her right arm was under me and clasped around my waist, her left hand resting upon and toying with my bare breasts. Propped up against the grassy mound, I was in a good position to gaze down upon the lovely girl as she pressed her lips gently on my cunt, letting the tip of her tongue glide along between the puffy love lips, fluttering now and then inside the red chink of my quim.

Oh, but Alex was a roguish little vixen! Time and again, when she felt I was on the verge of a spend, she would stop frigging me and wait until the gathering force of the climax had melted away. Nevertheless, she also wanted to come, so she carefully moved herself across me and lowered her thrilling young backside. Now we were entwined in the most voluptuous *soixante neuf* and her juicy crack was pressed against my mouth.

I parted her buttocks and licked and lapped around her sweet snatch whilst she bent forward and glued her mouth to my own sopping slit, sucking and nipping at the tender clitty in much the same way as I was working on her. She let out a gurgle of delight when I moved my tongue up and down between her wet pussey lips, kissing them tenderly between licks. Then I blew softly on her clitty feeling her tremble all over when I slowly circled it with the tip of my tongue. This excited Alex so much that after only about fifteen seconds I was swallowing her tangy cuntal juice as she came in a series of hysterical spasms.

Now she finally brought me off, licking my bedewed love lips at speed, flicking at the inner folds and turning the skin slightly outwards so as to better nibble my erect clitty. I savoured this delicious stimulation which brought on my orgasm very quickly. I came in great bursts which made me cry out as I spattered Alex's face with my spend. It left me breathless but fulfilled as we rolled around together on the dry grass.

Looking back on that lubricious afternoon, I realise how foolish we were to behave in such an uninhibited fashion. I shudder to think how embarrassing it would have been had someone seen us and reported us to the headmistress. However, more by luck than judgement, we managed to avoid detection and when we had recovered our senses, we dressed ourselves and walked briskly through to Hatching Green where we caught up with a group of other stragglers and sauntered back slowly with them to school. Miss Blundred was waiting for us and made some acid comments about how she had been on the point of sending out search parties for us.

After supper, Alex and I were quietly leafing through our geography textbooks in our study when we were honoured with an unexpected visit from Miss Dunaway. We rose from our seats when she came in, but as she shut the door she said: 'No, don't get up, girls, I don't want to disturb your work but I thought you might like to see some pamphlets I have just received from the Women's Freedom League [*The Women's Social and Political Union, the major militant organisation whose members became known as suffragettes, was founded by Mrs Pankhurst in 1903 – Editor*] because I assume that liberal-minded girls like you will be sympathetic to the cause.

'Let me know if you would like to join the movement. On the other hand, if you disagree with the sentiments expressed in them, I would ask you simply to return the pamphlets to me.'

She passed me a large brown envelope and hurried out of our study. I looked questioningly at Alex and remarked: 'Well, well, so Rosie Dunaway is a suffragist! To be honest, I've never given the matter much thought. But when you think about it, isn't it foolish that illiterate old fogies like Newman the gardener can cast their votes to decide who is going to be their next Members of Parliament whilst well-educated ladies like Miss Dunaway have no say in these affairs?'

I pulled a sheaf of pamphlets out of the envelope and tossed them across the table at Alex. 'Let's read these, my dear girl, they look far more interesting than silly old geography,' I said. This, dear reader, is how I was first introduced to the idea of sexual equality, a philosophy to which I have devoted my life.

Later that evening in the dormitory, Alex and I distributed the leaflets amongst the other girls. I am glad to say that everyone was in full agreement with sentiments expressed in the literature.

'Of course women must band together, though I'm not too sure about sharing *everything*,' remarked Babs Fawcett with a mischievous twinkle in her eye. I turned to Babs, an eye-catchingly attractive girl who was lithe and lovely as a fawn, and said sternly: 'Come now, Babs, one for all and all for one! Surely that must be our motto.'

'Maybe so, Sophie,' she rejoined as she winked at the other girls and went on: 'But I don't know whether you'll want to share your birthday present.'

'My birthday present?' I repeated and Alex chuckled: 'Well, you didn't think your friends would forget that you're seventeen tomorrow, did you?'

'Strictly speaking, you really shouldn't have your present until tomorrow but frankly we can't wait to give it to you,' added Babs as the girls crowded round my bed. 'So sit down and close your eyes whilst I get it.'

Someone switched down the lights as I obediently covered my eyes. I heard a great amount of giggling whilst I sat on the bed wondering what on earth my chums had in store for me. Then the sweet voice of Heather Adamson, a beautiful girl with a full, feminine figure who had already won a place to study history at London University in the autumn, whispered in my ear: 'Off with your nightdress, Sophie! You need to be naked to appreciate this particular gift!'

Curiouser and curiouser, I thought to myself as I peered through the darkness which was broken only by a small oil lamp at the side of the bed. I knew the other girls were probably all round us straining to see what was happening but I could only see Heather's flushed face and dark tresses of glossy hair when she gently lifted me up from the bed and began to unbutton her own nightdress. 'Don't be shy, Sophie,' she said. 'I'll take off my nightie too to keep you company, so to speak.'

I knew that Heather had taken a fancy to me but had up till now kept her distance. However, when she saw me survey her superbly large rounded bosoms, she cupped them together in her hands and rubbed her nipples, making the stalky red berries stand up between her long fingers.

She licked her lips and continued: 'Come and stand next to me and we can compare our pussies. I do love your pouting little crack. What a fine contrast our bushes make with your thatch of light blonde hair and my black curly moss. Let's go back to bed and I will frig you till your cunney is all nice and juicy.'

Now although this idea was not entirely without appeal, I prefer to decide for myself whether I want to take part in any such tribadic pastimes. I was slightly annoyed that my consent was taken for granted as Heather pushed me firmly down upon my mattress and covered my mouth with kisses. Nevertheless, I must confess that I did enjoy the feel of her hand between my thighs and I let out a tiny yelp of delight when she inserted the tip of her finger into my fast-moistening love channel.

'Is that nice?' she enquired unnecessarily, for she knew full well from my frenetic wrigglings how happy I was with this lubricious stimulation.

'Oh yes, Heather dear,' I panted as she frigged me to a spend and I coated her hand with my love juice. I lay back and let the blissful sensations seep through me when the sound of muffled giggling reminded me that we were not alone. I sat up and Heather slid off the bed as two more lights were turned up. I could see in front of the bed the figure of a young man dressed in a running singlet and athletic shorts with a blindfold around his eyes being led towards me by Alex.

'Darling, here's your birthday present,' she called out gaily. 'Now that Heather has put you in the mood, I'm sure you will enjoy it.'

I looked up and peered at the slender lad who I recognised as Phil Colnbrook, the head boy of Highcliffe, a boarding school situated some five miles away. The older pupils of both establishments meet twice a term, once at Highcliffe and once at Dame Chasuble's, for debates on topical subjects. Whilst we are well-chaperoned by Miss Randall and at least two other teachers, love laughs at locksmiths and many couples correspond and meet up secretly on half-holiday afternoons.

Among such couples were Babs Fawcett and Johnny Pilkington, the rugged captain of cricket at Highcliffe. They had exchanged *billets doux* and she had promised to regale us with the story of how she had first sucked his cock. Be that as it may, it must have been obvious to our respective friends that Phil Colnbrook and I were keen on each other. Although we had written each other long affectionate letters, the nearest we had come to consummating our friendship was a fifteen-minute session of spooning in Phil's study on our last visit to Highcliffe.

'Shush,' interjected Babs as I was about to speak. 'We also promised Mr Colnbrook a lovely surprise if he came here tonight dressed in as little as possible, didn't we, Phil?' She smoothed her hand across his chest and chuckled: 'Poor boy, you must be on pins and needles – tell us how you wangled your way out here tonight. It couldn't have been easy for you.'

'No, it wasn't,' he growled uneasily. 'So may I now please take off this blindfold and see for myself what all this is about?'

'Certainly you may,' Babs answered as she untied the knot of the scarf the girls had wrapped round Phil's head. He pulled it away from his eyes and then his jaw dropped when he saw me stretched out naked on the bed.

'My God! It's Sophie Starr!' he gasped and now realising exactly what the girls were giving me for my seventeenth birthday. I smiled at him and parted my legs so that in the low light Phil could make out the outline of my pink love lips in the thatch of tangled curls around my pussey.

'In person,' I murmured, moving my hand lazily across my thigh. 'I hope you're not disappointed.'

'No, no,' he mumbled, clearly torn between his powerful lustful passion and his embarrassment at being stared at by a gaggle of girls whilst a huge bulge formed between his legs. To put him at his ease, I reached out and let my fingers slip across to his knee, running them up his thigh and down again before – to the boy's clear delight – I squeezed his stiffie which was now straining the white cotton of his shorts.

'Oh Sophie, be careful, that's absolutely terrific, but I'm, oh gosh, er—' the sweet youth stammered out in great confusion and a crimson blush suffused his cheeks. 'You see, um, how can I put this—'

'There's no need to say anything at all,' I said reassuringly. 'Silly boy, I would be very disappointed if you didn't have a hard-on after looking at my naked body.'

A sudden thought struck me – perhaps his bashfulness arose because this handsome young man was still a virgin? The very idea of being the girl to assist Phil in his rite of passage into manhood whetted my appetite enormously. My pussey was buzzing excitely when I looked him straight in the eye and asked him bluntly if he still had to make his first journey across the sexual Rubicon.

He nodded shamefacedly and I murmured: 'This is nothing to be ashamed of, Phil. Why, stuck at Highcliffe, what chance have any boys to find themselves girlfriends?'

'Not a great deal,' he said quietly. 'Although one or two chaps have boasted that they found some girls in Courtfield village are willing to toss them off for a shilling.'

'Well, I can do that of course, but I had something even nicer in mind.' I heaved myself up from the bed and added: 'Phil, take off your singlet, if you please.'

His eyes glistened as he yanked the garment over his head and then I ordered him to sit down on the bed and take off his shoes and socks.

'Now stand up,' I commanded and, as he obeyed me, with one quick tug I pulled down his shorts. I licked my lips in anticipation as I gazed at his broad chest, narrow waist and muscular thighs. But, of course, what attracted my fullest attention was his succulent thick prick, which was standing stiffly up to his belly-button.

I grabbed hold of his red-headed champion and he let out a shocked little cry when I slid my fist up and down the warm, throbbing shaft. As if drawn by an invisible magnet, my lips were drawn to the rounded helmet of Phil's magnificent chopper and I kissed the smooth knob, swirling my tongue all over the mushroom dome before sliding my lips around it and lashing my tongue around the fleshy pole. Ah, the salty tang tasted so masculine. I closed my lips around his cock and eased them forward to take in more of the shaft inside my mouth. In fact I tried to take too much of his cock down my throat and began to choke, forcing me to pull my head away. I spluttered: 'Goodness me, Phil, what a big boy you are. I think I'd better just take you in hand for the moment.'

In reply he could only sigh. 'Now do you like my titties?' I went on. 'Why don't you suck them for me whilst I play with your prick? I would like that very much.'

'So would I,' he panted and his hands pushed my breasts together as his tongue came out to lick the erect red nipples. His mouth opened and he drew in each tittie in turn which sent wild vibrations shooting through me. Then I guided his hand down to my hairy quim.

How my cunney pulsed out love juice in a hot, sticky wetness whilst Phil's tongue continued to circle my rubbery nipples as his hand moved in and out of my sopping crack. He found my pulsating clitty, pressing it and releasing it quite delightfully. Phil may never have fucked a girl before but, as he later informed me, he had petted with the wanton assistant matron at Highcliffe who had showed him how to tickle a clitty.

My back arched in ecstasy as his skilful fingers slithered over my erect clit, sending me into deliriums of pure joy as

I achieved a magnificent spend. Instinctively I grasped hold of his huge prick and he panted: 'Oh please suck my cock, Sophie. I've never experienced that pleasure which I understand is simply divine.'

'I'll do my best,' I said, determined to give Phil the sucking-off he deserved. I slid across his body and brought my lips down upon his twitching todger. Letting my tongue run up and down the full length of his blue-veined shaft, I licked up a pearly drop of jism which had formed around the tiny 'eye' on his knob. Then I opened my mouth as wide as possible and he jerked his hips upwards to force some three inches of his hot hard chopper into my mouth. When he heard my helpless gurgle, Phil pulled back slightly so that his throbbing tool lay motionless on my tongue. I sucked greedily on this giant cock which tasted quite delicious. I closed my lips around it, working on the bulbous knob as I circled the base of his shaft with my hand. My head bobbed slowly up and down as I managed to take in every last inch of his gorgeous truncheon until his bell-end was almost touching the back of my throat.

I sucked his cock with relish and Phil was clearly in the seventh heaven of delight when I cupped his wrinkled pink scrotum in my free hand, feeling it tighten as the spunk boiled up in his balls. But I wanted his pulsating pole in my love channel and I pulled my head away from his glistening shaft and said somewhat pompously: 'Phil, this is your moment of truth because it's time for you to fuck me. However, before we begin I want you to know how honoured I am to be the first recipient of your sticky emission. Try and take things slowly though, there's no rush.'

He needed no further urging and I lay on my back and spread my legs as the excited boy rolled on top of me. I kept my hand on his prick and guided him between my yielding love lips. Of course, he slammed in and out of my juicy cunt at great speed and how my cunney tingled as his youthful thick prick pounded into me with such exciting force. As I expected, he came almost immediately, shooting fierce jets of creamy spunk into my dripping crack, but happily the young rascal's cock remained stiff after his copious emission. I closed my thighs, making Phil part his own legs and lie on top of me with his cock sweetly trapped inside my cunt for the muscles of my cunney were gripping his tool so tightly that Phil could not move his palpitating prick forwards or backwards.

Then I ground my hips round, massaging his cock as it throbbed powerfully inside my sopping slit. At my whispered request, Phil grasped my bum cheeks whilst I eased the pressure around his shaft. He began to piston his prick wildly in and out of my drenched quim and I panted: 'There, Phil, your big stiff cock is deep inside my wet cunt and you're fucking me – now come inside my love funnel and then you can call yourself a fully-fledged man!'

As if on cue, his body went rigid and Phil pumped out a deluge of jism deep inside me whilst I pushed my pussey up against him, burying his cock even deeper inside me. His creamy essence bathed the walls of my cunney to make my whole body glow with excitement as I convulsed into my own shattering spend.

We lay still for a while and then Phil slowly pulled out his shrunken shaft and apologised for not being able to make the fuck last longer.

'Don't be silly, it's quality not quantity which counts,' I said with all the authority of a girl who had only experienced less than ten previous pokings! To show my gratitude I licked his lovely cock clean, savouring the tangy mix of his sperm and my own cuntal juices.

In the excitement of the moment I had quite forgotten that we had been watched by the other seven girls who

shared my dormitory, but I was reminded of this fact by
Alex and Babs who now came forward and sat on the bed.
Both were stark naked and when I hauled myself up to get
a towel to wipe my face, they slid down on either side of
Phil and moved their soft nude bodies closer against him.

'Mr Colnbrook, how did you manage to get away from
Highcliffe tonight?' asked Babs as she idly flipped Phil's
limp cock onto his thigh.

'And how are you going to get back inside?' enquired
Alex as she kissed him lightly on his heaving chest. 'Is there
a handy drainpipe you can shin up? No names, no pack
drill, but Sophie and I know a gentleman who uses this
method to meet his *amorata* right here at Dame Chasuble's.'

'Good for him, but I wanted to stay the night,' grinned
Phil. 'So when I received Heather's note about it being
worth my while to meet her at the gates of Dame Chasuble's
at ten o'clock this evening, I paid a chum of mine five
bob to forge a letter to the headmaster from my Uncle
Fred. He lives only about ten miles away just north of
Wheathampstead, so I got a note asking if I could stay the
night with him to meet an old friend of the family who
would otherwise not be able to see me before he left for a
six-month stay in South Africa.'

Babs now squeezed Phil's prick in her fist and slid her
hand up and down the burgeoning shaft. She looked up at
me as I sat myself down at the foot of my bed and said:
'Sophie, as a suffragist, you must agree that we girls
should share and share alike. Does this apply to Phil's
cock?'

I couldn't help chuckling at the audacity of the cheeky
girl, but I had no real objection and so I laughed: 'Help
yourself, Babs. I'm no expert on the male physique but if
Phil can raise another stand, as far as I'm concerned, you
and Alex are welcome to make whatever sport you want
with it.'

'Thank you, Sophie, though there's only one particular game I want to play,' she rejoined as she continued to massage Phil's swelling shaft, drawing back his foreskin and making the mushroom helmet leap and bound in her hand.

Now Alex joined in the fun and a hoarse whimper of delight escaped from Phil's lips when the blonde beauty planted a loving wet kiss on his uncapped knob. She raised her head and commented: 'I think Phil has a very pretty cock. Babs, let's see if we can suck him up to shape.'

'What a splendid idea!' enthused Babs as she cupped his hairy scrotum in her hands and bent her head to begin licking the underside of his shaft. Alex concentrated on his knob, swirling her tongue around the sensitive dome whilst Babs opened her mouth and sucked in one of his balls.

'Oh, my God!' groaned the lucky lad who was transported to a state of ecstasy when Babs transferred her attention from his balls and worked her moist tongue along the length of his quivering cock. She held the base of his cock whilst she returned to licking his balls. Alex pumped her head up and down, keeping her lips taut as she sucked Phil's cock with evident enjoyment.

Then Alex pulled her lips away to look at the pre-come juice which was already oozing out of his knob. Judging that Phil would not be able to hold back for much longer, she clamped her lips back over his cock and slurped noisily over the purple bell-end whilst Babs continued to suck his balls. Moments later Alex was proved right as with an anguished cry Phil ejaculated his third spend of the night into her mouth. She rubbed his pulsating penis as she sucked and swallowed his copious emission, milking his cock of every last drop of masculine jism until his member softened and he withdrew the limp shaft from her mouth.

Dear Phil was now utterly *hors de combat* and the girls decided that the safest way to smuggle him out was for me to set my alarm clock for the ungodly hour of five in the morning to allow him enough time to dress (he had brought a set of clothes in a small travelling case) and leave the school without being seen. Afterwards, Phil could then catch a train back to Highcliffe where he would be able to sit down for breakfast with his chums.

The initial part of the plan worked well – at the appointed time I had just woken up after a vivid dream and was just about to turn over and go back to sleep when the alarm let out a shrill ring and I saw Phil's arm snake out and press the silencer.

'Hello there, Phil, so you weren't asleep either,' I whispered in his ear. 'Isn't it strange how we are able to set our own mental alarms to wake ourselves up when we have to wake up early? Come on, Phil, rise and shine!'

'There isn't any need to get up yet, Sophie, we've heaps of time,' he answered softly. 'So let's first take up where we left off last night? When all's said and done, it is your birthday, and how better to celebrate it than with a grand fuck?'

It was difficult to fault Phil's logic so I simply giggled when he kissed me lightly on the lips. Although I warned him that he could find himself in serious trouble if he were caught inside the precincts of Dame Chasuble's, I simply could not resist the darling boy. Our mouths meshed together and his tongue forced its way between my teeth. Inexperienced he may have been, but Phil soon had me squirming with erotic excitement as his hands roamed all over my breasts and he rolled my hard, elongated titties up against his palms.

'You're very naughty,' I breathed as he guided my hand down to his throbbing tool which I clutched tightly as his own hand descended below. His fingertips twirled through the thatch of pussey hair until my cunney was aching to be satisfied.

I pulled him over me and muttered fiercely: 'Fuck me,

darling! Slide every inch of your thick cock in my cunney, you sweet boy!'

Not surprisingly, Phil Colnbrook was more than happy to obey and I sighed with happiness when I felt his knob nudge its way through my love lips and sheath itself inside my cunt which was already so juicy that he slid in his lovely cock to the hilt.

I stuffed a pillow underneath my bottom as he began pistoning into me with great pounding thrusts. My arse arched up and down to receive his majestic penis as his prick plunged deeper and deeper until my legs left the bed to wrap themselves around his back. My hands clutched his shoulders whilst his trusty todger squelched its way through the clinging walls of my love funnel. A moan of exquisite pleasure escaped from my lips whilst waves of sheer ecstasy spread out from my crotch to every fibre of my being.

How I adored the masterful way he fucked me, allowing me just enough leeway to writhe and twist to his thrusts, yet holding me strongly enough to keep our bodies glued together. His head lay between my breasts and he nuzzled his lips against my titties, sucking each tight little rosebud until it was as erect as Phil's cock which was ramming so exquisitely in and out of my sticky honeypot. I could even feel his balls swinging heavily against my bum cheeks.

'H-a-r-g-h! H-a-r-g-h! H-a-r-g-h!' I panted as he embedded himself inside me with a jerking thrust which mashed my clitty against his pubic bone. This made my gratified pussey disgorge a further rivulet of love juice and I found myself in the midst of a swirling pool of sensual ecstasy. I let out a low howl, throwing my head from side to side as I shuddered into a truly glorious spend.

'Time for my final ride, I think,' Phil panted whilst he stroked his cock in and out of my seething slit, penetrating my cunt with lightning force and speed. This brought me to the brink of a second orgasm and then, with a wicked grin, he stopped still and held his position until the sensation subsided. He did this again and now my body was screaming for release. Then, with one final thrust, his body stiffened and I felt the throb of liquid fire as his climax juddered to boiling point.

'Ahhhh!' I gasped as my cunt was flooded with spunk. His hot sticky froth spurted inside me and brought on my second spend which came in a sudden delicious rush of blissful sensation.

He lay quietly on top of me, careful to keep his still beefy shaft inside my buzzing love tunnel until we had both calmed down. Then he rolled off me and as we cuddled up together, I said: 'Phil, it's hard to believe that Alex, Babs and I were your first conquests. Perhaps I don't have enough experience to judge your performance, but it seemed to me that you shagged us in a most assured, knowing fashion.'

'Thank you very much,' he said modestly. 'To be honest, I just followed the advice given in *Fucking For Fun*, Doctor Jonathan Elstree's monthly column in *The Oyster*, an awfully jolly magazine which I'm sure you would enjoy far more than *The Girls' Own Journal*.'

[The Oyster *was perhaps the rudest of all the 'horn books' illicitly published around the turn of the century – Editor*].

'I'm sure I would,' I chuckled, though when I felt his cock swelling up against my thigh, I said with mock exasperation: 'Goodness me, Phil, you're quite insatiable! But there really isn't time for another fuck, do you want to get us both expelled?'

He raised his eyes to the ceiling and stroking his stiff-stander he sighed: 'No, of course not, Sophie, although it does seem a shame to waste this hard-on. I suppose a quick sucking-off is out of the question?'

'Please don't tempt me,' I begged as he tried to place my

hand on his throbbing tool. I pulled my hand away and added: 'I'm sure your mentor in *The Oyster* would agree that it isn't worth fucking looking at the clock instead of the cock.'

'I'm well rebuked,' smiled Phil and he slid out of bed and padded out quietly to the bathroom. For a few fleeting moments I lay back on the pillow, thinking how exciting it would be to join him there, rubbing my soapy hands all over his body as we plastered our bodies together. Then Phil would double me over and spreading my bum cheeks, he would stand behind me and plunge his prick in me doggie-style, his hard stiff cock slicking its way in and out of my sticky honeypot.

My pussey began to moisten during this intense erotic fantasy and I gave my clitty a long lingering rub before I came to my senses. With a heavy sigh, I threw off the eiderdown and swung my legs over the side of the bed. I slipped on my dressing gown and waited for Phil to finish his ablutions because I knew that if I went into the bath-room and looked at his thick penis swinging between his legs, I would be unable to resist the temptation to turn my sensual daydream into reality.

After we had dressed, Phil and I crept out into the corridor and made our way out through the back entrance. Luckily, we were undetected (or so I thought at the time) and we hurried away until we were well clear of the school buildings.

It was a glorious summer morning and so when Phil and I reached the gates I looked at my watch and saw that I still had a good three-quarters of an hour to spare until I needed to be back in the dining room for breakfast. I remarked: 'I've time to walk with you to the railway sta-tion. The quickest way is through Farmer Hutchinson's meadow. He doesn't mind people taking the short cut so long as they keep to the footpath.'

'Good idea,' Phil agreed and, holding hands, we strolled through the lush grass when all of a sudden he stopped dead in his tracks and exclaimed: 'Sophie, look over there on your right – can you see what I see in front of that grove of silver birch trees?'

Looking at Phil with a slightly puzzled expression, I peered towards where he was now pointing with his outstretched arm whilst he gave a short laugh and added: 'Am I dreaming? Is this some kind of sensuous mirage?'

My eyes widened whilst I took in the extraordinary scenario which was taking place only some hundred yards away from where we were standing. No wonder Phil had wondered whether he was hallucinating. Standing in his shirtsleeves behind a small box camera set up on a tripod was a good-looking young man and some six feet away stood a pretty girl who I immediately recognised as we took a few steps closer to the couple.

Her name was Celia Parker, the eighteen-year-old daughter of a prominent local landowner who had attended Dame Chasuble's as a day girl but who had left the school the previous summer. She was dressed – or rather undressed – in a flowing white dress made of such fine material that Phil and I could clearly make out the sensual curvy outlines of her figure. As we watched, she took up a classical pose with one leg slightly forward and her arms flung out above her head. From our vantage point we could see the dark bulges of her breasts pressing against the wafer-thin transparent material of the robe.

The young photographer was unknown to me. Oblivious to our presence, he bent down behind the camera and peering into the viewfinder he called out: 'Hold it there, Celia! Good, that should make a lovely photo. Not that I can claim any credit with such a gorgeous model.'

'You press the button, we do the rest,' laughed Celia, repeating the famous Kodak slogan. She pulled off her robe and stood stark naked in front of us whilst the photographer reloaded his camera with a new plate.

What a perfect picture of female pulchritude she made and how Phil and I drank in the delights of her nudity. Her face was finely formed with light chestnut hair falling down in rolled ringlets onto her shoulders. Her breasts were luxuriantly large, hard and firm and tipped with two delicate nut-brown nipples that were already jutting out in excitement.

I waved to Celia as we walked towards them. The couple did not seem embarrassed in the least by our presence. In fact Celia greeted us with a happy smile and exclaimed: 'Hello there, Sophie! How nice to see you! I didn't expect anyone from Dame Chasuble would be up and about so early. Now you don't know Charles Prince, do you? Charles's a friend of my brother and secretary of the Cambridge University Photographic Club.

'Charles, this is Sophie Starr, a former schoolmate of mine.'

'Good morning, Sophie,' said the young man and I said: 'Pleased to meet you, Mr Prince. May I introduce my friend Phil Colnbrook of Highcliffe School. Phil, this is Celia Parker and Charles Prince.'

Phil gave them a slight bow and Celia smiled: 'You're a fair way away from Highcliffe, Phil. Are you a masochist or are you in training for some forthcoming athletic event? Mind, you don't look as if you've been for an early-morning run.'

'Oh no, he stayed the night in our dorm,' I said matter-of-factly and went on to describe in full lurid detail how Phil had crossed into manhood by fucking Alex Henderson and Babs Fawcett as well as myself.

'I don't believe you!' declared Celia robustly, but Charles shrugged his shoulders and said good-humouredly: 'I do, there's a contented air about them that makes me think they've been on the nest all night – which is more than we have, thanks to your dear parents not allowing me to stay over at your place.'

He turned to us and added: 'I had to stay in St Albans last night and get up at five o'clock and cycle all the way to Celia's house this morning.'

'It will be worth it if the Royal Photographic Society accept your photographs for their next exhibition,' cried Celia gaily as she lifted her hands to run her fingers through her hair, a movement which lifted her breasts. I quickly glanced down to see two tell-tale bulges forming in the front of the boys' trousers as they goggled at the gorgeous nude girl.

Charles took several more photographs and then, after putting a fresh plate of film in the camera, he walked over and whispered something to Celia who giggled: 'I'm game if you are, my dear, and I doubt if Sophie and Phil will have any objections.'

'Object about what?' I enquired and Celia replied: 'Taking some photos of Charlie and myself in the nude. We want to enter the competition in *The Oyster* for photographs of *tableaux vivants*. Count Gewirtz of Galicia [*one of the famous wealthy cosmopolitan friends of King Edward VII – Editor*] has generously donated the first prize of one thousand guineas and four runners-up prizes of two hundred and fifty guineas so I'm sure there will be a great number of entries.'

[*Tableaux vivants were theatrical entertainments in which a narration of Greek, Roman or Indian mythology, well-known historical events or even Biblical stories was accompanied by actresses dressed (or rather undressed) in poses to accompany the lecture. The girls usually wore body stockings but occasionally they posed bare-breasted on the strict understanding that they never moved. The ban on nudity on the British stage was not removed until the abolition of stage censorship in 1968 – Editor*]

'I don't mind taking some naughty photos, though I would expect to be given a percentage of any prize money,' I said and Charles nodded.

'I'm more than happy to give you ten per cent of anything we win – that might not sound very much but, to be quite candid, all you have to do is to press the button.'

'Sounds fair enough,' I agreed and took my place with Phil behind the camera whilst Charles ripped open his shirt and then sat down to remove his shoes and socks. He rapidly completed undressing and stood up naked, his cock swelling thick and hard.

Now I've never been one to dwell on the size of a man's prick but I readily confess that there is something about the sight of an erect cock which stirs me profoundly – and this was such a beautiful specimen, the shaft creamy pale and smooth with a tracing of pink running up the underside from his wrinkled ballsack to the moist ruby helmet flaring out from the pulled-back collar of foreskin. My pussey was already moistening whilst Charles walked towards Celia, holding his magnificent penis tightly in his hand, stroking the shaft until it stood up against his stomach. He called out to me: 'Sophie, shout out when you're ready to take a shot and we'll then try to keep still.'

He clasped Celia in his arms, his pulsing prick standing high up against his stomach like a blue-veined marble column and she gasped with satisfaction as she arched her hips forward to feel Charles' hot thick chopper against her flesh.

'Look towards me,' I cried. She rose up on the balls of her feet to experience the delicious feel of his rock-hard rammer directly against her pussey and after I snapped the voluptuous scene, Celia tilted her head to receive his mouth upon her full red lips.

In the next shot, Charles caressed the silky smoothness of Celia's back, his hands stroking deeply into her shoulders and down along her spine. Then their knees buckled and in a trice they were rolling around on the soft, warm grass. This took them out of my picture but Phil showed me how to take the camera off the tripod and, placing it in my hands, he said: 'If you want a first-class picture, you'll have to go down on your hands and knees. Then, once you have them in your sights, just remember to keep the camera steady when you're ready to take the snap.'

'Thanks for the tip,' I said gratefully. Following his instructions, I sank to my knees and watched Charles lower his body on top of Celia's with one of his legs dangling between her thighs. He heaved himself up to sit across her thighs, his legs gripping her hips as he cupped her jiggling breasts with his hands, letting his fingers trace patterns across the snow-white globes, gently tweaking the ripe erect nipples. Then he moved his body forward and I concentrated on catching the expression of lustful anticipation on Celia's face as she pulled his upwardly curved cock towards her mouth.

'Hold it there, please,' I instructed the lubricious couple. Charles slid the crown of his cock between Celia's waiting lips and I took an excellent shot of the nubile girl holding her lover's throbbing tool in a firm yet tender embrace whilst she moved her mouth along the fleshy shaft, licking, lapping, sucking, moving her mouth faster and faster as she placed one hand under his tightening ballsack.

I would have taken another photograph but then I felt my skirt being lifted up and I turned my head to see Phil kneeling behind me, his trousers and pants around his ankles and his naked cock stiffly waving upwards. Before I could say anything, the cheeky lad proceeded to roll down my knickers and slide his cock between my quivering bum cheeks.

'You naughty boy!' I scolded him, although I was hardly displeased by his passion and indeed I raised my buttocks slightly as I reached round for his cock and guided him home. With one vigorous shove the frisky young man began to fuck me doggie-style, burying his big cock inside my juicy cunt. His balls slapped nicely against my thighs as I fitted easily into the rhythm of Phil's fucking and I settled down to enjoy the delicious sensations as his shaft see-sawed in and out of my dripping crack.

In the meantime, no doubt worried that he would spend before I had finished taking the necessary pictures, Charles had withdrawn his glistening boner from Celia's sweet mouth. I heard her say to him: 'Lick out my pussey before you fuck me, darling.'

'What a splendid suggestion,' he answered, smiling his assent as he athletically sprang up. I focused the camera upon the mossy tuft of brown pussey hair at the base of Celia's belly as Charles knelt between her parted thighs.

Without further ado, he parted the crisp curls with his fingers to reveal her damp, inviting love lips which opened to reveal the red chink of Celia's cunney channel. It was obvious that Phil had been further aroused by this lascivious sexual play because he thrust into me at an even faster pace, clasping my breasts whilst I worked my bottom from side to side so that he could embed every inch of his palpitating prick inside my sopping snatch.

My buttocks rotated as Phil's rigid rod slammed home. It was clearly impossible for me to take any more photographs until we had completed this fuck, so I reached back and gently squeezed his balls. This made Phil come immediately and he spunked in a great shudder, a fountain of jism pouring out of his twitching cock into my agitated love funnel.

Now I could concentrate upon my photographic duties and I refocused the lens to see that Charles was now lying on his belly between Celia's legs, one hand under her backside to provide additional elevation and the other reaching around her lissome thigh so that he was able to spread her pussey lips with his thumb and middle finger. I did not interrupt them but simply snapped the raunchy pair. Celia purred with pleasure when Charles placed his lips over her swollen clitty and sucked it into his mouth where doubtless his tongue washed over the sensitive love button.

Celia became very excited and thrashed about as he increased the vibrations of his tongue, wrenching out tiny yelps of enjoyment as she wrapped her thighs around him as he slurped away on her juicy honeypot until he must have been swimming in a veritable sea of lubricity.

'Ooooh, that is heavenly! More! More! H-a-r! There I go, you've sent me off!' she shrieked, her body twisting and turning in a delicious climax whilst Charles gulped down the flow of cuntal juice which was pouring from her pussey.

When he had finished, he scrambled up to lie on top of her. Slipping his hands around her back to clutch her lovely bum cheeks, he remarked: 'I'm so glad you climaxed, my dear. Like most men, I find that sucking pussies can be hard work but it's well worth the effort when your partner achieves an orgasm. However, I trust your quim is ready for another spend because I'm dying to fuck you and drench your cunney with spunk.'

'Tell me first exactly how you would want to fuck me,' she begged.

Charles smiled as he answered: 'First I shall mount you and lie on your belly as I push my long thick prick between your love lips until every inch of my chopper is inside your juicy little cunt and when I feel the clingy muscles of your cunney grip my cock – but you'll see for yourself what happens from there.'

He moved over her surprisingly quickly, smoothing his hands over her breasts which sent Celia into fresh raptures of delight. Then, as promised, he crashed on top of her trembling body, hungrily searching for her mouth. They exchanged a burning kiss whilst they moved their thighs together until their pubic muffs were rubbing roughly together. I approached them to obtain some close-up shots and I managed to shoot an excellent snap of Charles's thick shaft probing the entrance to Celia's exquisitely formed crack. He lifted himself up on his hands and knees and I was able to shoot a picture of his wide-domed helmet forcing its way into the squelchy wetness of Celia's cunt.

Like a steel bolt, his prick rode thickly through her juicy honeypot, separating the folds of gluey skin and he pushed further and further inside until his cock was fully ensconced inside her love channel, pausing only when he was prevented from further progress by the jamming together of their loins.

'What a wonderfully tight wet notch you have, Celia,' breathed Charles, his lithe body rising up and down as he thrust his sinewy shaft in and out of her delectable honeypot.

'Thank you for the compliment but don't waste your breath,' she gasped in reply. 'No more talking, Charles, just fuck me. Oooh! Oooh! That's the way, you lovely big-cocked boy!'

He gritted his teeth and reached round to clasp hold of her bucking bum cheeks as they rocked in sensual harmony. His cock slithered in and out of her sopping crack as he pistoned himself deep, deep inside her. Celia's eyes were shining and such a beautiful colour suffused her cheeks that I thought to myself what a pity it was that this could not be captured on my photographs. I clicked the shutter one last time.

Charles must have felt his orgasm welling in his balls for

he now withdrew all but his knob from Celia's cunney. She whimpered in concern but then he plunged forward again to the hilt and repeated this delicious movement until the length of his shaft was coated in her aromatic love juice. As he lunged to and fro he panted in a voice husky with lust: 'There we go, Celia, can you feel my cock reaming out your pussey?'

'Yes, yes, y-e-s-s-s!' she screamed out and he added his fingers to rub her clitty whilst he continued to pound his rampant rod in and out of her slippery slit. This was very much to Celia's liking and very soon her entire body stiffened and she screamed out: 'I'm coming, Charlie, I'm coming! Flood my cunt with spunk, you randy rascal!'

Celia's cuntal spendings trickled down her thighs and his cock fairly vibrated as it slid in and out of her quim faster and faster. Then, with a hoarse cry, he jetted a torrent of creamy jism into her sated quim before slumping down on top of her. The couple sighed with happiness as they dissolved into that unique state of bliss which heralds the ebbing away of such a fervent fuck.

'M'mm, that was a gorgeous poke, darling,' said Celia as she cradled his head in her hands. 'Wouldn't it be wonderful if Sophie managed to capture some of our passion in her photographs?'

'It would certainly be the icing on the cake,' he laughed and as he rolled off her and scrambled to his feet, I looked at my wrist-watch and observed that Phil and I had to take our leave without delay or we would both find ourselves in the most horrendous trouble.

I handed the camera back to Charles who said he would send me a set of prints from the negatives. There was now no time for me to accompany Phil to the railway station for, unless I walked back briskly, I might miss breakfast and this was something I did not want to do. Since that day I have discovered that fucking sharpens my appetite and, in place of Benger's Peptonised Beef Jelly, I recommend a good poke to stimulate the gastric juices.

'I'll write to you very soon,' pledged Phil as we embraced and he too took off at a smart pace in order not to miss the next train to Highcliffe.

Fortunately I returned to Dame Chasuble's in time to take my place in the dining hall where I was forced to promise the girls that I would give them a detailed blow-by-blow account of my sensuous adventures.

Chapter Two

At the conclusion of afternoon lessons, my classmates cele-
brated my birthday with a grand tea held in the Common
Room with a *pièce de résistance* of a magnificent birthday
cake complete with seventeen small candles which, to great
applause, I blew out in one big breath.

Furthermore, later that evening I was given a further
unexpected birthday treat. How this came about is best
explained by recording the events which took place before
lights-out. My friends and I had listened to a lecture
complete with magic lantern slides, given by Babs Fawcett's
cousin Frank who, as an employee of the family firm of
coffee merchants, travels extensively to the Far East. He
was introduced to us by Miss Randall before we sat down to
supper. During the meal, Babs gleefully informed us that a
certain lady buyer at one of the large department stores in
London had told Frank that if he wanted an order to supply
the emporium with coffee beans, he would first have to give
her a good fucking.

'He has also enjoyed passionate affairs with Lady Angela
Sykes and two of the pretty young daughters of Lord
Dashwood,' she added with a giggle. 'And between
ourselves, I seduced Frank myself at a family gathering
during the Easter holidays.'

To a low murmur of agreement, Alex commented: 'I'm
not surprised, he's a very attractive young man.'

Indeed, it was easy to see why we were all so attracted to

Frank Fawcett. He was slim and tall with a shock of curly chestnut hair, deep brown eyes with a straight nose and full, sensual lips. He was also lucky enough to possess a beautifully even set of gleaming white teeth. These were set off so well by his bronzed complexion which he owed to his travels in countries with sunnier climates than our own.

Naturally we were all keen to hear how Babs lured Frank into her bed and after we had retired to the common room, Heather Adamson said to her: 'Come on, Babs, spill the beans! You must know that we're all dying to hear what Frank was like between the sheets.'

'You naughty cats!' exclaimed Babs, flashing her a wicked little smile. 'Well, I don't really mind giving you chapter and verse about it so long as everyone here promises never to breathe a word about it to Frank or anyone else in my family.'

After we had sworn faithfully to keep her secret, Babs continued: 'If you must know, the morning after the dinner party at my Uncle Arthur and Aunt Bertha's country house up in Oxfordshire, I pleaded a headache when they took their guests for a walk through the village. The truth of the matter was that I was feeling lazy and preferred to sit in the garden with the copy of *The Oyster* which was lying in a sealed envelope at the back of the wardrobe in my bedroom.

'So when everyone had left the house, I wandered upstairs to pick up my magazine. As I was crossing the landing, I heard what sounded like the creak of bedsprings coming from Frank's bedroom. The door was closed and normally I would have ignored the noise, but there had recently been a spate of house-breaking in the vicinity which is why I bent down to put my eye to the keyhole to see if anything was amiss – and goodness me, what a huge shock I got for my trouble!'

'Why, was there a burglar in the room?' I enquired and Babs shook her head. 'Oh no, It was only Frank, but what astounded me was that he was lying naked on the bed holding

66

a book in one hand and massaging his stiff, swollen shaft with the other! He had pulled down the white-skinned jacket from his knob which was gleaming in the bright morning sunshine as his hand slicked up and down his twitching tool.

'After the effect of the initial shock had worn off, I peered at his lithe muscular torso with interest and admiration but of course my eyes kept swivelling back to his thick erect prick and large wrinkled ballsack. A warm glow spread all over me whilst I watched him rub his meaty boner. When I felt a moistness spreading out from my pussey, I pulled up my dress and began to finger my cunney through the flimsy material of my knickers. I felt randier and randier whilst I gave my pussey a thorough fingering, but then I heard the footsteps of one of the servants on the stairs and realised that I would have to move on in a few seconds. Instinctively I turned the handle of Frank's door which opened to my touch and without further ado I marched straight in.

'Poor Frank's face was a picture! In an instant all the colour drained from his cheeks as he dropped the book and with only limited success, he attempted to cover his cock and balls with his hands.

'"God Almighty, what are you doing here, Babs? I understood that everyone was going out for a hike," Frank spluttered wildly. I couldn't help laughing out loud as he squirmed with embarrassment. Then I took pity on him and remarked: "Well, It's elementary, my dear Frank, as Sherlock Holmes would say. One must never assume anything and if you decide to lie down in the nude and frig your cock, commonsense should tell you always to take the precaution of first locking the door."

'"It's hardly an onerous chore," I added as I slipped the bolt. Then I walked purposefully towards him and sat down on the bed to take a closer look at his proud prick. My blood was up and I did not waste time in any preliminary foreplay.

Without as much as a by your leave, I pulled his hands away to reveal his beefy truncheon which was no longer erect but still thick with unslaked passion.

'"Babs, what the deuce—" he began but his voice trailed off when I reached for his cock. It immediately sprang up to its fullest extent in my hand. I gave his rock-hard boner a friendly squeeze before releasing it and then I unbuttoned my blouse and slid the garment off my shoulders. Frank looked on open-mouthed whilst I continued undressing until I too was naked. My cousin's cock throbbed with desire as I lay on my back. Opening my legs, I slowly drew my forefinger down the slit of my tingling quim. Then I grabbed hold of his pulsing prick and pulled him across me, letting the knob rub against my bushy mound.

'To his credit, Frank somehow managed to stop himself sliding his helmet between my puffy love lips and he whispered hoarsely: "Babs, are you certain you want me to fuck you? It's not that I don't want to, mind, but you must say now if you want me to stop because in a few seconds it will be too late, though if I do continue, I'll take care not to come inside you."

'"But I do want you to fuck me, Frank," I assured him, sliding my hand up and down his quivering cock. "And as I shall be starting the monthly curse tomorrow or the next day, you can shoot off inside me."

'As I finished speaking, I eased his knob inside my love channel, spreading my thighs well apart to enable him to push his full length into my juicy cunt. Once he was fully embedded, I urged him to fill my pussey with his spunky cream.

'"Aaaah!" he panted as his shaft slid into its desired haven. Every last nerve in my body thrilled in exquisite rapture as I heaved up to meet his thrusts, winding my legs around him so that his heavy ballsack banged against my bum cheeks as he pistoned his prick at a pacey rate of knots in and out of my squelchy snatch. Any inhibitions Frank may have felt were now forgotten as he fucked me with deep long plunges that almost mashed my clitty against his pubic bone. My cuntal juices were already flowing so freely that when he suddenly stopped reaming out my cunt and held his prick quite still inside my quim, it sent a series of tiny electric shocks speeding through my trembling frame.

'When these spasms subsided and I lay gasping for breath, Frank began stroking into me again, moving with lightning speed for perhaps a full minute until I screamed out my orgasm. Then I gloried in the rush of liquid warmth as, with every throb of his quivering cock, jets of his creamy spunk shot into my sated love funnel.'

'Sounds as if you had a great time together,' said Heather with a twinge of envy in her voice. Babs chuckled: 'Gosh, I'll say we did, but it was impossible to continue because the housemaids wanted to make up Frank's bedroom. So we had to get dressed and, as fate would have it, we never managed to find any privacy for the remainder of our stay.'

'Well, I've a good idea,' I declared thoughtfully. 'Why don't we arrange for you and Frank to get together again after his talk? Alex, you wouldn't mind letting them use our study, would you?'

'Of course not! To make things more comfortable, I'll pop up to the dorm and sneak a couple of pillows into our study,' replied my pretty blonde friend. She stood up and looked at her watch. 'Look, you had better make your way to the lecture room if you want to get the best seats. Save one for me because I'll meet you there.'

Miss Randall and Frank were already on the platform when we filed into the crowded lecture room. From the knowing expression on her face when she stood up to say a few words before Frank's discourse, I am sure that Miss Randall was aware that it was Frank's good looks rather than an interest in coffee which had drawn such a large attendance! Certainly, none of the girls could have had any idea of the sensational happenings which occurred shortly after the magic lantern was switched on . . .

However, at first all went well and Frank proved himself to be a fluent speaker. He began by telling us that magic powers were attributed to coffee soon after its introduction in Europe during the sixteenth century. In the Netherlands, plants were carefully kept alive in greenhouses and many were offered as rare gifts to visiting dignitaries. He went on: 'One Dutch sailor was even convinced that coffee would make him immortal but unfortunately he died soon afterwards after falling down a flight of stairs in a drunken stupor!'

Frank slid the first slide into the lantern which showed an Amsterdam café with some Dutch words scribbled in chalk on a blackboard. As he explained: 'This is an old Dutch tradition. When the café opens up in the morning, a waiter puts out a sign that says "the coffee is ready".

'Of course, the Dutch are great coffee drinkers and in France breakfast is unimaginable without a large cup of *café au lait* whilst lunch and dinner are concluded by sipping a demi-tasse of *café noir*. In Germany, coffee is the centre of an important social ritual in the afternoons known as the *kaffee-klatsch*. This refers to the generous amount of gossip exchanged between the ladies who gather around the coffee-pot. But from my own experience, I can tell you there is nowhere in the world where you can order so many delicious varieties of the beverage accompanied by a wide selection of cream cakes as you will find in the coffee-houses of Prague and Vienna.'

Now at the start of the Spring Term, Miss Randall had purchased a new magic lantern which has a double changing stage raised and lowered by a brass lever so that framed slides can be shown without any gap between them, with such a quick action that the change of slides is almost imperceptible. So the picture on the screen changed immediately to a coffee plantation in the East Indies as Frank continued: 'Coffee berries grow on shrubs which bear white jasmine-like flowers all year round. The berry, consisting of a fleshy pulp and two seeds joined by even planes side by side, is hand-picked as soon as it is ripe although it takes eight years before the fruit of a shrub can be harvested for the first time. The annual yield of one shrub is a scant two pounds of coffee beans.

'The best yield comes from *Coffea robusta* but the finest flavours are obtained from *Coffea arabica* which is produced in Central and South America as well as in Africa.' He changed the slide and after a few seconds of shocked silence, it was at this stage of the proceedings that pandemonium broke loose!

For what appeared on the screen was not a picture of Costa Rican peasants harvesting the coffee crop, but a hand-tinted colour photograph of a beautiful naked mulatto girl seated on the lap of her equally nude Negro lover – but she had lifted her bottom for the camera so that the viewer was given sight of the man's huge thick stiffie, about half of which was already implanted inside her cunney. Her arms were around his neck and her face was turned up, beaming with the satisfaction she was clearly experiencing in her well-plugged pussey.

'Great Scott!' gasped Frank. He hastily moved on to the next slide, but this brought no relief because it showed two pretty young girls in a loving clinch, their bodies pressed tightly together with their arms wrapped around each other's chubby bum cheeks.

The lecture-room now resounded to cheers and laughter from the audience until Babs' highly embarrassed cousin pulled the slides out of the machine and Miss Randall marched up in front of the screen. In a voice that would have done credit to a barrack-square sergeant-major, she called out: 'Quiet! Quiet! This lecture is now terminated – you will all go back to your studies and common rooms and remain there until bed-time.'

Alex, Babs and I filed out with the rest of the girls but we lingered in the corridor after Miss Randall swept imperiously past us. We slipped back inside the room where a red-faced Frank was packing his slides into a travelling case.

'Congratulations, darling! You really are a devil! I would never have believed that anyone might have the nerve to pull off a crazy jape like that,' cried out Babs with genuine admiration, but Frank looked up at her in astonishment and exclaimed: 'What are you talking about, Babs? That sort of wheeze is all very well among close friends but I wouldn't go in for the kind of stunts which will cause embarrassment to so many young ladies. Anyhow, I'm hardly likely to play a practical joke which puts me in such a highly discomfiting situation. After all, how the deuce am I going to apologise to Miss Randall?'

Babs' face fell and she muttered: 'Oh, I'm sorry, Frank, I thought you might deliberately have placed one or two naughty slides in the magic lantern to spice up your talk.'

'No, that would not be my style at all,' he replied coldly but then his face broke out into a grin and he added: 'Though to be honest, Babs, it did cross my mind as to whether you or one of your friends might have been responsible for interfering with my slides.'

This remark gave Babs enough ammunition to go onto the attack. 'Frank! How could you even think such a thing?' she said indignantly, wagging a reproving finger at her cousin. 'Anyhow, I can't think of anyone who might be able to lay her hands on such rude slides, although I'm sure that everyone except Miss Randall preferred the outrageous pictures to boring old photographs of coffee beans.'

Now it was Frank's turn to apologise which he did with good grace. Babs introduced Alex and myself to her cousin before inviting him to join us for a drink before he left the premises.

'Thank you, that would be very nice, but I had better first make my peace with Miss Randall,' grinned Frank and I chipped in: 'Fine, let me show you where her rooms are and then I'll wait outside to take you back to our study. We'll make you a nice cup of coffee if that's what you prefer, but Alex smuggled in a bottle of cognac at the beginning of term and you'll need a nip to steady your nerves after being carpeted by Miss Randall.'

'I expect I will,' agreed Frank and we helped him load his slides into his case, which Alex and Babs took with them as I accompanied him to Miss Randall's quarters. I expected to hear raised voices as I stood outside the headmistress's door, but in fact all I could make out was Frank's fulsome apologies for inadvertently showing his audience slides fit only for houses of ill-repute.

To my surprise, he emerged five minutes later with his handsome face creased in smiles of relief. 'Well, it's plain that you didn't get hauled over the coals after all,' I observed and he nodded: 'Not in the slightest, Sophie. I must say that Miss Randall is a very understanding lady. After I gave her my word that I had never seen those slides before in my life and had absolutely no idea as to how they came to be in my possession, she said: "Well, if I accept what you say – which of course I do – then that means we have both been the victims of a foolish practical joke. Whilst I would not put it past some of my more exuberant pupils to perpetrate such an outrageous prank, I cannot see how they could have done so because I don't believe your bag ever left your side since you arrived here."

' "In that case I owe you a further apology on behalf of the idiotic acquaintance of mine, whoever he may be, who

73

switched the slides," I replied and we shook hands and decided it would be best to forget all about the unfortunate incident.'

'Good, I'm very glad that we've also escaped censure,' I commented as we reached the door of our study where Alex and Babs were impatiently waiting to greet us.

Alex's bottle of cognac was immediately opened to celebrate Miss Randall's decision to draw a curtain over the whole affair of Frank's lecture. Of course, we still wanted to know how the rude slides had found their way into his case.

'You must have some idea as to who put them there,' remarked Babs and Frank grinned ruefully and said: 'Yes, there can be only one explanation. The truth is that I had a rather wild time last Saturday afternoon with Giles Horrabin, an old chum of mine from my 'Varsity days.'

'Giles Horrabin,' said Alex thoughtfully. 'Now that name rings a bell somewhere. Oh yes, didn't he have a fling with Lady Horne? I remember seeing them pictured together in *The Tatler* at the Berkeley Square Ball.'

He nodded: 'That's the chap, although there was nothing between him and Lady Horne except their shared passion for music. Giles has a fine tenor voice and Lady Horne is an accomplished pianist who has recently accompanied him at several charity concerts in London.

'Mind, Giles is a great cocksman too. I was hardly surprised when he arrived unannounced at my apartment at noon last Saturday with two pretty chorus girls from the new revue at the Holborn Empire. Of course I could have sent him away for I had planned to spend the evening working on the script for tonight's lecture. However, he also brought with him a luncheon hamper from the Army and Navy Stores and insisted on dragging me out to Regent's Park for a picnic.'

'Not that I needed much persuasion for it was a warm, sunshiny day, perfect for eating *al fresco*, whilst Dolly and

Paula proved themselves to be light-hearted carefree companions and we had a very jolly time. Anyhow, at about five o'clock we staggered back to my place – my flat is just off Prince Albert Road. Unfortunately Dolly stumbled over a loose paving stone and although she didn't fall, the poor girl strained her back. She was forced to lean heavily upon my shoulder until we reached Charlbert Mansions.

[*If anything it is surprising that Dolly was the only casualty on this journey for in 1907 a picnic luncheon basket for four people from the Army and Navy Stores contained Veal and Ham Pie, Roast Lamb and Mint Sauce, Roast Fowl, Cut Ham, Salad, Cheese, Cake, Pastries and Bread Rolls plus four bottles of champagne, one bottle of sherry or whisky, two bottles of claret and half a dozen bottles of mineral water! Linen and cutlery were also provided and the cost (including the hire of the hamper) was £3 6s 7d or £3.33! – Editor*]

'Once inside Giles and Paula disappeared into my bedroom whilst Dolly hobbled to the bathroom. When she returned I enquired whether her ankle now felt any easier. "Yes, thank you," replied the pert little red-head. "But I've strained a muscle in my back and I'd be really grateful if you would massage it for me."

'"By all means," I replied as I hauled myself to my feet. "Although it's only fair to warn you that I have never massaged anyone before."

'"Never mind, I'm sure that a resourceful chap like you will make an excellent masseur," smiled Dolly who had obviously shed her underwear in the bathroom, for before I could say Jack Robinson she slipped off her dress and stood in front of me stark naked except for a pair of frilly cream knickers. However, I was only given a brief glimpse of her delectable bare breasts because she then turned her back on me and lay face downwards on my new Chesterfield sofa.

'"Just rub my back, Frank," she murmured and as the saucy girl swiftly wiggled down her knickers to expose her gloriously rounded buttocks, she deliberately parted her thighs so that I was given full view of her pussey as well as her tiny wrinkled bum hole.'

'I'll wager your cock was now as stiff as a board,' Babs chimed in as Frank swigged down his third large cognac and he replied: 'Of course it was, but for all I knew Dolly could have simply wanted a massage and I had no desire to force any unwanted attentions upon her. So all I did was to take off my jacket and kneeling over her, I put my hands on her shoulders and gently rubbed the smooth warm flesh with my fingertips.'

'However it turned out that Dolly did want more than a massage,' I said drily and Frank chuckled: 'Yes, I'm glad to say she did, although she did compliment me on the lightness of my touch. After I had smoothed my hands all the way down her back and over the soft rounded hillocks of her backside, she purred: "M'mm, that was very relaxing, Frank. Now I can think of something else you can do to finish off the treatment, but you'll have to take your clothes off first. I don't have to spell it out, do I?"

'For reply I began kissing her, starting at the nape of her neck whilst I frantically tore off my shirt. I rained kisses down Dolly's back as I divested myself of the rest of my clothes. Just as I pulled down my pants, she turned over to sprawl upon her back, running her forefinger down the prominent pink love lips which jutted out from the unruly mass of auburn curls around her crotch.

'She flung her legs invitingly open and the soft globes of her breasts acted like magnets to my roving hands. Our lips pressed together in a passionate open-mouthed kiss from which she broke away to gasp: "Fuck me, Frank! Oh, I must have your cock inside me right now!"

'Throwing her arms around my neck, she thrust her tongue back into my mouth with all the wild abandon of uninhibited lust. I jabbed my hips forward to sink my shaft in her waiting cunt. But I missed the moistened opening so Dolly placed her hand around my throbbing tool and directed my knob between the puffy love lips. Once safely inside, I plunged deep inside her clingy crack, stretching the resilient love funnel to its utmost as together we rode the wind.

'What a glorious fuck this turned out to be! It was nothing less than sublime ecstasy to hold Dolly's creamy bum cheeks and suck her erect rosy titties whilst I slewed my cock in and out of her supple, lubricious cunney. How she yelped when she felt the tip of my prick touch the innermost wall of her juicy cunt. She clamped her thighs around my waist, squealing with delight as I pumped away, her body bucking and twisting in time with my pistoning chopper to maximise her pleasure.

'"Ahhh! Ahhh! Keep ramming in that fat cock," wailed Dolly as she writhed in delicious agitation. Our pent-up ecstatic bliss reached its peak. After only three or four more rapid, impetuous thrusts of my trusty tool, her body jerked upwards and her fingernails clawed up and down my back whilst she shuddered her way through a fulfilling, all-embracing climax.

'I spunked only seconds later, my cock spouting a stream of milky jism into Dolly's sopping slit which mingled with her own copious rivulets of cuntal nectar that were already running down her thighs. When I was spent I collapsed down upon her, almost fainting with fatigue after this session of short but torrid love-making.

'When we had recovered our senses, Dolly and I marched into the bedroom to watch Giles fuck Paula doggie-style and we later joined in to make up a "whoresome foursome" but that's another story.'

He finished his drink and Alex refilled his glass whilst Babs produced a pack of playing cards and suggested that we teach Frank the rules for our special form of pontoon which we often played in the dormitory after 'lights out'.

Frank pretended to be horrified at the idea and re-monstrated: 'Babs, you shock me! My goodness, Dame Laetitia Chasuble would surely turn in her grave if she knew that games of chance were taking place within this august seat of learning.'

She shook her head and giggled: 'Dame Laetitia shouldn't be too upset because we don't play for money and the rules couldn't be any simpler. On each deal, all the losers must take off an article of clothing. Whoever is naked first leaves the game until there is only one person left with any clothes on.'

'And presumably that person is the winner, but if you don't play for money, what is the reward for her achieve-ment?' Frank enquired. I answered: 'Well, she has the choice of which players she would like to share her bed with for the rest of that night but we don't have to wait till then if we begin the game now.'

Frank must have realised there and then that this was a game in which he had to come out on top because if he won the game, he could have whichever one of us he wished to fuck. On the other hand, even if he lost, Frank knew that the winning girl would pick him to give her a good poking!

Babs shuffled the pack and dealt out two cards to herself and the other players. 'Twist or stick?' she asked Frank and he said: 'I'll stick with these, thank you.'

'What about you, Sophie?' she demanded and, having the ten of spades and the nine of hearts in my hand, I also refused the offer of a further card. 'You too, Alex?' said Babs and when Alex replied that she would twist, Babs flicked over the three of hearts onto the table in front of her. However, to my amazement, Alex threw down her cards and announced that she had 'bust'!

'Bust! Wait a minute, that means you must have twisted on nineteen,' I exclaimed with a frown. 'Oh come now, Alex, that's cheating.'

She looked at me with wide-eyed innocence. 'Take that back, Sophie, how can it be cheating to take a gamble?'

Nevertheless Babs joined my protest and after a short heated debate it was agreed that players could not twist when holding cards worth eighteen points or over. Well, as luck would have it, I was fortunate enough to lose several hands in succession and I was wearing only my knickers when dear Babs dealt me the nine of spades and the six of clubs and when the next card turned out to be the eight of diamonds, Alex and Babs sportingly congratulated me on being the first to lose all my clothes.

'Babs, why don't we pop round to Heather's study for a chat?' suggested Alex, giving me a broad wink as she added: 'I have the feeling that Sophie would appreciate the opportunity of entertaining Frank on her own for half an hour or so.'

'I'm sure she would,' said Babs drily as she heaved herself up from her chair. After she had reluctantly followed Alex out of the room, Frank licked his lips when I stood up and slowly rolled down my knickers. Little more needs to be added but Frank then pulled me into his arms and kissed my naked breasts with a wild, avid hunger. The handsome boy kissed me on the mouth, long and deep, until my hands came around his neck and we were both shaking with passion. We sank down upon the carpet and I helped Frank to tear off the rest of his clothes. I pulled down his drawers and I gasped with wonderment at Frank's colossal cock which sprang upwards from a mossy thatch of dark curls at the base of his belly.

I just had time to notice how his thick shaft curved slightly to the left as it stood sprightly to attention against his lean muscular torso before Frank gathered me back into his arms and said in a husky voice: 'Sophie, you are truly the most exquisite creature I have ever seen. What beautiful breasts you have, so firm and yet so gently rounded.'

As Frank spoke his hands caressed the contours of my bosoms, making me purr with pleasure. He continued to massage the soft globes, rolling my engorged nipples into erection between his clever fingers. My pussey soon became decidedly damp, moistening like a dew-drenched flower in eager anticipation of what I knew would soon follow.

In no time at all I had melted away under his loving touch. After we had exchanged the most passionate of kisses, he whispered in my ear: 'How delicious your cunt looks with such gorgeous pouting love lips protruding through your silky bush of pussey hair. May I pay homage to this divine little quim before I fuck you?'

Now to be honest, I would not have minded in the least if Frank had wanted to fuck me without this admittedly pleasing titillation – but fortunately I decided that, if nothing else, politeness demanded I accede to his request. I say fortunately because Frank showed himself to be an adept master of cunnilingus. Indeed, if there were to be a contest in this art at the forthcoming Olympic Games [*which were held twelve months later at the White City, London in the summer of 1908 – Editor*], I am certain that Frank Fawcett would be in contention for a gold medal!

He began by placing one of the pillows Alex had brought in from the dormitory beneath my bottom. Then he pushed my knees up to my breasts before parting them, thus exposing my light auburn bush which exactly matches the colour of the long tresses of silky brown hair which tumble across my shoulders.

Then he kissed my knees and the insides of my thighs as his lips made their inexorable way down towards my pussey. I clasped my legs around his head and let out a yelp when I felt his tongue gently slide through the labia. Soon I was moaning with delight as the first tingles of delicious sensuous rapture coursed through my cunney.

By now my clitty was peeping out and Frank placed his lips over the fleshy love bud and sucked it into his mouth whilst he slid one hand under my bottom to pull me even closer to him. With the other, he spread open my cunney lips with his thumb and middle finger.

'Oh Frank! You clever boy!' I gasped when he found the tiny magic button under the fold at the base of my clitty and instantly began to twirl his tongue all around it. Of course the faster he vibrated his tongue, the more excited I became. I began to gyrate as if possessed as Frank's tongue flicked quickly across the grooves of my cunney walls, licking and lapping my love juices which were now flowing freely. With each stroke I arched my body in ecstasy to press the trembling erect clitty against the tip of his darting tongue.

'I'm there! I'm there!' I cried out thickly and I exploded into a thundering climax, flooding Frank's face with cuntal juice as I spent quite exquisitely in great tumbling bursts. Dear Frank lapped furiously away, filling his mouth with my tangy spendings which he swore was nectar to his taste as he gulped it down.

Frank then rolled me over onto my tummy and pulled me up by the hips so that the dimpled cheeks of my backside presented themselves provocatively to him. I reached round with my right hand and grasped his hot throbbing shaft and placed his cock into the cleft of my bum, expecting him to push his knob through between my yielding love lips and into my waiting quim.

However, my lusty lover had other ideas and he pulled away to scramble to his feet and pad across the floor to the dressing table where he picked up a tube of Nataline, an oily lubricant which gives a shiny gloss to the hair. Squeezing a liberal amount on his erect cock, Frank announced: 'I want to fuck your bottom, Sophie, and greasing my cock will make it more pleasurable for both of us.'

'But Frank, I have never had a cock up my bottom,' I faltered. 'Won't it be painful for me?'

'A little uncomfortable at first, perhaps,' he said honestly as he came back and positioned himself behind me. 'And if you find that you cannot take my cock in your snug little rear dimple, you have my word that I'll pull it out straightaway. Trust me though, Sophie, for I think you'll have your senses opened to a delightful ravishment.'

'Trust me, I'll be very gentle,' he added as he angled my legs further apart to afford a better view of my tiny wrinkled rosette. Then he separated the luscious globes of my buttocks and, despite Frank's promise, I drew my breath in sharply when I felt his knob sliding into the starfish-shaped entrance of the tiny orifice.

'Ow! Ow! It hurts, no more, Frank, I can't take any more!' I yowled as he pushed firmly forward but, as Frank had forecast, after a few short jabs of his cock, the sphincter muscle gradually relaxed and I began to enjoy the frigging of my big strawberry titties. He drew his arms around me, pushing firmly into my bottom and indeed the initial discomfort gave way to a new, most exhilarating sensation as his stiff shaft stirred me up to the very highest pitch of sensual excitement. His pulsing chopper now slid in and out of the snug sheath, plunging in and out of the widened rim, pumping and sucking like the thrust of a steam engine whilst he diddled my cunney with his fingers. I reached back and spread my cheeks even further, my bum jerking to and fro in time with Frank's rhythm until he lathered my back passage with jets of creamy jism and we spent together in perfect accord.

With an audible plop, Frank withdrew his beefy semi-stiff cock, leaving my puckered nether-hole slightly sore after this first ever insertion of anything more than a finger. 'There, that was fun, wasn't it?' he asked cheerfully and I replied: 'Yes, it did hurt somewhat at first but in the end the experience was very enjoyable.'

'There, I told you so,' said Frank with a satisfied grin. 'Of course the other great advantage for a lady is that this form of fucking allows her to enjoy as much cock as she wishes without any worry of becoming *enceinte*. Did you not feel my cock throbbing away inside you just like it would if it had been inside your cunt?'

'Yes, I suppose so and I'm truly grateful for the initiation,' I answered slowly. 'Although whilst I wouldn't mind an occasional poke *à la Greque*, I think I really do prefer being fucked in the more traditional manner.'

Frank smacked his lips again as he fisted his hand up and down his meaty shaft. When it was again standing stiffly against his stomach, he chuckled hoarsely: 'Fair enough, Sophie, but in that case you must let me pay my respects to your neglected pussey.'

I lay back and parted my thighs as he carefully lowered himself on top of me. We both sighed with satisfaction when Frank eased his blue-veined truncheon through the soft folds into my dripping crack. At first we lay motionless with his thick cock filling my clingy love funnel to capacity, billing and cooing like two turtledoves. Then I arched my hips upwards and Frank started to pump his prick in and out of my squishy cunt, moving in and out of my sopping snatch in slow, rhythmic thrusts.

'Wooooh! Wooooh! Keep going, you randy rascal,' I breathed blissfully and not for the first time I wondered whether in this life there could be any other sensation which even approached the ecstatic joy of the loving penetration of one's cunney by a fine stiff prick?

Whatever the answer, Frank's shaft slid deliciously to and fro, his big cock stretching my sheath to the limit, not hurting in the slightest, but instead transporting me to the heights of sheer ecstasy. He was not so very experienced in *l'arte de faire l'amour* yet Frank used his tool like the baton of an orchestral maestro, varying the angle and speed of his pistoning thrusts. We fucked away happily until the climax of this superb love-making when he spurted his warm cream with such intensity that I could imagine it splashing off the rear wall of my cunt. Indeed, so abundant was his spend that the frothy seed trickled down my thighs as he pulled out his quivering cock. His bell-end rubbed itself amorously between the puffy love lips of my sated cunney until I also achieved a thrillingly powerful orgasm and only then did he withdraw his softening shaft which was glistening from our mingled love juices.

As we lay back exhausted, struggling for breath, Alex and Babs came trooping in. Neither of the girls batted an eyelid when they saw our naked bodies sprawled out on the floor. They exchanged a meaningful look and Alex exclaimed: 'Oh Sophie, you won the game fair and square but I hope you haven't over-tired poor Frank's cock. I was looking forward to sucking him off.'

'And so was I,' pouted Babs crossly as she bent down. Holding his shaft between her thumb and index finger, she teasingly flipped Frank's limp cock onto his thigh and asked him: 'Are you able to oblige us, cousin?'

'Give me five minutes and I should be able to get another hard-on but I'm afraid I'll never be able to satisfy you both,' he replied sadly.

'Well in that case, I waive my claim and Alex can have her wicked way with you,' said Babs generously. 'After all, we'll be able to get together at Mr Jeffrey Martin's party up in Oxfordshire on the first weekend after we break up.'

Babs explained that she and Frank had been invited by the famous barrister to a reception and ball marking the coming of age of his nephew in the absence of his parents who were unable to come back to Britain from Canada (where his father is the Deputy High Commissioner) for the occasion. And, by coincidence, who should this lucky youth be but Frank's best chum, Giles Horrabin, the reckless prankster who had switched the slides for Frank's lecture – though naturally neither Frank, myself nor Alex and Babs were displeased with the results of Giles's jape.

However, she then clicked her fingers and went on: 'Meanwhile, I'll tell you what happened to me at the last party I attended before coming back here for our last term. It was a charity affair at the Park Lane Hotel and my parents had paid for me to stay the night at the hotel with my older sister Kirsty. But little did they know that Kirsty's fiancé hired a room at the hotel so they would be able to spend the night together. This gave me the opportunity of consummating my flirtatious romance with young Lord Roger Tagholm who had been pursuing me with love letters since we were introduced at Hurlingham Tennis Club.

'As the strains of the last waltz died away, Roger kissed my hand and asked whether I would like to finish the evening by taking a short stroll with him in Green Park. "No thank you," I replied and then, lowering my voice, I explained that I was staying the night at the hotel and added: "But if you would like to have coffee with me, come up to room four hundred and forty three in ten minutes' time. I'll leave the door on the latch."

'Roger's eyes sparkled as he eagerly accepted my invitation. He walked out of the ballroom with me into the foyer where, for the benefit of the other guests milling around us, we shook hands and he said loudly: "Good night, Miss Fawcett, I will come back at ten o'clock in the morning to take you to Paddington Station."

'"Good night, Lord Tagholm," I replied. I stepped into the lift and instructed the attendant to take me to the fourth floor. Once in my room I quickly undressed and five minutes later I was sitting at my dressing table naked except for a scanty pair of lace knickers. As arranged, I had left the door on the latch. I wondered how Roger would manage to dodge the hotel staff as I dusted my breasts with my favourite French powder.

'In fact I was so diligent in coating my bosoms with this delicately scented talc that my sensitive nipples soon hardened up into miniature red bullets. I cupped the full roundness of the soft spheres in my hands, letting my fingertips rest enticingly on the swollen titties. Then I heard the door close and I glanced up and saw Lord Roger Tagholm standing in front of it. He was holding a tray with a bottle of champagne and two glasses upon it and looking stunned at the sight of my bare breastes.

'"You clever boy, I could do with a night-cap," I said cheerfully. "But don't just stand there – why don't you bring the tray over here and put it down on the table. You'll get a much better view of my titties if you stand just behind me."

'"Indeed I will," he readily agreed and when he moved across the room I was excited to see how the front of Roger's trousers was distended by a large bulge between his legs.

'"Shall I open the champagne now?" he enquired and I said coyly: "In a moment, my dear. First, would you mind giving me your honest opinion on a personal matter? Do you like my breasts, Roger? It looks to me that you are genuinely fascinated by my creamy globes."

'Roger gulped and beads of perspiration formed on his forehead when I began to stroke my erect titties. I closed my eyes in sensuous satisfaction and what a delight awaited me when I opened them again a few seconds later! For Roger had torn down his trousers and drawers and was fondling his splendidly thick prick! Unashamedly he was rubbing his hand up and down his shaft. Each time he pulled his foreskin to and fro, it made a sexy slurping noise from the pre-come juice which had already leaked out from his uncovered purple knob.

' "Let me take over, Roger," I cooed as I reached out for his pulsing prick and held it lightly between my fingers. Then I slipped my other hand underneath to feel his wrinkled pink ballsack but alas, this sent the hapless boy over the top and in a trice a fierce torrent of sticky white froth was spurting out from his knob in a looping arc before splashing down on my heaving breasts.'

Alex and I would have liked to know what happened next, but Babs' reverie was interrupted by Frank, whose prick had now regained all its former strength and was standing up between his thighs as stiff as a poker.

'Someone suck me off, please,' he begged and Alex immediately fell to her knees and leaned over him to kiss the uncapped ruby helmet before opening her lips wide to take the mushroom dome inside her mouth. Alex sucked gently, savouring the texture of Frank's thick prick, rolling her tongue over the rounded crown. He let out a long ecstatic groan as she let the tip of her tongue travel down the underside of his shaft to catch a sticky drop of jism.

Now Alex nibbled round the ridge of his knob before clamping her lips around Frank's majestic member. She slurped noisily upon her luscious sweetmeat and carefully squeezed his balls to heighten his enjoyment. Soon Frank's body went rigid and she frantically gobbled his knob when she sensed that his orgasm was upon him.

A throaty growl escaped from Frank's mouth as he climaxed. Alex swallowed his copious emission with relish, milking his cock of every last drain of seed. Then she raised her head and, sweeping the silky tresses of golden blonde hair which had fallen over her face, she kissed Frank's softening shaft and said to me: 'Sophie, doesn't his spunk have such a nice clean taste? It isn't as salty as Terry Jackson's jism.

'But I suppose that a real fuck is now out of the question,' she sighed, looking down at Frank's forlorn prick and not wishing to embarrass our guest, I said firmly: 'Well of course it is, Alex. Even a virile cocksman like Frank has to sheath his sword after three frenetic spends.'

'Thank you, Sophie,' added Frank, nodding his head in gratitude. 'As my biology tutor taught us whilst I was studying for my degree, energy levels rise and fall far more dramatically for boys during a fuck and we really do need some time afterwards to recuperate. It's a fact of life and whilst I appreciate that no girl likes her partner to fall asleep immediately after a poke, she shouldn't feel rejected if he needs time to recuperate after a long session of love-making.'

In any case, even if Frank could have coaxed his cock up for a fourth joust, there would have been little time for either Alex or Babs to enjoy a poke as I looked at my watch and saw that it was only ten minutes to 'lights out'. So we hastily dressed ourselves and bade farewell to Frank, though as will be seen, the three of us were to meet up with him only a few weeks later at Giles Horrabin's twenty-first birthday party, full details of which will be set down in due course.

Little happened of interest during the following few days but two weeks later, just before the end of term, Babs and I were among a group of girls who journeyed over to High-cliffe Boys School for a debate with their Current Affairs Society. As luck would have it, Alex contracted a nasty summer chill and was unable to join the party, but of course I was looking forward to seeing Phil Colnbrook and hoping that we might be able to sneak away for some canoodling after the splendid supper which was always produced for us on our visits to Highcliffe.

As the reader of this memoir may remember, I recorded the fact that Babs Fawcett had been in regular correspon-dence with a lad named Johnny Pilkington, Highcliffe's ruggedly handsome captain of cricket. They were both looking forward to meeting up again and cementing their friendship by way of a passionate poke.

Indeed, the evening before our trip Babs came into my study and asked me whether I thought there would be any opportunity to indulge ourselves during our short stay at Highcliffe.

'I wondered whether you and Phil Colnbrook had made any plans to slope off somewhere,' she remarked, but shaking my head I replied: 'No, although I did receive a note from Phil to say that he would try and find a private place where we would not be disturbed for an hour or so. If he's successful, you're very welcome to join us.'

'Oh thank you, Sophie, you're a real pal,' exclaimed Babs, kissing me on the cheek. 'Johnny is so thrilled at the thought of losing his virginity. Truth to tell, I'm equally excited by the thought of plucking his cherry. Here, read this letter I received from him this morning.'

She brought out an envelope from the pocket of her dress and, handing it to me, she remarked with a giggle: 'Read this and you'll see how he really is on pins and needles at the prospect of a good fuck.'

I sat down and read Johnny Pilkington's epistle which ran as follows:

My Dearest Babs,
You may recall from my last letter how I had been given permission to spend the weekend at my parents' country house in Buckinghamshire to attend a family gathering in honour of the fiftieth birthday of my uncle, General Sir Kelvin Juffkins of the Grenadier Guards. This leave was given at my father's request as opposed to mine and I was feeling really cross when the dog-cart came round to take me to the station on Saturday morning because I would far rather have stayed at Highcliffe and captained the First Eleven in the important cricket match against Beddingfield College.

However, as is often the case, when one doesn't look forward with great anticipation to an event, one is often pleasantly surprised to find it extremely enjoyable and this is exactly what occurred to me. For if I had rebelled against my parents' wishes, I would not have made the acquaintance of Miss Maggie Fairbridge, a girl with a similar appetite for rumpy pumpy as myself and who made the weekend a highlight of the summer for me.

In all honesty, Babs, let me say here and now that what happened should in no way affect our friendship as Maggie is my Aunt Felicity's personal maid and our different stations in society as well as my Aunt's residence being in far-away Shrewsbury preclude any further relations between us.

Anyhow, we first came into contact with each other on the Saturday afternoon. It was raining quite heavily and I was wondering whether the bad weather would force the postponement of the match against Beddingfield. As I sat alone in the library idly thumbing through the morning newspaper, there was a tap on the door and Maggie entered the room dressed in her black maid's dress with a well-filled sparkling white blouse.

'Sorry to disturb you, sir,' Maggie apologised as she bobbed a graceful curtsy. 'But Lady Norrice-Grant instructed me to see if there were copies of Bradshaw's in the library because she wants to check the time of her train home on Monday morning.'

[Bradshaw's Railway Guide was a comprehensive railways timetable first published in 1839 which ceased publication in 1961 – Editor]

Now even though my father's sister has been as rich as Croesus since the death of her wealthy husband, my Aunt Felicity is notorious for her hatred of spending a penny more than is absolutely necessary, and wrong though it was to make fun of this characteristic with her maid, I pointed to the relevant shelf of reference books and grunted: 'Let me guess, the old trout wants to know the time of the first cheap excursion fare even though she could probably buy the actual train with her monthly dividends cheque from Baring's Bank!'

I was rewarded with a smile and I heaved myself out of my chair and went on: 'It must be pretty awful working for Aunt Felicity. Is it true that when she last opened her purse a moth flew out of her handbag?'

Maggie rewarded my witticism with a little giggle and she replied: 'Well, that wouldn't surprise me, sir, although you couldn't really call your aunt a miser. She gives generously to charities and yet she scrutinises the household accounts so carefully that the cook had to explain to her why last month's milk bill was fourpence ha'penny more than usual!'

'Life's too short for such pettiness,' I said grandly and then I bent down to pick up a folded sheet of paper which had fluttered to the floor as Maggie pulled out the copy of the book she required from the shelf.

'Good grief, whoever could have drawn this picture?' I gasped, hardly believing the evidence of my own eyes for I unfolded the paper which presumably had been erroneously left in Bradshaw's by the last person to use the guide.

For in my trembling hands was a well-crafted carbon pencil sketch of two pretty girls lying naked on a bed working priapic-shaped dildoes into their cunnies. They were being watched by two young men peeping round the door with wide smiles on their faces and who were handling their pricks which they had pulled out of their trousers whilst they looked at the lascivious lasses playing with themselves.

'Oooh, what a naughty scene!' exclaimed Maggie, but she did not turn away in disgust – rather the opposite in fact, for she put down her book to take the paper from my *unresisting hands to study it more closely. 'Master Johnny, you know who drew this picture, don't you?'*

'No, of course I don't,' I replied and she laughed: 'Why, it's General Juffkins, I recognise his style from the sketches he made of me on his last visit to Lady Norrice-Grant. Now the general is a generous man, he paid me a gold sovereign to pose in the nude for him.'

It would be an understatement to say I was shocked at this news but this was nothing to what was to follow, for then Maggie winked at me and went on: 'When the general left, he presented me with a few of his drawings as a parting gift – come up to my room if you would like to see them. Lady Norrice-Grant is playing bridge this afternoon and I don't have to bring her this book till six o'clock.'

Naturally I could hardly wait to see more of my uncle's artistic handiwork and I was not to be disappointed. Minutes later I was sitting on Maggie's bed gazing at an equally sensuous sketch of a girl who looked very much like Maggie kneeling between the legs of a bespectacled gentleman in clerical garb. Her lips were clamped round the randy clergyman's thick stiffie whilst her hand cupped his balls.

'That's our vicar, Reverend Gibson,' she said to me nonchalantly. 'The lucky man is very well endowed, don't you think?'

Then Maggie confirmed her identity as the model in the picture by adding thoughtfully: 'I really had to open my mouth wide to cram his big cock down my throat.'

I was unable to contain myself and I burst out: 'My God! Wouldn't I give anything to be in his place!' I bit my lip and my face flamed a bright shade of crimson immediately after this heartfelt plea left my lips, but I need not have worried because Maggie placed her hand on my straining shaft and said with a mischievous chuckle: 'Well, Master Johnny, I don't see any reason why you shouldn't, your cock seems good and ready for it!'

She proceeded to unbutton my trousers and released my throbbing tool which she gently fisted up and down in her hand as our mouths met and crushing her to me, I kissed her lips, softly at first and then deepening the pressure when her tongue darted between my teeth. I helped her undress and she tugged down my trousers and drawers to the floor.

Maggie continued to rub my cock until we were both naked and we fell onto her bed and writhed about in each other's arms with my prick leaping and dancing between Maggie's thighs.

'Fuck me, Master Johnny!' she panted, thrusting her wicked tongue into my mouth with wild abandon.

However, I was so excited at the thought of losing my virginity that I could not find the entrance to Maggie's quim! I jabbed my hips backwards and forwards, moaning in frustration as I failed to sink my shaft but Maggie opened her legs wider and clasped hold of my cock and directed the knob towards her cunney and I whimpered with joy as I thrilled to the sensation as my helmet slid between the puffy outer lips of her cunt.

Once I was fully inside her I began to fuck her with long, simple strokes, glorying in the electric tingle that spread up and down my spine as I slowly withdrew my glistening chopper before plunging it back in her wet love channel.

Maggie spread her legs and bent her knees so that her heels rested upon the small of my back whilst I continued to marvel at the blissful sensations produced by her clingy cunney muscles upon my twitching todger. My previous fumblings must have alerted Maggie as to how inexperienced a player I was at this finest of all sports, but she was an excellent teacher, slowing me down and then telling me to quicken the pace of my plunges as her love juice lubricated the tender walls of her cunney, making my shaft squelch merrily in and out of her sticky honeypot.

Now she twined her legs around my waist and instructed me to put my hands under her hips as I pushed forward and buried the entire length of my cock inside her sopping crack. As I did so Maggie rubbed her clitty against my rigid rammer and her soft moans turned into a rising scream as she cried out: 'Ahhh! Ahhh! Push on, Master Johnny! Yes, that's the way! Now empty your balls, you big-cocked boy!'

With wild abandon I began to pump in and out of her cunney at great speed, feeling my ballsack smack against her bottom as together we scaled the heights of ecstasy. I crashed huge shoots of jism into Maggie's cunt and this brought down her flow of pussey juice which flooded her luscious notch as I collapsed down upon her soft curves.

Although my cock soon stiffened up again, we had no further time to continue and much to my disappointment, it proved impossible for Maggie and I to sneak off somewhere for some more rollicking fun.

But just writing about what happened is making my shaft swell, especially when I think how dandy it would be if we could enjoy a good poke when you come over to Highcliffe for the inter-school debate.

Love and best wishes,
Johnny

I passed the letter back to Babs and remarked: 'Well, if Johnny Pilkington can fuck half as well as he can write, you're in for a fine time this afternoon, you lucky girl.'

'Yes, that's what I thought,' said Babs happily. But, as Fate would have it, when we arrived we found from Philip Colnbrook that poor Johnny was confined to his bed, having been struck down by the same feverish chill which had afflicted Alex!

Nevertheless, as shall be seen, it turned out to be a most satisfactory day for us both in the end, although Babs' face fell as she imparted this sad news to us. However, she brightened up when Phil went on: 'Babs, I would very much like you to meet Lawrence Reuben. He's a close chum of mine with whom I think you will have something in common as he's all for the suffragettes. Anyhow, I hope I'm right because I've taken the liberty of placing him next to you at lunch.'

Fortunately, Phil's attempt at matchmaking proved to be one hundred per cent successful. Babs and his friend Lawrence took to each other from the moment they were introduced. Lawrence was a swarthy good-looking young chap with riotous curls of black hair which, as a senior prefect, he was able to wear long, just touching his collar. He had also been blessed with liquid dark eyes which swept over Babs' body as he kissed her offered hand.

There was but the merest whiff of a summer breeze in the air to complement the glorious sunshine, and Dr Harold Ossulton, the progressive headmaster of Highcliffe, had ordered luncheon to be served on the immaculately tended front lawns. Not surprisingly, Phil and I spent most of our time at luncheon canoodling under the table. On a number of occasions, I slid my hand onto his lap to squeeze his stiff cock. But we left off our petting to do full justice to the trout which had been freshly caught only the previous afternoon from one of the local rivers. That was followed by roast lamb which melted in the mouth.

Meanwhile, Lawrence and Babs were getting on famously discussing the many conflicts in the field of industrial relations. Babs was saying: 'What riles me most is that some employers and leader writers in the Tory newspapers pretend to believe that all the strikes and lock-outs are due to a few agitators who refuse to let well alone. The truth, though, is that this constant industrial strife is due to the fact that many members of the working class are toiling fourteen hours a day for a mere pittance and living in accommodation which would disgrace any decent race of savages.

'Don't you agree with me?' she asked and clearly her new beau was not paying proper attention to her words, for he mumbled: 'No, I mean yes, ah, most certainly. Really, you make a most interesting point.'

'I'm delighted that you think so, Lawrence,' said Babs sweetly. 'Yet I have the distinct impression that my conversation is boring you.'

Phil and I could not help chuckling to ourselves. Lawrence blushed scarlet with embarrassment, but he quickly recovered his composure and exclaimed: 'Oh no, Babs, far from it! Please forgive my rudeness for which I humbly apologise. It would be foolish not to deny that whilst you were speaking my thoughts were elsewhere.'

Babs patted his cheek and smiled: 'Don't worry, my dear, I'll overlook it because unless I am very much mistaken, they were probably between my legs if that nice big bulge in your trousers is any guide to where your thoughts had strayed.'

These brazen words caused great merriment. Lawrence threw back his head and laughed aloud at her brazen words, unaware that Dr Ossulton was walking up to our table from behind him. He gave a start as the headmaster placed a hand on his shoulder and said: 'Reuben, I'm glad to see you and your party are all enjoying yourselves. May I share the joke or could I or another member of staff be the butt of your jest? No matter, I came to tell you that it seems ridiculous for you to be cooped up in the hall on such a lovely afternoon, so I have postponed the start of the debate until four o'clock. This will still allow us enough time for a lively discussion and I suggest that you and Colnbrook use the extra hour to take these two young ladies for a walk round our grounds.'

'Thank you, sir, that's a splendid idea,' said Lawrence, rising to his feet. 'But if you don't mind, we'll stroll down to the ruins of the old Abbey. I think the girls will find this more interesting than our cricket fields.'

'By all means,' said Dr Ossulton affably and after he sauntered away to another table, Lawrence grinned: 'Actually there isn't much to see but at least we'll be away from the rest of the crowd.'

'Where are these ruins?' I asked and Phil replied: 'Oh, they are only a mile away, although we'll have to climb up Lempert Lane to get to them.'

'Well, I'm game,' said Babs and I nodded my agreement as I heaved myself off my chair. Even after our delicious luncheon, a slow uphill walk was hardly onerous. Phil explained how the Abbey had been ransacked for its treasure when Henry VIII dissolved the monasteries.

'The Abbot was an unpopular fellow who squeezed as much as he could in taxes on the local people and had fathered three children by local girls into the bargain,' he remarked as we ambled through the ruins.

Truth to tell, I have never been able to extract any interest from any ruined site – even the excavations at Pompeii held little fascination for me because I find it impossible to conjure up in my mind how an ancient building might have looked from a pile of old stones. Be that as it may, it was certainly pleasant enough to sit on the grass and look down at the quiet wooded hills around us. Naturally we paired off with Phil and myself cuddling up together and watching with some amusement as Lawrence hesitantly put his arm around Babs' waist as she lifted her head and whispered something I could not catch into his ear.

I wondered what on earth Babs could have said for her words had caused Lawrence to frown and I heard him say with some slight apprehension: 'Well now, I wouldn't mind but I'll have to find out if Phil's game. Frankly, I'm rather doubtful that he'll want to take part in such a frolic.'

But my curiosity was immediately satisfied when Lawrence ambled across and, squatting down next to us, he said: 'Phil, Babs is very interested to know if we have ever been caned. I told her that as prefects we are now the ones who wield the rod, but she says she would be very grateful if we would demonstrate how the punishment is inflicted. So I've come to see whether you would take part in a little charade to show her how it's done.'

'If you like,' answered Phil with a shrug of his broad shoulders. 'But only if I play the prefect and you take the part of the wrongdoer!'

'How about tossing up for the prefect's role?' suggested Lawrence, pulling out a penny from his pocket.

Phil nodded: 'Fair enough. I'll call tails.' Lawrence spun the coin and looking down gloomily on the ground, he announced: 'Tails it is, you win.'

'Of course not,' agreed Phil, giving me a large wink as he scrambled to his feet. 'I'll just hack off a cane from one of the ash trees in that grove over there.'

'All right, though don't swish too hard, Phil, there's no need to whop me like a cheeky third-former,' muttered Lawrence. He turned on his heel and sloped off back to Babs whilst Phil grinned: 'Wait here for me, Sophie, I'll just run across and pick up an ashplant and then we'll have some fun.'

He returned a couple of minutes later with a suitable stick under his arm. We walked over to where Lawrence and Babs were sitting on a log. When we reached them Phil cleared his throat and roared: 'Stand up, Reuben! How dare you kiss a pretty girl in such a wanton and lewd manner! Prepare yourself for punishment!'

Lawrence looked at him apprehensively as he reluctantly heaved himself up and I took his seat next to Babs as Phil continued: 'Come on then, take off your jacket and pull down your trousers, we don't have all day.'

Phil swished the cane menacingly as Lawrence did as he was told. When he tucked his shirt round his waist, Babs and I were given a glimpse of his cock before, on Phil's curt word of command, he turned round to bend down and touch his toes. Something was different about Lawrence's shaft, I thought to myself, but I had little time to consider the matter because Phil had slipped off his jacket and was ready to administer the caning. Babs and I just had time to admire the dimpled swells of Lawrence's tight rounded buttocks when Phil lifted the ashplant and it whistled through the air and landed firmly upon his friend's quivering bum cheeks.

'Ow! Ow! Ow!' he cried, but I don't think Phil really inflicted too much damage because Lawrence turned round and waggled his tongue at us as he comically screwed up his face.

But when we began to giggle, Phil growled: 'You impudent boy! I'll teach you to make fun of me!' And then he swiftly laid on five fierce cuts which made Lawrence yell out in earnest as his bum cheeks turned a bright shade of red. Phil was skilled in the use of the rod. He did not swing the cane high in the air but laid on the strokes with a flick of the wrist, taking care never to strike twice in the same place.

'You rotten so-and-so, I thought we agreed to act out the swishing!' said Lawrence angrily as he straightened up and faced his tormentor. He grabbed the cane from Phil and turning to Babs and I said: 'Don't you agree that Phil deserves some of his own medicine?'

'Absolutely so,' we chorused. Not wishing to be thought cowardly (and doubtless thinking it a good excuse to remove his trousers in anticipation of a poke) Phil shucked off all his clothes except for his shirt. He bent down and Lawrence lifted his shirt before applying three stripes to Phil's naked posterior.

To my surprise, Lawrence had no sooner finished when Phil turned round and lifted his shirt to display his thick shaft which was swelling up to a fine stand before our very eyes. In seconds his tool was fully erect against his belly, the coral head pressing against his navel.

'M'mm, that juicy chopper looks good enough to eat,' murmured Babs. I said to her: 'Be my guest, darling. You were kind enough to let Alex and myself enjoy your cousin Frank's delicious cock the other evening and so I'm delighted to be able to offer Phil's prick in return. I'm sure Phil will have no objection to your sucking him off, will you, dearest?'

'None whatsoever,' he replied without hesitation. Phil's eyes lit up as Babs dropped to her knees in front of him and wrapped her fingers around his throbbing stiffstander. She peeled back his foreskin and swirled her tongue over his wide purple helmet before opening her mouth and plunging her face forward to allow Phil's thick cock deeper entry between her lips. Babs loved sucking cocks and her hands as well as her mouth were soon moving up and down the engorged shaft, co-ordinating the rhythm so that as her mouth came down on his cock for a suck, her fingers slid towards the base where she jiggled his balls in the palms of her hand. Then I noticed that Lawrence's love truncheon was also bolt upright. As I peered at his prick, I realised what was different about it when he started to pull his hand up and down his pulsating shaft – there was no foreskin to slide back from his bare knob!

My surprise must have shown on my face for Lawrence smiled at me and said: 'Sophie, you haven't seen a circumcised cock like mine before, have you?'

Of course, that was it! I should have realised from Lawrence's Biblical-sounding name that he was Jewish and thus had his foreskin removed eight days after his birth.

[*Circumcision became fashionable amongst the upper classes in Britain during the 1930s when it became known that it was practised in Royal circles. Prince Charles was circumcised but since the 1960s the operation has lost much of its popularity although the procedure is much favoured on medical grounds in most American states. It remains, of course, a fundamental observance even amongst secular Jews and Muslims – Editor*]

I licked my lips as I hastily began to undress and when I yanked down my knickers he gazed in lascivious rapture at the hairy furrow between my thighs. Stretching myself down on the grass and using my rolled-up clothes as a pillow, I cried out: 'Come on then, Lawrence, I want to see how it feels having a circumcised cock stuffed in my cunney!'

He was upon me instantly. I guided his ruby knob between the pouting lips of my pussey and threw my legs around his waist and drummed my heels on the small of his back.

Lawrence was lucky enough to possess a beefy prick. As far as I was concerned, it was clear from the start that circumcision makes not a jot of difference to a boy's performance one way or the other, not that I had any complaints about Lawrence's love-making ability! He fucked me quite beautifully and his cock was so huge, so filling, so utterly delicious that I spent as soon as he drove in his beefy todger! I groaned in sheer delight and matched him thrust for thrust, jerking my hips upwards to meet his downward jabs as he pumped in and out of my sopping quim.

'Fuck away, Lawrence!' I cried out uninhibitedly. 'Yes, yes, yes, I'm there, you've made me come! Now spurt your spunk, you dear boy!'

These lewd instructions sent Lawrence off into a wild frenzy. He had tried to keep his strokes nice and slow but now he changed up a gear, really banging his cock into me fast and hard, his balls slapping against my bum cheeks with every forward lunge as he pistoned into my sated cunney with all the energy he could muster. Then I felt his body stiffen and seconds later my love channel was filled with his creamy emission. I cried out in ecstasy as my body shook with the force of my own exquisite climax.

As the delicious sensations died away, I turned my head to see that our friends had also stripped to the buff and were engaged in an 'upside downer' as this form of fucking was commonly termed by my chums. Babs was crouched over Phil whose stiffie was waving like a flagpole in a high wind. I watched her spread her cunney lips apart with her hand as she slowly sat herself down to be spitted by Phil's thick cock as she directed his knob through the gateway of her pussey lips into her clingy cunt.

Phil let out a satisfied growl as he felt Babs' cunney juices wash around his willing shaft. His hands slid round to clasp her chubby buttocks as she wriggled to work the full length of his throbbing tool inside her. Then she began to bounce merrily away on his rock-hard rammer and Phil released her bum cheeks to play with her jiggling titties.

'Those two seem to be having a really good time, don't they?' I chuckled. Lawrence, who was clearly of a studious disposition, nodded his head and replied: 'Yes, I've never tried the so-called female superior position myself but Professor Gottlieb highly recommends it in *A Young Person's Guide To Procreation*, a book which our headmaster keeps under lock and key in the school library but which can be issued to senior sixth formers in their last term at Highcliffe.

'The professor advocates the position as an occasional change to one's regular pattern of love-making, though not too often. It can be quite tiring for the girl who has to lift herself up and down with her legs in a somewhat cramped position.'

'Well that may be, but I adore fucking this way,' called

out Babs who had listened to Lawrence's little discourse. 'It gives my cunney a good going-over – especially when I have a nice fat cock like Phil's inside my crack to give my clitty a good rub as well!'

She wriggled her bottom from side to side whilst Phil jerked his hips up and down and then she caught his rhythm and lifted herself up and down in time with his upward thrusts.

'You see what I mean,' Babs gasped as she bounced up and down on Phil's thighs. 'Oooh, harder, Phil, harder! A boy also enjoys this style of fucking because he has to do little more than lie back and let the girl do most of the work. Now in my view—'

But at this point she was interrupted by a hoarse growl from Phil who could no longer hold back the gush of spunk shooting through his shaft. He creamed Babs' cunney with a copious emission of sticky white jism.

'Oh, I'm sorry about that,' he apologised. 'I tried hard but I simply couldn't wait for you any longer.' Babs raised herself off his limp prick, patted his cheek and said: 'Never mind, Sophie will finish me off in her own special way, won't you, darling?'

'With pleasure,' I answered as Babs laid herself down on her back and I crawled across to her and knelt between her parted thighs. I wasted no time and she purred with pleasure when I kissed her elongated titties and opened up her sticky honeypot with my fingers.

Babs spent as soon as I began to frig her erect clitty. It crossed my mind that although there is no guarantee that a girl will achieve an orgasm every time we fuck, we are fortunate in that we possess the capability to climax again and again. Members of the so-called superior sex need more and more time to recover from a single good spunking after they reach the age of twenty. Indeed, only the other week one of the most noted cocksmen in Europe, Count Gewirtz of Galicia, admitted to me that at best he is now able only to fuck five times a night.

However, Babs was still raring to go. She gurgled delightedly when I slid my mouth down from her titties across her snowy white tummy and into her moist bush of pussey hair. Without any preliminary licking or lapping, I immediately took a huge suck on her puffy love lips, holding her still whilst I nibbled on her fleshy clitty and Babs threshed about like a wild animal under this erotic oral stimulation.

She yelped out in dismay when I released my suction hold and moved my tongue up and down her juicy crack. She shuddered all over when I jabbed the tip of my little finger up her bum-hole which brought on a pungent flow of love juice from Babs' cunney which I licked up and swallowed before raising my head up and dragging myself on top of her writhing body which was twisting from side to side in a paroxysm of sensual fervour.

'Now I'm going to fuck you,' I whispered as I pressed my quim hard against Babs' slit, positioning myself in such a way that our clitties touched each time I pushed my hips forward. I opened up her juicy snatch with my fingers and managed to insert my own stiff, protruding clitty inside her cunt, closing her cunney lips over it and then holding them tightly together in my hand.

'Oooooh! Oooooh! Sophie Starr, you really are a wicked little puss,' breathed Babs rapturously. She responded to my efforts by heaving and jogging herself upwards faster and faster until the tingling ripples of pleasure which had been coursing out from my cunney became even stronger and my body floated in a sea of sensuous sensation as we climaxed together in a wonderful simultaneous spend.

Our voluptuous exhibition had excited the boys so much that they both sported tremendous hard-ons and though Babs and I would have liked nothing better than one last fucking by their thick love truncheons, there was alas no time left for any further fun and games.

Fifteen minutes later, the four of us strolled into Highcliffe's library where the debate was to take place. We were in good time for Lawrence, Babs and myself to take comfortable seats in the front row. Phil had been asked to second the proposition that 'This House deplores the excesses of the modern novelist' and he left us for the table facing the audience to closet himself with Cecilia Buckman-Webbe from my school who had been chosen to propose the motion.

At four o'clock precisely Dr Ossulton entered the hall and, rapping the table, asked Cecilia to open the proceedings. I should add that the idea behind these debates was not merely for speakers (except those from the floor) to indulge themselves by riding their favourite hobbyhorses. The main speakers were given no choice on whether they wished to support or oppose the matter under discussion. This often meant taking up cudgels on behalf of causes that one did not personally favour, which had the advantage of making the participants aware of both sides of an argument and hopefully made us more broad-minded and receptive to reasoned discussion.

However, this was not one of the occasions when the proposer of the motion spoke against her own personal belief. Cecilia Buckman-Webbe (a tall, angular girl who hailed from a wealthy family of landowners up in North Yorkshire) was one of the small narrow-minded group of girls in our year who thoroughly disapproved of the 'goings-on' which the rest of us enjoyed. Nevertheless, we respected Cecilia for she held to a 'live and let live' philosophy and never reported the shenanigans in the dormitory to Miss Randall. When she stood up, I applauded her politely before settling down to listen to her speech.

She began by saying that writers like Ouida and George Moore were guilty of poor taste and flagrant want of reticence. Then she continued: 'Yet in spite of these unnecessary passages which add nothing of value to the narrative, I would have to agree that we must overlook these blots as their novels are inspirational records of vibrant, passionate humanity.'

'How kind of her,' breathed Lawrence quietly as Cecilia went on: 'But there are many lesser writers eager to make their mark in the crowded market-place who, instead of breathing the pure atomsphere of imagination, freely playing around the truths of life and of love, force the reader instead down into the gutter. I regret to say that women have often been the worst offenders. Is it not quite revolting that a writer of the calibre of Mr Charles Nettleton should be able to conceive of a woman describing her feelings for her husband to his young sister in these words: "*My love for Henry is a purely sensual one*"?

'This is only a mild specimen of the gutter school but there are many other stronger examples which cannot be quoted here.'

'What a pity, they might have prevented me from dozing off,' commented Babs in a *sotto voce* murmur, earning herself a glare from Miss Dunaway who had accompanied our party to Highcliffe.

Cecilia finished her oration with a flourish by stating: 'This fashion of vulgarity will not last; there is nothing so ephemeral as the startling.'

She sat down and Dr Ossulton invited the main speaker against the motion to address us. I raised my eyebrows when a strapping blond youth rose to his feet. The lad possessed a soldierly smartness in his manner and, noting my interest, Lawrence whispered that we were about to hear from Randolph Ponsonby, a scion of General Ponsonby of the Honourable Artillery Company.

Ralph spoke well and I am sure won over many in the audience by his amusing dissection of Cecilia's speech. He cleverly switched his attack to the consequences of her argument. His basic thesis was that the so-called immoral novel is written as a reaction to the spirit of the age which refuses to face the facts of human nature and falsifies them to the young. As he roundly declared: 'The so-called excess of the modern novelist is a natural reaction from this curious overblown Puritanism which would circumscribe the writer's freedom even more and lead to censorship by self-appointed guardians who believe we are unable to think for ourselves. And it is astonishing how ridiculous people can be when it comes to censoring literature.

'For instance, Elizabeth Browning's beautiful poem *Aurora Leigh* was banned in New England where it was condemned as "the hysterical indecencies of an erotic mind" – and before you smile at the foolishness of our American friends, think of our own Dr Bowdler who thought it necessary to remove swathes of what he considered to be impolite text from the works of Shakespeare. Furthermore, I understand that even in these early years of the new twentieth century, a public librarian in Staffordshire has banned classics such as Flaubert's *Madame Bovary* and Ibsen's *Ghosts.*'

It was clear from the thunderous applause at the end of his speech that Randolph would win the day, despite a good rearguard performance by Phil who insisted that the fashion of dwelling upon unclean topics was the hallmark of a poverty of mind.

I raised my hand when Dr Ossulton called for speakers from the floor and commented that a book worthless to some may convey something of value to others. Then I shocked the headmaster of Highcliffe by adding: 'If there is a lack of reticence in the modern novel, this has been caused by an immoral prudery in our society which will not face the facts of human nature itself and attempts to falsify them to the young.'

Perhaps because the sun was still shining down and we all wanted to get back into the fresh air, there were few other contributions. After calling for a vote on the motion (which was defeated by a large majority), Dr Ossulton brought the meeting to an end.

This left Babs and myself with a little over an hour to kill before meeting up with the other girls for the journey back to our own school. We toyed with the idea of a further session of fucking with Phil and Lawrence but reluctantly decided that there really wouldn't be enough time. So instead the boys showed us around the school. Lawrence took Babs to see the school's well-stocked library, whilst Phil escorted me across to the newly erected gymnasium. He turned to me and grinned: 'Sophie, have you heard the rumour about your Miss Dunaway and our sports instructor, Mr Clee?'

'No, and I'd be surprised if there were any truth in it because I happen to know that Miss Dunaway already has a beau,' I answered, thinking back to my recent exploits with Terry Jackson.

Phil shrugged his shoulders and declared: 'That may be so, but I'm sure that she is also involved with Nicholas Clee. A chap whose word can be trusted happened to pick up a *billet doux* from her off the floor of the gym which must have slipped out of Mr Clee's pocket during a training session with the fifth form. He says it was pretty hot stuff.

'Anyhow, let's pop in for a moment. I'd like to pick up a pair of plimsolls which I left in the changing room this morning.'

He pushed open the door and I followed him up a short flight of stairs to the changing rooms. I was about to speak when suddenly Phil turned round and placed his finger in front of his lips. Then he beckoned me up to squeeze alongside him on the narrow step and whispered: 'Well, what did I tell you? You won't get any plainer evidence than this!'

With my head peeping round from the foot of the stair, I looked across the changing room. Sure enough, for the second time in only a matter of weeks I spied Miss Dunaway *in flagrante delicto*. She was sitting on a bench with a fresh-complexioned young man wearing only an athletic vest and a pair of football shorts whilst he dextrously unbuttoned her blouse and skirt.

'Nick, are you sure we won't be discovered?' she asked anxiously, but he shook his head and replied: 'No, no, Rosie, I asked Dr Ossulton for the gymnasium to be made out of bounds this afternoon. I can promise you that we're quite safe from any prying eyes here.'

My eyes were agog as the couple dissolved into a fierce amatory clinch. The gym master undressed Miss Dunaway so skilfully that in no time at all she was sitting clad only in her knickers. Then Mr Clee rose to his feet and pulled off his vest whilst Miss Dunaway herself yanked down his shorts and he stood naked in front of her.

'My, I do believe your cock has grown since the last time I saw it,' giggled Rosie Dunaway as she fisted her hand up and down his swollen shaft. 'Tell me, what are you going to do with your lovely thick prick?'

'What am I going to do with it?' he echoed hoarsely. 'Well, what do you think, Rosie? I'm going to fuck you, my girl! We're going to slide down onto that mat I've laid down on the floor and you'll open your legs and I shall mount you. To begin with I'll lie on top of you and prise open your pussey with my helmet and push forward until my shaft is fully inside your tight little notch before I pull it out and tease the lips of your pussey with my knob. Then I'll lift your bottom with my hands and I'll crash my cock back inside your cunney and pump in and out of your clingy moist sheath, fucking you faster and deeper till my balls are slapping against your bum cheeks. You'll jerk upwards at every stroke and after a while we'll come together and gushes of spunk will cream your love channel whilst your own pussey juice dribbles out of your cunt.'

'Oooh, that sounds wonderful,' breathed my English teacher, smacking her lips as she slid down onto the mat and Nick Clee followed her to the floor, kneeling between her parted legs. Without further ado she pulled his head down to her breasts and he turned his face from side to side, kissing each engorged stalky tittie in turn whilst his right hand reached down so that his fingers could play inside the silky forest of dark hair which covered her prominent mound.

My hand stole down to rub my own moistening pussey as I watched them kiss. I saw Nick Clee's hand cup one of Rosie's large bare breasts, making her raised-up red nipples grow before my eyes as he fondled each beautiful bosom in turn. She slid her hand up and down his big blue-veined boner, capping and uncapping the wide mushroom knob.

Then Rosie released his cock and leaned back with her head resting against the wall as he parted the puffy lips of her pussey which protruded through her glossy bush. Rosie twisted and turned as she rolled her belly on his throbbing stiffie whilst he continued to suck her engorged titties.

Now she threw back her pretty head and moaned with passion as Mr Clee brought her up to the very highest peaks of unfulfilled desire, pressing his fingertips against the sodden slit of her cunt, flicking at the erect fleshy clitty which was already peeking out. Only then did he take hold of his huge chopper and make Rosie yelp with delight as he propelled inch after inch of his hot pulsing prick inside her cunt.

For a moment or two Mr Clee stayed still with his shaft totally embedded inside Rosie's clingy quim, but then he slowly pulled out his cock and then drove back in again, pushing his full length inside her sticky honeypot.

'Faster, Nick, faster!' she panted, urging him on by closing her feet together at the small of his back to force the very last quarter-inch of cock into her tingling quim. She raised herself to meet his stroke and drummed her heels upon the base of his spine as he pistoned his prick in and out of her juicy sheath, his body jerking to and fro in a frenetic rhythm which I correctly guessed heralded his approaching spend.

'I'm going to come, Rosie, I can't stop!' he cried out as he plunged home one final time, spurting his copious ejaculation of creamy jism inside her cunt as he sank down upon her.

'M'mm, what a delicious fuck,' sighed Rosie as the wiry Highcliffe sports instructor rolled to one side and scrambled to his feet. He held out an arm to help Rosie up to sit on the bench. She kissed the tip of his still semi-erect shaft and added: 'I suppose we had better get dressed, Nick, or have I time to suck your lovely cock?'

'I'm afraid not,' he replied with a smile as he picked up his trousers and rummaged through the pockets until he found a small package wrapped in coloured paper which he passed to her and added: 'Rosie, I want to give you a present. I saw this in the window of a little shop in St Albans last week and I really would love you to have it.'

'Nick, it's very kind but you shouldn't buy me things,' declared Rosie as she picked up her knickers and pulled them on. 'Remember what we said when we first fucked? We agreed not to become closely involved and to keep our relationship solely on the physical level. Otherwise I could not look Terry Jackson in the eye and you will feel guilty when you meet up with your fiancée during the summer vacation.'

'Oh Rosie, surely you are not saying that it is only the inability to enjoy the company of members of the opposite sex which has drawn us together?' persisted Mr Clee. Rosie puffed out her cheeks as she slowly exhaled a deep breath before answering: 'No, of course not, because if I just wanted a cock I could have simply used my dildo or requested the services of one of the young tradesmen who occasionally come to the school. So clearly I am very fond of you.

'But that's as far as it goes. To be frank, I was about to tell you that I don't think we will ever fuck each other again. I haven't told anybody yet, not even the headmistress, but my application to join the staff at Cheltenham Ladies College has been successful and I shall hand in my notice to Miss Randall tomorrow.'

Mr Clee gave a wry little laugh as he pressed the package into Rosie's hand and said: 'Well, I'm truly sorry that we won't be making love any more. I shall be forced to take myself in hand every night and think back to the glorious fun we had together. Still, I'm truly glad that you are joining the staff of such a prestigious academy. Come to think of it, you can now accept this little gift as a memento of our friendship.'

Rosie leaned forward and kissed him lightly on the cheek and said: 'Thank you, Nick. On those terms I am delighted to accept your gift.'

'Good show, but you don't have to wait till you get back to Dame Chasuble's to open it,' he chuckled. Rosie tore open the package. Although Phil and I were too far away to see what was inside it, Rosie satisfied our curiosity by exclaiming: 'Oh, what a pretty silver brooch. Thank you very much, Nick. I will think of you every time I wear it. Tell me though, what are these four tiny flags? They look like naval signals.'

With a broad smile on his handsome face, Mr Clee said

admiringly: 'They are indeed naval signals, you clever girl. It's a copy of the very brooch the King gave to Mrs Keppel shortly after they first met and it reads "Open your hatch as I am about to fire my torpedo!"'

[*This is actually an inaccurate translation of the original gold, rose diamond and enamel nautical brooch given by the then Prince of Wales in the summer of 1900 to the woman who was to become his favourite mistress. This message on the flags read, 'Position quarterly and open, I am about to fire a Whitehead torpedo, ahead.' – Editor*]

Not wishing to eavesdrop, I quietly stole away from the scene and met Babs who was holding a sheet of paper in her hand. I looked at her enquiringly and she said: 'Sophie, I misjudged Lawrence. He's a very sweet boy who has a very romantic nature. Look, Sophie, whilst I was leafing through a book, he sat down at a desk and penned a little poem which he dedicated to me. Would you like to read it?'

'Of course I would,' I said but Babs refused to let me see Lawrence's verses until later that evening in her study. We had just come out of the bathroom and were wearing only our dressing-gowns when she passed me over a sheet of paper and I read out loud the following:

> *Come, sweet Babs and dwell with me,*
> *Under the shade of the old oak tree,*
> *No-one could happier be*
> *Than I if kindly blessed with thee.*
> *I know the lessons I have learned from you,*
> *Sweet tuition in the paths of love,*
> *Sure I'll remember what I ought to do*
> *When I am under and you are above!*
> *Enter at once, dear lover to my bower,*
> *Each movement will give me bliss,*
> *'Tis joy for me to know I have the power,*
> *With you to share sweet rapture such as this!*

How often have I praised your quim's tight grip!
Each time we fuck is better than the last,
Now from your sheath my prick will never slip!
Your legs and mine entwined shall keep it fast,
Only your love such joy can give,
United thus, forever I could live.
Nor envy those who boast a mistress's love,
Give me your cunt, I ne'er will rove!

'What do you think of it?' asked Babs and I replied: 'It certainly is a spirited and evocative piece of writing, but I don't think John Masefield [*the Poet Laureate – Editor*] has too much to worry about.'

We dissolved into peals of laughter and as I passed back the paper to Babs, she slipped it into her pocket and said thoughtfully: 'Yes, Lawrence Reuben is a clever chap and he is a good fuck too. But until the end of term that will be the last cock either of us will see.'

The thought of our randy afternoon must have fired Babs' blood because as we sat down on the small sofa she suddenly reached out and slid her arm inside my robe and cupped one of my breasts in her hand as she continued: 'Actually, I often find that I can spend just as well without the aid of a cock, can't you?' And then as if as an afterthought she added: 'Oh, I hope you don't mind my squeezing your nice big nipples.'

'Not at all,' I answered huskily because I was also becoming fired up by the insistent tweaking of my titties. Very soon the pair of us had chucked off our robes and cuddled together in a naked embrace.

'My, your pussey is getting wet,' Babs giggled, moving her hand down to let her fingertips brush through my hairy bush and then running her forefinger along the length of my crack. Then she took my hand and placed it firmly on her own moist pussey as she lay back on the sofa. Spreading her legs to let me kneel between them, she panted: 'Please be a dear and bring me off, Sophie! I'm absolutely dying for it.'

This was a request I was only too happy to grant. I began by kissing Babs' titties as I moulded her jouncy big breasts in my hands, mashing them together so that her nipples were practically rubbing together as I began to suck them. The lissome girl began to writhe with pleasure and she gasped out: 'Oh yes, that's delicious, darling! Now suck my pussey and make me come!'

I wiggled my head down and started to lick Babs' wet opening. She thrust her hairy pussey hard against my mouth, quickly moving into the dark folds of her cunney until I uncovered the erect nub of her clitty. I took the fleshy bud between my teeth as Babs moaned and bucked her hips at the exquisite torture as I began to work on her inner walls, scouring the delicate membranes and using the tip of my tongue like a tiny prick, penetrating again and again into her tingling love tunnel.

Babs' squeals of pleasure increased in frequency and she clutched the back of my head. I continued to lick remorselessly at her soaking slit as I felt her tremble all over at the approach of her spend. She bucked and twisted as her orgasm shuddered through her groin and when it had passed I raised my head and climbed on top of her so that our two nude bodies were pressed together nipple to nipple, pussey to pussey.

'Now let me be the gentleman,' she whispered. We changed positions with Babs lying on top of me. Fondling my breasts she dipped down to swirl my hardened titties between her lips, sending chills of unslaked desires up and down my spine. As her knowing fingers inched towards my cunney, I felt my thighs stiffen and my hips involuntarily thrust forward in tantalising anticipation of what I knew was soon to follow.

With her index finger, she traced a dainty path through

my pussey bush and settled on my quim, around which she drew hard little circles until I was squirming with delight. 'O-h-h-h!' I moaned in a half-strangled voice. As she slid a finger up to the knuckle between my yielding love lips into my sopping slit, she breathed into my ear: 'Oh Sophie, frigging you like this is making me randy again. Just wait a moment, I've something here which will pleasure us both.'

She jerked herself upwards and I yelped in disappointment as she pulled her finger from my cunt and dived down to draw something out from the pocket of her discarded dressing-gown. What could this be, I wondered, as Babs brought out an engraved silver box from which she took out an exquisite wooden dildo, upon which was carved a lascivious scene of a girl lying on a bed holding an erect cock in each of her hands.

'My sister Veronica lent me this ladies' comforter which was given to her by Sir Martin Windrow,' explained Babs as she caressed the two-headed artificial prick. 'It was fashioned by Baum and Newman, the famous Derbyshire manufactory in 1903, supposedly from the shafts of two great cocksmen, His Royal Highness King Edward VII, God bless him, and his crony Sir Richard Segal, the merchant banker.'

'Have you ever used a double-headed dildo before?' she enquired as she took out a small jar of orange-flavoured oil which she poured liberally over both of the knobs before shaking the last drops all over my pussey. 'No? Well in that case, you're in for a treat, you lucky girl. Open your legs and prepare to be fucked by the royal tool of His Royal Highness, the King of Great Britain and Emperor of India.'

I giggled as I obediently lay back. Babs went to work on my pussey with a will, kissing my titties as she pressed the knob modelled on His Majesty's bell-end between my pink love lips, working it in slowly but surely until I called out that I could take in no more. With the godemiche now fully embedded inside my cunt, Babs lifted herself up and sat herself down astride my thighs. She fingered herself with one hand as she vibrated the wooden cock which was stuck inside my sated quim. Then she tilted it slightly upwards and raising herself up she inserted the opposite knob of the dildo inside her own sticky snatch.

'Isn't that dreamy?' she enquired as she reached round my sides and pulled me forward until our bodies were pressed tightly together, separated only by the stem of the dildo. I wrapped my arms as tightly as I could around Babs and, as we rocked to and fro, we achieved a wonderful rhythm which allowed the wooden cock to slide thrillingly in and out of our juicy honeypots, sending pulses of sheer ecstasy to every nerve-centre in our bodies. As our excitement grew, our fucking became even more frenzied.

'Ahhh! Isn't that scrumptious? Didn't I tell you how enjoyable this kind of frigging can be?' gasped Babs as she slid her fingers up and down my back with gentle, titillating strokes which sent chills of desire sweeping all along my spine. We continued to fuck ourselves on this extraordinary artificial cock, arching ourselves like two excited kittens as we encouraged the wooden knobs to prod through the pink petals of our pussies into the grooved walls of our cunnies. Indeed, Babs and I diddled each other so superbly that we spent simultaneously, shuddering in the joys of our mutual come as love juice poured out of our cunts and seeped into the cushions of the sofa.

'Crumbs! That's torn it! What will the maids think when they come in to clean the study?' I asked anxiously but the ever-resourceful Babs replied: 'Don't worry, Sophie. I'll just go back to my study for a moment and bring back my bottle of Professor Boodle's All-Purpose Elixir which I recommend you should always keep handy. Just a few dabs of this wonderful cleaning liquid will take out the stains and no-one will be any the wiser.'

She was as good as her word and, to my great relief, the Professor's Elixir proved itself as efficacious as Babs had promised. I went to bed without any concern about being embarrassed by questions from Mrs Uxbridge, our formidable housekeeper. Yet although there was no reason why I should not have enjoyed a sound night's slumber, I woke up shortly before six o'clock. Dawn had broken, bright sunlight was streaming through the thin curtains and my body stubbornly refused to go back to sleep.

I decided to take an early-morning walk before my morning shower. I slipped on a blouse, my tennis skirt and a pair of plimsolls before making my way quietly out of the dormitory, taking care not to wake anyone else who was still fast asleep. The front door would still be locked so I walked down the stairs to the servants' quarters where I would be able to leave via the tradesmen's entrance. However, as I walked down the stairs I heard two of the young servants who came in daily from a nearby small village gossiping to each other. I recognised the dulcet tones of Dorothy, a pretty slip of a girl who could be no more than sixteen, who was saying: 'So there we were, Bella, just the two of us and Charles Prince lying down on his back on the grass without a stitch of clothing on him.'

'Oooh, the dirty beast! You should have run back here and told Mrs Uxbridge. She would have telephoned the police station,' said her companion. I waited at the foot of the stairs, wishing to hear more of this conversation, for those readers with a good memory will of course recall that Charles Prince was a friend of Celia Parker and the photographer whom Phil Colnbrook and myself had helped take some *risqué* pictures on the morning of my birthday.

I could hardly wait to find out why on earth Charles should have been lying naked out in the open air. Fortunately Dorothy had time to relieve my curiosity by saying: 'Why would I want to do that? Come on, Bella, he wasn't doing any harm and he was terribly apologetic when he saw me standing in front of him. The fact is that Charlie had been for an early-morning run and had got so sweaty that he took off his clothes and went for a dip in the stream. The poor chap didn't have a towel so he stretched out to dry himself off in the sun, not thinking that anyone would be coming by so early in the morning.'

'My, my, it's Charlie now, is it,' teased Bella mockingly. 'But he was "sir" to me and the rest of the girls when he came round with his camera to take the photographs of the junior forms!'

'Oh, go on with you, do you want to hear what happened or not?' exclaimed Dorothy. 'Well, I stood there gaping at Charlie's cock which was standing up between his thighs, swaying back and forth like the grass in the warm breeze. He's very well-hung with a really beautiful shaft, all pale and smooth with a trace of pink running all the way up from his balls to his knob which was flaring out from his pulled-back foreskin.

'Charlie's eyes were closed as he wrapped his fingers round his stiffie and began to pump his hand up and down it. What a waste, I thought to myself as I slipped down on my knees beside him. With one hand I pulled his fingers off his throbbing tool and laid it on his tummy. He woke up with a start and cried out: "Hell's bells! Who are you and what are you doing?"

'"My name's Dorothy, Mr Charles, and I'm a maid-of-all-work at Dame Chasuble's Academy. As to what I'm doing, well, I don't really have to tell you, do I?"'

'You cheeky monkey, I'd never have had the nerve to toss off a young toff like Charlie Prince let alone answer him back,' commented Bella with a laugh. 'So what happened then?'

Dorothy gave a husky chuckle and answered: 'Charlie smiled at me and said to me: "Well, please carry on,

Dorothy. I never thought I would be pleasured so nicely this morning but I've always held to the motto of never looking a gift horse in the mouth, especially one as pretty as yours!"

'He winked at me as I curled my fingers round his thick prick which was now as hard as a rock. As I slid my hand up and down the blue-veined shaft, I moved myself forward and leaned across to lick the smooth-skinned dome with the tip of my tongue. Charlie let out a yowl of delight when I began to suck his cock, keeping my lips clamped around his shaft as I took him into my mouth, rolling my tongue around his knob. It didn't take too long for him to spend. I swallowed every drop of his sticky jism as his prick started to shrink back to its normal size.'

'Very nice too, Dottie, but are you going to see Mr Prince, oh, beg your pardon, Charlie again?' The shapely young girl nodded vigorously as she replied: 'I should say so! We've arranged to meet at the Hare and Hounds tomorrow night at nine o'clock. And between you and me, I can hardly wait, it's been two months now since I've had a good fuck!'

I waited for the two maids to walk off before I sauntered through to the tradesmen's entrance and then, finding myself in a sheltered spot in a clump of silver birches, I lay against the trunk of one of the trees. After throwing up my skirt, my hand stole to that magic place between my legs as I thought about Dorothy's lewd encounter with Charlie Prince's cock and how I had seen the handsome young man slew his throbbing tool in and out of Celia Parker's juicy cunt.

My fingers pressed against my moistening slit as I closed my eyes and another lascivious image now floated across my mind, this time of when Terry Jackson had seduced me and how his hot pulsating prick had slid so deliciously into my clingy cunt . . .

I was wearing no underwear so my fingertips had free access to my pouting pussey lips which I spread open and then I pressed a finger into my squishy quim, filling my love channel with it. Then, with my finger coated with cuntal juice, I pulled it out and ran the tip up and down my puffy pussey lips before concentrating on my erect little clitty. I rubbed slowly at first and then faster and faster as I imagined how lovely it would feel to have a thick stiff cock pounding in and out of my sticky honeypot, be it the shaft of Terry Jackson, Charlie Prince or Phil Colnbrook. Soon an ecstatic moan escaped from my lips as I gyrated my hips and frigging my clitty at an even more furious pace, I swiftly achieved a delightful spend.

Naturally, I made no mention of this little episode to my friends when I returned to the dormitory, but as fate would have it, I was shortly to meet Charles Prince again, albeit after the end of term which also heralded the completion of my schooldays.

Chapter Three

I detest snobbery and even my bitterest enemies could not accuse me of trying to conceal my personal background. It is of no more importance to me that my dear father is but a small shopkeeper in the cathedral city of St Albans than it is that my mother was born into the wealthy Wellsend clan of South Hertfordshire. She was shunned by her family because she married my father who was considered 'beneath her'.

Nevertheless, I will not pretend that I do not prefer the lazy carefree life of the so-called upper classes and I will not deny that when I deemed it to be of use, I have deliberately dropped the Wellsend family connection into a conversation. The first time I used this ploy was in obtaining an invitation from Alex's parents to spend a week at their home on the outskirts of Oxford. Now I am not saying that Sir Brindsleigh and Lady Maria Henderson would not have allowed Alex to bring me home if they had known that I hailed from humble stock, but I am sure that mention of my mother's family banished any doubts Lady Maria might have entertained about my suitability as a guest in their beautiful country house in Sutton Green some six miles west of Oxford's dreaming spires.

Be that as it may, I was delighted to have the chance to spend a week in the beautiful town of which Keats wrote: 'This Oxford, I have no doubt, is the finest city in the world – it is full of old Gothic buildings – spires – towers –

quadrangles – cloisters – groves and is surrounded with more clear streams than I ever saw together.'

So when I arrived at Henderson Hall just before noon, I could hardly wait to unpack and climb into Sir Brindsleigh's twenty horse-power Rover motor car which would speed Alex and I into Oxford. When I thanked him for driving us into town he replied: 'It's no trouble at all, m'dear. I enjoy driving although the roads are getting pretty clogged with cars these days. Anyhow, the trip will give me the opportunity to meet up with an old business acquaintance from London who is staying at the Randolph Hotel.'

He started the car and added: 'Alex, I'll drop you two off at Carfax and meet you back there at half past six this evening. I suggest that you take a light luncheon at that pleasant little restaurant we went to last week and then take Sophie for a stroll down the High Street.'

Sir Brindsleigh was a keen motorist and I must admit to being slightly concerned as he pressed his foot on the accelerator. We whizzed at almost forty miles an hour down the narrow country lane to the Oxford road.

'Hold on to your hats,' cried Sir Brindsleigh as he successfully executed a violent swerve to miss a clutch of squawking Buff Orpingtons. Glancing back at us he snorted: 'Damned stupid farmers, fancy letting poultry out on the highway. Lucky we weren't going really fast.'

[*Sir Brindsleigh Henderson may have been too carefree a driver even in those far-off days but his Rover Twenty was one of the most reliable of the mid-Edwardian motor vehicles. One of these 3.5 litre cars won the 1907 Tourist Trophy race in the Isle of Man at an average speed of twenty nine miles per hour – Editor*]

Thankfully we arrived in Oxford without further mishap. Alex and I alighted safely at Carfax, the hub of the town where the main thoroughfares intersect. We waved goodbye to Sir Brindsleigh and then Alex proposed we saunter through the High Street towards Magdalen Bridge. But just as we approached Brasenose College she said: 'Are you ready to eat, Sophie? Just across the road there's a very nice restaurant where Papa and I had a delicious lunch a few days ago.'

'Lead on, there weren't any refreshments available on the train and I'm feeling quite peckish,' I replied and so we crossed the road into Harpers, a brightly furnished establishment of only a dozen or so tables, most of which were already occupied. Luckily, there was one free table for two by the window to which we were escorted by a plump middle-aged gentleman who looked more like a University don than a waiter. I find it slightly intimidating to give commands to an older person, especially one of such distinguished appearance, but Alex said to him briskly: 'We'll order straightaway, please, as we don't have too much time. What does the chef recommend today?'

'There's a very good Italian vegetable soup to begin with, miss,' he replied solemnly. 'And I would follow that with a nice piece of turbot with anchovy sauce. Then you might choose between rack of lamb or perhaps you would prefer duckling with new potatoes and green peas?'

'I'll have the duckling,' I said promptly and Alex nodded: 'So will I, and shall we both have the soup and the turbot? Yes? Good, and we'll have a bottle of that excellent sparkling Moselle I had here last week. I think it was an '03 Zeltinger.'

I am certain that the old waiter thought us two most forward young ladies even to come into the restaurant unaccompanied by any male escorts, let alone to order any wine, but if he did he said nothing except to murmur: 'Very good, miss.'

We enjoyed an excellent meal although it was hardly the light luncheon suggested by Alex's father. Anyhow, we were finishing our repast with a delectable gooseberry tart and cream when all of a sudden I spied a familiar figure looking at the menu which was written up on a card pasted in the window.

'Alex, look behind you,' I cried out excitedly. 'Isn't that Charles Prince standing on the pavement?'

'Charles Prince? Oh, you mean the photograph chap who Miss Randall asked to take pictures of the junior classes back at Dame Chasuble's last term?' said Alex. She turned her head and peered outside to where I was pointing. Then she exclaimed: 'Good heavens, so it is! I wonder if he is still going steady with Celia Parker? Well, what a coincidence seeing him here! Why don't we ask him to have some coffee with us?'

'Oh yes, I saw him quite recently,' I said, rising to my feet. 'On my birthday, as a matter of fact. Of course he might not want to join us, but I'll say hello to him and see what he says.'

In fact Charles was only too happy to sit down for coffee with us and the waiter (relieved perhaps that there was now at least one gentleman at our table) trundled up with an extra chair for him.

'How nice to see you again, Charles. May I ask you what brings you to Oxford?' I asked and he smiled: 'Probably for the same reason as you. It's one of my favourite towns and I never get tired of walking round the colleges and going for a row on the river.'

'And you always bring your camera with you, I'll be bound,' Alex chimed in and Charles nodded: 'But of course, and this trip will be particularly exciting because I plan to try out my new cinematographic camera and take some moving pictures.'

'Will you really? Gosh, that sounds fascinating! Are you going to make one of those short films they show in the music halls? I've only seen one myself and that was at the Empire, Leicester Square when my parents took me to

London for the day last year. The final act in the show was five minutes of jerky film called The Biograph.'

'Ah yes, the Biograph. It isn't all that impressive, is it? On the other hand, the art of moving pictures is still in its infancy, Sophie,' he said earnestly. 'I predict that the three-minute film will soon be overtaken by full-length dramas which will be screened in special cinematic theatres. And I'll lay odds that some clever chaps will transform the medium by inventing processes for adding colour and sound to the film.'

'I think you might be straying into the realms of fantasy,' smiled Alex but Charles shook his head vigorously and replied: 'No, no, I'm convinced it will be only a matter of time. Remember how people scoffed at the idea of the telephone and the phonograph when they were first mooted?'

'Only time will tell,' I said placatingly. 'Right now, tell us about the scenario for your film.'

'I don't really have one,' he confessed with a wry shrug. 'But I thought that the river would be an excellent background for any story that I might dream up and so I'm going to spend the afternoon looking around for a suitable location. Um, I don't suppose you ladies would be interested in coming out for a punt on the Cherwell?'

Well, I liked the cut of Charles's jib so although Alex and I had planned to look round the colleges after lunch, I decided that if my friend was agreeable, I would postpone my sight-seeing tour to another day. As I expected, Alex was agreeable. When I exchanged an enquiring glance with her, she signalled her approval with a nod and a smile so I replied: 'Thank you, Charles, that would be very nice. But wouldn't we be in the way?'

'Far from it,' he said promptly. 'Not only would I thoroughly enjoy the pleasure of your company, but it would really be most helpful to hear your opinions on any ideas that might occur to me during the afternoon.'

The waiter brought us our coffee as Charles went on: 'I'll pass on the coffee, if I may, as I want to hurry back to my hotel and tell them to make up a picnic tea for three people. Then I'll come back here for you in about forty-five minutes if that will be convenient.'

'That sounds fine,' said Alex. 'But we've finished our lunch so why don't you meet us in front of the Radcliffe Camera instead?'

'Why not indeed,' said Charles and, after gulping down his coffee, he walked out briskly to make all the necessary arrangements. When the waiter brought the bill, I wanted to pay my share but Alex would have none of it, insisting that I was her guest as she took out half a sovereign [*or 50p – an amount that one hundred years later seems extraordinary value for the meal described by Sophie and shows how much one could buy before inflation robbed us of our currency – Editor*] from her purse and placed it on the waiter's plate. She waved him away when he returned with her change. His gratitude at her munificent gratuity was such that he almost bowed us out of the restaurant.

I was so pleased that Alex took me to the Radcliffe Camera, a domed eighteenth-century edifice which housed a large medical library. She explained that it was built with funds provided by Queen Anne's physician, Dr John Radcliffe, and whilst the building was interesting in itself, what it best offered visitors was that on payment of tuppence they are allowed to climb to the gallery at the base of the dome from which one is given a truly magnificent view of the towers and spires of Oxford.

'Charles should have brought his camera up here,' I observed as Alex pointed out some of the prominent places for me – and then looking down to the High Street, I added: 'Oh look, there he is, getting out from that hansom cab. Let's go and meet him.'

It was fun to ride in a horse-drawn cab down to the river and when I mentioned this to Charles, he commented: 'Yes, they are disappearing fast. I understand that there aren't more than a handful left in London. So we won't hear any such stories like the tale about the late Queen who was being driven around Windsor Park in a small laudulet by a stableman when the horse emitted a tremendous fart. The stableman went as red as a beetroot and croaked: "Oh, I do beg your pardon, ma'am," and the Queen is supposed to have replied mildly: "That's all right, Smithers. If you hadn't have said anything, I would have thought it was the horse!"'

We roared with laughter and Alex asked if there was any truth in this amusing story. 'I don't honestly know,' Charles grinned as we came up to a boat-hire establishment on the banks of the Cherwell. 'However, as the Romans say, *Se non è vero, è molto ben trovato!*' Then seeing the blank looks on our faces (for neither Alex nor I spoke Italian) he translated: 'Even if it's not true, it's well told!'

Charles slipped the cabbie a florin and instructed him to come back to the landing stage at five o'clock to take us back to town.

Unfortunately there were no punts available but Charles did manage to hire a rowing boat for the afternoon. This hardly mattered for, unlike the Isis, the Cherwell is not the river for energetic rowing. The river is simply a sweet maze of water especially devised for the enjoyment of lazing around although, in all fairness, I must record that Charles was an expert oarsman and rowed us away from the jetty with strong, even strokes. Then he dropped the pace and, settling myself against the pile of soft cushions thoughtfully provided by the boat's owners, I soon felt my eyelids droop. I was aware only of the soft rhythmic splash of the oars, the golden sparks of afternoon sunlight which tipped each tiny ripple on the water and the low murmur of voices punctuated by bursts of giggles as Alex and Charles became better acquainted.

The gentle rocking of the boat finally lulled me to sleep from which I was woken by Alex's soft hand shaking my arm. Her sweetly sibilant voice broke through my slumber.

'What is it? Where are we?' I murmured drowsily and she chuckled: 'Wake up, Sophie! You've been asleep for half an hour, you lazy creature!'

However, when I opened my eyes I was shocked to find that the lovely girl had partially disrobed. She was wearing only a semi-transparent camisole fashioned from the softest Belgian linen through which the contours of her jutting breasts and luscious big titties were clearly visible, together with a pair of tiny French knickers cut from the same sheer fabric which showed the curves of her tight little bottom and the outline of her fluffy triangle of pussey hair.

My eyebrows were raised even higher when I sat up and looked across to Charles to see that he had stripped down to his drawers. As I admired his lithe muscular physique, the good-looking young man swung the oars to guide us towards the shore and I noticed a large swelling in his lap when I glanced down at his crotch.

'We've come down a little tributary of the river to a small island where I thought we would have our tea,' said Charles as he jumped out of the boat and pulled it up onto the bank. 'Actually, it's private property owned by Lord Chiddingfold but Edward, his eldest son, is a good friend of mine and there won't be any bother about us trespassing – especially as I believe that the Chiddingfolds are spending the summer up in Scotland.'

He helped us out of the boat onto the soft grass and, with a mischievous twinkle in his steely blue eyes, he said: 'I do hope you don't mind my taking off my clothes. It's so much more comfortable to row in just a pair of shorts in this heat.'

'No, of course I don't mind and indeed I think I'll join

Alex and take off some of my clothes too,' I replied as I began to unbutton my skirt. So Alex and I were clad only in our underwear whilst Charles went back to the boat to carry the picnic hamper back to us. Charles had also eaten a good lunch so none of us were very hungry. We could only nibble at the dainty cucumber sandwiches and tiny fruit tartlets, but then he took three tall tumblers and filled them to the brim with sparkling champagne which had been kept cold in a small ice-box inside the hamper. Handing us both a glass, he leaned back and took a well-deserved sip as he looked at his half-naked harem through amused, appraising eyes.

Gazing back boldly at him, I raised my glass and took a long cool draught of the refreshing drink, giggling gently as the fizzy bubbles tickled my nose and delicious tremors of sensual langour ran through my body. It didn't take us too long to finish the bottle and it was soon abundantly clear that the champagne had gone to Alex's head for, brushing back her honey-blonde tresses from the front of her face, she sighed: 'You know something, Charles, I would love to have a little swim. How I wish I had a bathing costume because the water looks so lovely and cool.'

'There's really no reason why you shouldn't go in for a quick dip,' said Charles encouragingly. 'As I said to you, this place is always deserted and we could see anyone approaching a mile off.'

Alex winked at me wickedly and said: 'Sophie, do you fancy coming in the river with me?'

Now it wasn't difficult to guess that apart from splashing about in the river, my pretty friend wanted to know if I wanted to join in some saucy business afterwards. However, the idea of frolicking with Charles Prince appealed to me and so I returned Alex's wink and replied: 'Yes, I'll join you, darling, but we can't let our underclothes get wet.'

I heard Charles draw in his breath sharply as I took hold

of her outstretched hand and pulled myself to my feet. Then I slowly pulled down the straps of my slip from my shoulders, baring my soft creamy breasts which jiggled seductively as I turned away from Charles and tugged down my knickers to expose my curvy bum cheeks as the gentle breeze wafted around my nude body.

Alex followed my example and, with a seductive rustle, she slipped out of her flimsy camisole. With a fine theatrical flourish, she wiggled down her panties and, completely and utterly naked, her lissome body gleaming in the sunshine, unabashedly displaying her pert boyish bottom, slender waist and pert uptilted breasts to Charles who stared at her open-mouthed as she pirouetted daintily in front of him.

Naked as nature intended, we ran hand in hand to the water's edge, squealing like children as we gaily splashed each other before striking out into the rivulet for a swim. Despite our calls for him to join us, Charles stayed on the island, silently watching us from his vantage point and clearly fascinated by the sight of this happy pair of alluring frolicsome kittens.

About ten minutes later Alex and I made our way back to him, pink-cheeked and sparkling-eyed after our aquatic exertions. Thousands of jewel-clear drops of water clung to our lissome nude bodies which we deliberately shook off over Charles, eliciting a cry of protest. We flopped down on the rug next to him, drying ourselves with the fluffy white towels which had been provided by the owners of our boat in the event of customers taking an unwanted tumble into the Cherwell.

'Charles, I'm surprised you didn't fancy a quick dip to cool yourself off,' I remarked. We folded our towels into pillows and lay back to let the warmth of the sun dry off any remaining moisture from our bodies. He smiled wanly and replied: 'Yes, I'm sure I would have found it most refreshing, Sophie, but the problem is that I can't swim.'

'You can't swim!' I echoed in amazement for it was hard to fathom out any reason why a healthy young chap like Charles should labour under such a handicap. 'With the greatest of respect, that's utter nonsense! Everyone has the innate ability to swim and it's only the degrees of strength and technique which distinguish the expert from the novice.'

He looked doubtfully at me but Alex chipped in: 'Sophie's quite right, my dear. Our games mistress at Dame Chasuble's used to reassure any nervous girls by telling them that all one needs is having the confidence to relax.

Charles stroked his chin thoughtfully whilst I pressed home the attack. 'Why don't you let Alex and I help you?' I asked, taking hold of his hand. 'In any case, the river's so shallow that you would easily be able to stand even at its deepest level.'

'Well, if you think it will help—' he said hesitantly, but Alex clasped his other hand and helped pull the reluctant lad to his feet. She said brightly: 'I've a marvellous idea! If you succeed in conquering your fear of water – because that is all that's stopping you swimming – Sophie and I will suck your cock! There, isn't that a great incentive?'

Despite his nervousness, Charles burst out laughing and answered: 'Alex, I can't think of anything better – except actually fucking you, of course.'

The thought of gobbling Charles's prick made me tingle all over and I giggled: 'That could also be arranged, although in that case I would feel somewhat superfluous to requirements.'

'Not necessarily,' said Charles as he divested himself of his drawers. Naturally our eyes were drawn to his erect mushroom-domed shaft which was standing high and proud against his flat hairless belly.

For a few magical moments the three of us fell silent, breathing in the undeniable odour of sexual arousal which now began to suffuse the air.

'Alex, perhaps we should get Charles in the right frame of mind before his swimming lesson,' I said softly, not waiting for an answer as I slipped to my knees and planted a huge wet kiss on the ripe ruby plum of his uncapped helmet, juicing it with saliva whilst I slipped my hand underneath to squeeze his wrinkled pink ballsack.

Lovingly I began to give his pulsing prick a thorough leisurely suck, slowly bobbing my head up and down the smooth warm shaft which was twitching so violently that I was afraid he would soon be on the verge of a spend. I switched my attention to his scrotum and he let out a heartfelt little cry of delight when I lapped around the deliciously sensitive area between his balls and bum-hole.

Alas, this proved so exciting to Charles that he gasped out: 'Oh God! I'm coming, Sophie! Suck my cock again, you wicked vixen!'

I just had time to slide my lips over his knob and flick my tongue over its slitted end when I felt his body stiffen. As I gave his helmet one final slurp, his balls began to pulsate and a stream of hot love juice spurted into my mouth. Charles' cock throbbed wildly as I held it lightly between my teeth. I sucked and swallowed his creamy emission until I felt the spongy helmet soften and then I rolled my lips around it, nibbling away at the rounded bulb until his shaft shrivelled into limpness.

To be honest, I would have loved him to poke me after he had recovered his strength. My pussey was now so damp that I was simply aching for a good shagging, but I could hardly deny Alex her turn to sample Charles' goodies and she slid down on her back next to our gallant young stallion.

She ran her fingers through the fluffy blonde triangle of flaxen pussey hair at the base of her belly and giggled sweetly: 'Well, Charles, the merchandise is on display – do you wish to make a purchase or shall I wrap it up again and send it back to the factory?'

He answered with a low growl as he rolled over and covered Alex's curvy body with his own, immediately sliding his hands under her legs to squeeze the jouncy globes of her peachy bottom.

'Ahhhh!' she gurgled happily when Charles pressed his lips to her invitingly horned-up titties, licking and lapping at the delightful little pink paps. Then he lowered his head and kissed her pussey whilst he released his hands from her bum cheeks to speed upwards to her breasts where he tweaked and rubbed her engorged nipples between his fingers.

Now it has been my experience that, unlike their Continental counterparts, Englishmen are not skilled in the delicate art of muff-diving. However, as I watched Charles Prince at work, it was patently obvious that this virile youth was an honourable exception to the rule.

Alex was yelping with delight as his tongue ran along the edges of her pouting pussey lips before flicking inside to lash itself around her erect clitty, which made the lubricious lass shiver with sensual desire. Then Charles hauled himself up and was about to plunge his rampant shaft into Alex's welcoming love funnel when the hot-blooded girl grasped his thick prick and gasped: 'Oh Charles, please let me suck your lovely big tool before you fuck me.'

This was my first exposure to the grand practice of *soixante neuf* and I watched intently as, nothing loath, Charles nodded his agreement and continued to lick out her sopping slit whilst Alex curled herself round until her face was level with Charles's cock. His back arched in ecstasy when he felt the wet warmth of her soft lips around the ridge of his uncapped knob. Alex teasingly planted a quick series of butterfly kisses on his bell-end as she slid her hand up and down his sturdy shaft before she tightened her hold and sucked his purple bell-end into her mouth.

At the same time, Charles busied himself in providing a

similar oral stimulation to Alex's sopping slit. I craned my head forward to see his tongue shoot out and move slowly around her pouting pink cunney lips. Her rounded bum cheeks jiggled saucily from side to side whilst Charles sucked on her pussey and I saw rivulets of cuntal juice beginning to trickle down her thighs.

This excited Alex so much that, after one last slurping suck, she pulled her head up from his twitching tool and panted: 'Oooh, that's lovely, but now finish me off with your cock!'

She threw herself down on her back and parted her legs wide, exposing the red chink of her cunney between the puffy love lips which protruded from her fluffy blonde bush of pussey hair. Charles did not reply but, with a gleam in his eye and his stiff shaft sticking out like a bar, he answered her call and clambered upon her nubile curves.

How they sighed and moaned in the ecstasy of the moment when his blue-veined boner slid smoothly into her welcoming love funnel. Their lips met in the sweetest of kisses! My own hand strayed down to my pussey and I began to rub my clitty whilst I watched Alex jerk her tight little bum cheeks up and down to absorb as much of Charles's thick prick as possible. Then she let out a tiny choking cry of delight as he embedded his cock inside her juicy cunt and his balls slapped against her bottom.

I slid down on my knees, frigging myself faster and faster as, with her big titties jiggling as she writhed from side to side, Alex cried out: 'Oooh! Oooh! Charlie, that's incredible, I've never been so full of cock! Oh, I'm going to come! H-a-r-g-h!'

Alex rotated her hips, answering his powerful thrusts with upwards jerks of her own until Charles's lithe torso tensed. He shuddered violently as the first gush of sticky spunk surged out of his cock.

'Aaaah! Aaaah! Do more, I'm coming too!' she howled as she clawed at his shoulders and crossed her legs across his back. The virile young man pumped spurt after spurt of cream jism into her tingling quim whilst I held my breath. My fingers raced in and out of my cunney until the initial wave of a small but satisfying spend spread through my body.

During this excitement a bank of grey cloud had slowly made its way over the sun. When we had recovered, we dressed ourselves and after clearing up the remains of our picnic we set off back to town.

'I'm afraid we didn't think of any ideas for your film,' I remarked to Charles as he pushed us out from the shore with the blade of an oar.

'True enough, Sophie, but it was hardly a wasted afternoon as far as I'm concerned,' Charles grinned as he laid down his oars and went on: 'Actually, it reminds me of an exciting sensual experience I enjoyed last summer when my parents took me to Venice. Well, one afternoon I was invited by our Italian hosts to take a cruise on the canals with Signora Tardelli and her beautiful eighteen-year-old twin daughters, Claudia and Francesca. They squeezed themselves in on either side of me whilst their mother sat with her back to us in the front of the gondola in order to give me a running commentary (for like her daughters, she spoke perfect English) on the beauties of her magical city.

'To be honest, I must confess that I found it hard to concentrate on anything but the two gorgeous girls who were naturally most properly dressed. Yet it was noticeable that Claudia had neglected to push back into place a tendril of silky dark hair which had escaped its coiffure and which was lying against her cheek. Francesca had undone the top three buttons of her blouse to reveal the swell of her lush breasts. We chatted away gaily and I must admit that when the girls smiled I could imagine their full red lips closing around my uncapped purple knob and their even white teeth nibbling the length of my shaft, which had already begun to thicken and was tenting upwards in my lap.

'Summoning up all my reserves of willpower, I succeeded in banishing all lewd thoughts of fucking these ripe creatures from my mind. Instead I gave all my attention to Signora Tardelli's interesting narration as we passed by the Doge's Palace on the Grand Canal. I genuinely admired the splendours of the magnificent buildings but then, just like today, the weather became cloudy and one of the girls spread a large rug over our laps. My attention was suddenly distracted from the sights by what I thought might be an insect crawling up my leg. I wriggled slightly to try and shake it off. However, this proved ineffectual and I could not slide my hand onto my thigh because I was closely hemmed in by the twins. I could say nothing for I had no wish to cause a panic by telling them that there might be a spider under the rug!

'I tried to distract myself by listening to Signora Tardelli who was extolling the beauty of this church and that tower. The girls occasionally added a word or two of further explanation, apparently unaware of my growing discomfort.

'The movement was now around my crotch and I realised that it was caused by soft fingers caressing the bulge in my trousers, kneading and squeezing my cock – yet although either Claudia or Francesca was responsible, it was impossible to tell which of these pretty dark-haired minxes was secretly frigging me because both were showing complete detachment. Claudia was talking to her mother in Italian whilst Francesca was telling me something about the history of St Mark's Church.

'This state of affairs went on for some little while and then the mysterious fingers deftly unbuttoned my trousers and, plunging through the slit in my drawers, slid themselves around my aching shaft. I looked at Claudia, then at

Francesca and finally back again to Claudia but they acknowledged my fevered glances only with an innocent smile such as one would give on catching a friend's eye in a crowd. There was not the slightest suggestion that one of these sweet young girls was secretly playing with my cock beneath the cover of the rug.

'I would have given anything to find out which of the girls was responsible, though as both were stunningly beautiful it hardly mattered. I sat there seething with lust whilst the soft skilled hand worked firmly up and down my twitching tool with such discreet strokes that barely a ripple of movement showed on the surface of the rug. Appropriately enough, at this time we were passing a square where Signorina Tardelli turned herself round and told me a tale about the great lover Casanova who used an apartment for his assignations nearby, unaware for some time that a jealous rival used to spy on him through a peephole in the wall of the bedroom.

'Then she added: "My dressmaker lives very near here and I would like Guiseppi to come with me to her apartment and carry back two frocks she altered for me." So the gondolier guided the boat to a quiet private mooring stage where he helped Signora Tardelli alight. As they walked away, the twins burst into a fit of giggles and Francesca kissed me lightly on the cheek and said: "Oh Charles, will you forgive us? Claudia and I have been teasing you unmercifully. But before Mama returns, let my sister and I – how do you say in English – relieve your feelings."

'It was as well that the gondola was moored in a quiet spot and that dusk was now falling, for with these words Francesca threw off the rug and held my naked shaft in her hand as she drew in her breath and looked at her sister. "*Dio mio*, what a magnificent prick!"

'"Yes indeed," Claudia agreed. "I am very much looking forward to being fucked with it after dinner tomorrow night. But in the meantime . . ."

'Her voice tailed off and then, as if planned, their two pretty faces were lowered in unison towards my lap. Two tongues began to lick my cock whilst two hands, one from the right side, one from the left, reached inside my drawers and brought out my balls which they squeezed gently whilst their questing lips met at the moist top of my knob. Tongue touched tongue, jostling together wetly as they lashed down my gigantic erection. I found this erotic play so exciting that very soon a fountain of warm white spunk burst out of my cock and jetted into their mouths and over their faces. I spent copiously in a shuddering joyous ecstasy.

'With my seed still sticky on their lips, each sister kissed me open-mouthed, thrusting her tongue between my teeth. "There we are, Charles," said Claudia gaily. "Francesca and I may tease a little but we are not so unkind as to leave you without *any* satisfaction. But now you had better button yourself up because Mama and Guiseppi will be back very shortly."

'Since then I've always had the fondest memories of Venice,' Charles observed. He smiled at the remembrance of this horny affair as he carefully steered us out of the tributary and back into the Cherwell proper. 'I never managed to fuck Francesca. Unfortunately, at the dinner in question, she was unable to join Claudia and I for a midnight romp because her Mama had paired her off at the dinner table with Prince Oskar of Saxony.'

'Lucky old Oskar,' I remarked and Charles chuckled: 'Not really, the charms of this gorgeous girl were wasted upon him. I'm afraid he would have been more interested in the young gondolier!'

'What a waste of pussey,' commented Alex and he nodded: 'My feelings exactly. Still, one must live and let live and I can't believe that a stupendously attractive girl like Francesca will ever find herself short of a willing cock.'

The hansom cab was waiting for us when we reached the mooring stage and as we reached the Randolph Hotel where Charles was staying, I looked at my wrist-watch and said: 'Wasn't this where your father was meeting his friend? It's only a little after half past five and if he is still here we could save him making the journey to meet us at Carfax.'

'Yes, that's a good idea,' said Alex and she turned to Charles and said: 'I'd like to introduce you to my father.' She saw an embarrassed frown form on his face and she giggled: 'Don't worry, dear, I'm hardly going to say "Daddy, do meet Charles who fucked me so nicely this afternoon." No, you silly boy, I thought you might like to dine with us if you haven't already made any arrangements for this evening. Our chauffeur will drive you home.'

Charles's face cleared and he replied: 'No, I have nothing planned so I would be delighted to dine with you.'

'Oh look, there's your father's motor car so Sir Brindsleigh must still be in the hotel,' I said, pointing to the shiny green vehicle parked near the entrance to the hotel.

'Excellent,' said Alex, as the cab came to a halt. Once inside the foyer of the hotel she said: 'Sophie, I need to visit the ladies' room. Would you and Charles find out where my father is and I'll see you back here shortly.'

'Of course,' I rejoined and on asking at the reception desk, I was given the curious information that Sir Brindsleigh could be found in room twelve as opposed to any of the spacious public lounges, bars and restaurant.

When I conveyed this news to Charles he stroked his chin thoughtfully. Then he proposed that I went up and saw Sir Brindsleigh by myself, as he thought it would be best if he stayed there and waited for Alex. He added: 'When she comes back we'll come up together and she will be able to introduce me to her father.'

This seemed a reasonable suggestion and so I went up to room twelve by myself. I knocked on the door and I heard Sir Brindsleigh's fruity voice sing out: 'By Jove, Chrissie, your friend has been able to make it after all. Open another bottle of champers whilst I let her in.'

For sure, whoever Sir Brindsleigh Henderson expected to be waiting outside, it certainly was not any companion of his daughter's. He threw open the door and revealed himself to be stark naked. His chest was covered with matted brown hair and below his corpulent belly his prick stood up as stiff as a poker. Behind him I could see a girl dressed in a chambermaid's uniform. Sir Brindsleigh had undone the buttons of her blouse and her jutting breasts had freed themselves of any covering. They stood out, naked and mouthwateringly ripe for the touch of lips or fingers.

It was difficult to know who was the more surprised, Sir Brindsleigh or myself, as we gazed in awe-struck astonishment at each other. Then I heard footsteps from the top of the stairs. When I saw Alex and Charles turn the corner I rushed forward to meet them and said breathlessly: 'I'm afraid Sir Brindsleigh is not quite ready to leave yet. He suggests that we go downstairs and he will meet us in the bar in about fifteen minutes' time.'

'By all means, we're in no rush,' said Charles who later that evening told me that from the harried look on my flushed face he had guessed that I had caught Sir Brindsleigh in some kind of embarrassing situation. But Alex could not read between the lines and said to me in a puzzled voice: 'All right, if that's what Daddy wants us to do, but whilst I'm up here I'll just tell him about Charles.'

She took a step forward but I deliberately blocked her path. I said the first thing that came into my head: 'No, don't do that, my love, he wouldn't appreciate any interruption right now. I'll tell Sir Brindsleigh that we'll see him in the bar and join you a little later after I've visited the ladies' room. Charles, will you order me a glass of lemonade shandy, please?'

'Of course,' said Charles and, taking Alex's hand, he gently guided my still slightly perplexed friend back along the corridor to the stairs. Meanwhile I rushed back and hammered on the door of room twelve which of course was now closed. This time, it was opened only a fraction by the girl who, on seeing me, turned her head towards Sir Brindsleigh and called out: 'Brinnie, it's that young lady again. Have you a message for her?'

'Just see what she wants, Florrie,' I heard him mutter fiercely, but then I heard further footsteps coming down the corridor and so I pushed past Florrie. Confronting the naked baronet I said: 'I'm sorry to barge in but you wouldn't have wanted anyone else to hear our conversation. Anyhow, I've seen so much already that it hardly matters. Don't worry, sir, I don't tell tales out of school. I said to Alex and the young gentleman with whom we spent the afternoon, that you are finalising some business arrangements and will meet us in the bar in about a quarter of an hour.'

'That is really very good of you, Sophie,' he said gratefully. 'I really appreciate your understanding attitude.'

'Thank you, Sir Brindsleigh,' I said, but not wishing my motives to be misunderstood, I added: 'May I speak candidly?'

The baronet shrugged his shoulders and replied: 'Pray do so, Sophie. I think that whenever one has anything unpleasant to say, one should always be quite candid.'

'Well, to speak with perfect frankness, it's only for Alex's sake that I'm keeping your guilty secret,' I said in a severe tone of voice. 'I know that fucking is great fun but I don't think it right for a married man to indulge in bedroom sports with anyone else but his wife. How would you like it if you discovered that Lady Henderson was bedding your butler?'

I thought that question would be difficult for him to answer, but in fact he replied immediately with a bitter little laugh. 'You don't realise how germane that question is, my dear. If you must know, I have already had cause to think about such a situation – only the person involved was a good-looking young footman!'

'Oh,' I said feebly and sat down on the bed as Sir Brindsleigh continued: 'You see, about a year ago I found myself beset by some crushing monetary worries. Last year I purchased ten thousand shares in a Latin-American railway which my brother, who is a City stockbroker, had recommended as a sound investment. I would realise a huge profit if I bought the stock within the week. Alas, only two months later, the company declared itself bankrupt and my shares are virtually worthless. I could hardly tell Lady Henderson what had happened because she had often warned me about taking financial advice from my brother who she felt had a reckless streak in his character – and what was worse, I had taken cash out of a joint account by forging her signature on a cheque.

'So I said nothing to my wife and tried not to show my concern, but it had to show itself somewhere and it did so in the bedroom. To be blunt, I found myself physically unable to make love to Maria. At first she thought I was simply suffering from some kind of mild nervous complaint which would soon disappear of its own accord. Frankly, I didn't believe she was that concerned because Maria has never been a great one for bed but, about a couple of weeks later, I was sitting in the study one afternoon wondering if I would ever find a way to clear my debts (for I had borrowed a substantial sum from the bank to buy these wretched shares) when there was a knock on the door and Florrie here walked in and asked if she could have a private word with me.'

I looked at him quizzically when he paused to clear his throat. He gave a thin smile as he continued: 'Oh yes, Florrie used to work at Henderson Hall. Well, I looked up and said curtly: "Shouldn't you speak to Lady Henderson rather than me?"

'"Oh no, sir," she said pertly as she walked up to my desk. "In fact, it was Her Ladyship who suggested I should come here."

'"Very well," I sighed wearily. "What's this all about?" She looked at me with a saucy glint in her eyes and—'

To my surprise he gave a low chuckle and turning to Florrie who was sitting on a chair opposite me, he grunted: 'Why don't you tell the rest of the story for Miss Sophie whilst I have a little wash and brush up before getting dressed?'

'Okay,' said Florrie cheerfully as she pushed her breasts back inside her blouse and buttoned up the garment as she took up the story. 'Well of course, he didn't know that Lady Henderson had confided in me that for some reason Brinnie hadn't been able to manage a cock-stand for more than a fortnight. "I was brought up very strictly, Florrie," she said. "I had no experience of intimate matters before I met my husband and my mother's advice before my wedding night was to lie still and think of England.

'"I certainly don't propose to give such guidance to my daughter because it has proved impossible for me to shake off the shackles of my upbringing. However, even though I could never take part in them, I am given to understand that there are certain sexual acts which men find extremely arousing. It occurs to me that one way to restore Sir Brindsleigh's jaded appetite might be to allow him to take part in these pursuits.

'"Now I know that you are well versed in such matters for only yesterday I saw you engaged in some curious love-play with Sutherland, the new young footman. He was standing against the side of the motor-house with his trousers down and you were kneeling in front of him holding his erect member in your hand.

'"I don't know exactly what you were doing to him but from the blissful expression on his face Sutherland was clearly enjoying the experience. So I want you to perform the same service on my husband. Perhaps it will revive his interest in again affording me my conjugal rights."'

'Good heavens! You say that Lady Henderson actually told you to fellate Sir Brindsleigh,' I gasped and Florrie shrugged: 'Well, I don't know what fellating is but I gave him a good sucking-off if that's what you mean.'

'Yes, that's exactly what I mean,' I grinned and she went on: 'So that very afternoon I went to my room and took off all my clothes. Then I slipped on my dress and I must say it felt quite funny walking around like that. I couldn't help wondering how excited Sutherland and the other men in the house would be if they only knew I hadn't put on any underwear!

'Anyhow, I went straight to Brindsleigh's study. You heard him explain how I told him that I needed a private word with him. So I sat down and said: "It's like this, sir. You know how keen your lawyer friend Mr Jeffrey Martin is on art. Well, he's written me a letter asking me if I would model for him when he comes up to stay at Henderson Hall next week."

'"Has he now?" asked Brindsleigh. "Well, I have no objection and if you have the time I suggest that you accept his offer. Mr Martin is a generous chap and when he leaves us, I'm sure he will give you a nice present for all your time and trouble."

'"Oh, I'm sure he would, sir," I agreed and then I added shyly: "But you see, he wants me to pose in the nude."

'"In the nude!" exclaimed Brindsleigh. He put down the papers he had been holding in his hand and patted my arm. "Well, Florrie, don't worry yourself about it, you can leave this matter to me. I'll write a stiff letter here and now to Mr Martin telling him never to make such an outrageous proposal to you or any other servant ever again."

'"No, please don't do that, sir," I begged him. "I'm very flattered, especially when there must be lots of girls in London who would love to pose for Mr Martin. The reason I'm here is that I don't know whether my figure is good enough for him. What I'd really appreciate is for you to give me your honest opinion on the matter."

'But before poor Brindsleigh could say another word, I slipped off my dress and stood naked in front of him. His jaw dropped and he spluttered out: "Florrie! what do you think you're doing? My God, what would my wife say if she came in?"

'"Actually, she wouldn't say a word, sir. It was her idea that I came to see you," I said coolly. I slid my hands under my breasts and pushed them out towards him. "Tell me honestly now, don't you think my titties are a bit small for Mr Martin?"

'Then I swung round and, turning my head over my shoulder, I added: "And what about my bum? Are my cheeks tight enough for him?"

'"Of course they are," he said in a choked voice as I padded across and knelt down in front of him. I rubbed my palm over his lap and, despite what Lady Henderson had told me, I could feel a meaty shaft stiffening up under my touch. So I pulled open his fly buttons and out sprang his stiff cock. Now I've always been turned on by a thick cock and Brinnie here has one of the biggest I've ever seen!'

'Oh come now, don't exaggerate,' interrupted Sir Brindsleigh modestly but Florrie stuck to her guns. 'No, what's right is right. I've seen quite a few pricks in my time but yours is a real beauty. It must have been ten inches from top to base and I loved the way his tool throbbed when I slipped my fingers around it.

'Anyhow, shaking some stray hairs from my face I bent down to taste this rock-hard monster. I felt Brindsleigh shudder all over as I sucked his knob slowly, working around the ridge of his helmet. Then I washed my tongue all over the smooth mushroom helmet before putting my lips around his shaft as far as it would go, sucking hard for an instant before letting it out of my mouth. I cupped Brinnie's balls and bobbed my head up and down as I gobbled his cock with relish.

'"Whew, Steady on, Florrie!" he panted, his shaft twitching violently as I held it lightly between my teeth. "I'll spunk in your mouth if you carry on like that for much longer."

'I was enjoying myself too much to let him finish so quickly so I slowly drew it out of my mouth and distracted him by tonguing just the very tip of his knob. But from the way Brindsleigh's boner was twitching in my hand, I could tell that he couldn't hold back much longer, so I started to frig myself with my fingers whilst I swirled my tongue over his helmet. Sure enough, his tool began to jerk even more strongly. He squirted a salty fountain of jism into my mouth which I gulped down and I brought myself off as I milked his cock of every last milky drop.'

Sir Brindsleigh broke in to add a final coda to Florrie's tale by saying how this highly enjoyable episode might not have directly eased his financial difficulties but it certainly showed him that any problems he was having with his wedding tackle were only in his mind.

Florrie grinned: 'And Lady Henderson was delighted to hear that Brindsleigh was on the road to recovery. The very next morning she slipped a sovereign in my hand and told me in so many words that Brindsleigh had made love to her for the first time during the night. He had been so passionate that she could scarcely believe that it was her husband's think tool pounding into her pussey.

' "I would be grateful if you would continue his treatment," she said to me, which of course I was happy to do. But when I told Lady Henderson that I found it embarrassing to fuck the master of the house where I worked, she recommended me for the position of senior chambermaid at this hotel. It has worked out very nicely because the pay is better and I don't have to work such long hours.

'Brindsleigh fucks me here every week except at the wrong times of the month when he has to make do with a sucking-off. We always go out somewhere first for a slap-up meal and then come back here and have some wild rumpy-pumpy. I've taught him there's much more to fucking than simply lying on top of a girl and pumping away for three minutes!'

'So all's well that ends well,' I remarked and Sir Brindsleigh smiled: 'Very much so, Sophie. Shortly after Florrie gave me the gobble she just described to you I was fortunate enough to find myself in the happy position of being able to pay off all my debts – not that I can claim any credit for the fortunate cause which enabled me to do so.'

'Brinnie, you're being too modest,' Florrie insisted as she rummaged through the pile of clothes and picked up her knickers. 'What happened was that his Aunt Philothea kicked the bucket last month and left him thirty-five thousand pounds in her will. She said that Brindsleigh was the only person in the family who had always been kind to her, many years before there was any chance of gaining anything from her estate.'

It was nice to hear that this story had such a pleasant ending and as the couple finished dressing, I reflected that this interesting episode showed how important it is never to jump to conclusions. On the face of it, the evidence appeared to show that Sir Brindsleigh Henderson was guilty of cheating on his wife, but in fact he was poking a pretty chambermaid with the full approval of his spouse!

Clearly Sir Brindsleigh was genuinely fond of Florrie for he tenderly kissed her farewell and insisted that she take the five pound note he had left in the small envelope on the dressing table to buy herself a nice 'unbirthday present'.

'My Aunt Vanessa often sent me such gifts when I was at school and very welcome they were too,' he explained whilst he accompanied me downstairs to the bar. 'I've followed her example because from my own experience, it's great fun receiving this kind of unexpected present. Now more to the point, Sophie, can I take it that you will not expose the little white lie to my daughter about what I have been engaged in doing this afternoon? I plan to tell her that I was involved in a discussion with dear old General Goldstone about how best to construct a set of dwellings for artisans out at Stanton Harcourt.'

'I shall say nothing to contradict you, sir,' I promised and permitted myself only a slight smile as he apologised to his daughter for keeping her waiting, blaming the General for his late arrival for their meeting. Alex introduced Charles to her father and we exchanged a satisfied nod as it soon became clear that Sir Brindsleigh – who was also a keen amateur photographer – was most impressed by him. So much so, in fact, that even before Alex could suggest it, Sir Brindsleigh invited Charles to dine with us at Henderson Hall that evening.

'Thank you, sir, that's very kind of you,' Charles replied as he rose to his feet. 'Would you excuse me now as I need time to bathe and change.'

'By all means, my boy,' said the genial Sir Brindsleigh. 'I'll have Mutkin pick you up at seven-thirty if that's convenient with you. Of course he will drive you back here afterwards. Come, ladies, we might as well go home now. Charles, we'll look forward to seeing you later.'

Perhaps it was because he was still recovering from his energetic afternoon with Florrie, but Sir Brindsleigh drove back to Henderson Hall just as fast but braking and swerving far more erractically than on our earlier journey into Oxford.

'Does your father always drive at such high speed?' I asked Alex quietly as I looked anxiously at the speedometer needle hovering around the fifty-five miles an hour mark. Clouds of dust were thrown up from the road as we shot through the tiny village of Standlake.

'You're right, as usual he's driving much too fast,' she said grimly. She was about to lean forward and ask Sir Brindsleigh to slow down when some two hundred yards in front of us a uniformed police constable suddenly stepped out from behind a tree and signalled us to stop.

'Hell and damnation!' muttered Sir Brindsleigh as we screeched to a halt beside the policeman who walked slowly over to us and said: 'Good afternoon, sir. Have you any idea at what speed your vehicle was going? I timed you since you passed my colleague up the road and you were travelling at more than fifty miles an hour.'

'Stuff and nonsense,' snorted Sir Brindsleigh. 'I was driving at no more than forty. Anyhow, what of it? There's no-one else on the road.'

'Maybe not but there would probably have been an accident especially if a horse and cart had come out from that turning behind me or if an old lady had tried to cross the road just as you came thundering through,' retorted the constable. He took his notebook and pencil from his pocket. 'Anyhow, you'll be charged with furious driving, so I'll need to have your name and address.'

Sir Brindsleigh glared at the constable as he pulled out his wallet and, thrusting his card out of the window, he demanded to know which court he would have to attend if he were to be summonsed. He counted most of the local magistrates amongst his close friends.

'The case'll be heard at West Oxfordshire Police Court

over in Witney,' replied the constable as he wrote down the registration number of the new Rover and added with unconcealed relish: 'If you're acquainted with Colonel Topping, the chief magistrate, you'll know that he hates motorists, especially those who drive too fast and frighten his horses.'

'Is that so?' muttered Sir Brindsleigh as he engaged the clutch and as we sped away he called out: 'We'll see about that, officer.

'Bloody speed traps! I was in full control of the car, the visibility was good and there wasn't any traffic around,' grumbled Sir Brindsleigh and Alex said sympathetically: 'Never mind, father. It's only the third time you've been caught this year.'

'The fourth, actually,' he scowled angrily. 'And if I get any more summonses in the new few weeks, some dolt like this Colonel Topping fellow might try and ban me from driving for six months.'

I had noticed that an Automobile Association badge had been affixed to the Rover's radiator and I said: 'It's a great shame that there wasn't an Automobile Association scout on patrol who would have warned you to slow down in time.'

[*Animosity between the police and the growing army of motorists – there were almost 85,000 cars in Britain by 1908 – was at a height during these early years. The AA was formed in 1904 by the racing driver Charles Jarrott who employed a cyclist to warn fellow motorists of a speed trap on the London to Brighton road – Editor*]

'Quite so, Sophie, but I'm afraid the damage is done,' he said gloomily. We drove on in silence (and at a greatly reduced speed!) for two or three minutes until Sir Brindsleigh clicked his fingers and said to Alex: 'My dear, I've just had a thought. Do you think Monty Skinner might know this fellow Topping? After all, Monty's the deputy lord lieutenant of the county and he might even have appointed the wretched chap to the bench.'

Fortunately, her father could not see Alex nudge me with her elbow and roll her eyes skyward as she answered: 'Well, you could call him on the telephone when we get home, but I don't really see how that might help you.'

Sir Brindsleigh raised his eyebrows. 'Don't you, my dear? Well, the point is that Monty might persuade Colonel Topping to instruct the police to drop the case. H'm, I wonder if he plays bridge. If so, Monty could bring him over here one afternoon while Jeffrey Martin is staying with us and I'll do my level best to see that the blighter wins every damned rubber.'

Alex pretended to be shocked and, clapping her hand to her cheek, she tut-tutted reproachfully: 'Father! Surely you wouldn't cheat at cards!'

'My driving licence is at stake and I'll do whatever's necessary to keep it,' he replied grimly. Then he broke into a chuckle and continued: 'Anyhow, it's about time we opened that pack of magician's playing cards you bought me from Gamage's last Christmas. Don't look at me like that, Alex. Far from taking his money, Colonel Topping will have the satisfaction of telling his friends how he trounced – and here you must forgive my immodesty – one of the leading players in England at the bridge table!'

Then he turned his head to me and added: 'Sophie, please answer honestly, do you believe that it would be so very wrong to put this harmless little subterfuge into practice?'

Despite his exhortation for me to be frank, I could hardly have replied as I would have wished, which would have been to tell Sir Brindsleigh if he hadn't been driving so recklessly, he would not have found himself in his present awkward situation. But in any case, I had no desire to take sides in an argument between my friend and her father. All I said in reply was that an alternative plan for him might be not to appear in person in front of Colonel Topping, but instead simply to write a grovelling letter of apology to the magistrate.

He grunted an acknowledgement of my suggestion as we approached the gates of Henderson Hall. To my relief the subject was dropped and Sir Brindsleigh brought the Rover to a halt and honked the horn to alert one of the servants of our arrival.

A footman came bustling out of the house to open the car doors for Alex and myself and, after exchanging a brief word with Lady Henderson, we went straight upstairs to change for dinner. Unfortunately, the plumbing in the guests' bathroom was playing up and Alex generously invited me to use her own en-suite facilities.

'I do hope Daddy won't try to wriggle out of this summons for speeding, Sophie,' sighed Alex as we began to undress. 'I'm rather worried that he will end up by making things much worse.'

'You mean that Colonel Topping could take umbrage at what he feels is an attempt to pervert the course of justice?' I queried. Alex nodded as she pulled down her knickers and walked naked past me into the bathroom.

'Exactly, and if my dear father gets into any trouble I won't neglect any opportunity to say "I told you so",' commented Alex as she turned on the taps. I tugged my chemise over my head and folded it neatly over a chair.

'Don't worry, he might yet see sense,' I said comfortingly as I followed her into the bathroom where Alex was pinning up her blonde tresses into a bun before stepping into the wide circular bath-tub. Her uptilted bosoms caught my eye. They jiggled saucily a she lifted her arms to complete the task and seeing the direction of my gaze, she chuckled: 'My breasts are nice, aren't they, Sophie? Boys are always

complementing me on their size – they must be attracted to
large titties in the same way that we enjoy looking at really
big pricks.'

'Yes, I suppose so,' I said slowly. 'Although I know you
would agree that quality is more important than quantity.
After all, there's no joy in having a poke with a chap who is
hung like a horse but simply rams his tool in and out like a
steam-hammer.'

Alex turned off the taps and motioned me to join her in
the tub where there was plenty of room for me to sit down
beside her. She passed me a bar of soap and commented:
'You're right there, darling. Only yesterday my maid
Belinda was telling me that Windrow, our new footman,
only has a five-inch cock. But he is such a clever and considerate lover that she almost always spends when they fuck
– which proves that technique is much more important than
anything else.'

As she delivered this little homily, Alex stood up and
sponged her smooth white belly which was dimpled with a
sweet little button in the centre. My nipples began to
harden as I watched the rivulets of water slide into her fluffy
blonde bush of pussey hair only inches away from my face.
The temptation was simply too strong to resist and,
scrambling up on my knees, I kissed the soft wet skin of her
tummy and then ran my lips lower into her damp flaxen
thatch. For an anxious moment I thought that Alex didn't
want to be sucked off and might push me away, but in fact
she pulled my head closer to her and gasped: 'Oh yes,
Sophie! Lick me out and make me come!'

I clasped hold of her bouncy bum cheeks and buried my
face between her thighs, licking around the edges of her
pretty crack. Then I moved down the smooth-skinned
creases of her pussey, lapping at her pouting love lips which
slid open under the probing of my tongue.

'Wooooh!' gurgled Alex as I nibbled away at the erect

tender clitty which was now protruding out between her pussey lips. When I paused to draw breath she cried out: 'Don't stop, darling, don't stop! Be a good girl and finish me off with your fingers.'

She need not have worried that I would have left her in limbo. I prised open Alex's cunney lips with my forefinger, sinking it deep inside her cunney. Then she began to tremble all over when I slowly eased in a second and third finger. I didn't have to frig the lovely girl for very long before her pungent pussey juice was running all over my face. I licked up her tangy spend as she melted away into a delicious climax.

By now my own pussey was tingling with desire but there was no time to continue our frolic. This did not bother me too much for I knew that with any luck we would find an opportunity for a post-prandial fuck with Charles Prince. I enjoy an occasional tribadic romp, but as far as I am concerned, there is nothing in the world which can compare with the thrill of a thick throbbing stiffie threading its way into my love channel!

And I am delighted to record the fact that I was not to be disappointed – even though it would happen that the shaft which would slide into my cunney some four hours later was not that of Charles but of Lady Henderson's nephew, a handsome young undergraduate named Alan Greene.

However, I could never have imagined the events of that extraordinary evening. When Alex and I had finished dressing, we made our way to the drawing room where aperitifs were being served. Charles had arrived a few minutes before Alex and I came downstairs and he looked very smart in his gleaming white shirt, black bow tie and well-tailored dining jacket. Certainly he was one of those fortunate men who possessed that certain *je ne sais quoi* which makes them quite irresistibly attractive to the opposite sex. My pussey was already moistening at the thought of what Alex and I might get up to with him after dinner when Lady Henderson came up to me and said: 'My dear Sophie, may I have a little word with you in private?'

She drew me aside and said quietly: 'When I happened to see my nephew in Oxford the other day, I invited him to dine with us this evening. I am sure you will find Alan to be a charming young man and I would be grateful if you would allow him to take you into dinner.'

'Of course, Lady Henderson,' I answered promptly. It was impossible for me to refuse this request, even though it meant leaving Alex to sit next to Charles at the table.

Now I might have felt disappointed but as my grandmother liked to say, virtue brings its own reward. I liked the look of Lady Henderson's nephew when he came into the room a few minutes later. She brought the good-looking young man over to me immediately and said: 'Alan, this is Miss Sophie Starr – Sophie, I would like you to meet my nephew Alan Greene. He is reading English Literature at Worcester College whenever he can find time to tear himself away from the distraction of the cricket field.'

I smiled at Alan whose curly brown hair set off a hand-some face with clear blue eyes, well-proportioned features and a smooth unblemished complexion, and remarked: 'If it's English Literature and cricket, Mr Greene, I suppose you're familiar with Rudyard Kipling's *Just-So Stories*.'

His brow wrinkled in concentration for a moment or two and then returning my smile he said: 'Oh, I think I know the couplet you are referring to: *Then ye returned to your trinkets; then ye contented your souls/With the flannelled fools at the wicket or the muddied oafs at the goals.* I take it that cricket has no appeal for you.'

I shook my head and answered: 'No, I wouldn't say that, because I've never watched a cricket match, although my Uncle Albert is very keen on the game. He once played for Hertfordshire against a team captained by the famous

W G Grace. Uncle Albert opened the bowling and swears that the famous batsman was clearly leg before wicket on his fifth ball but when he shouted "Howzat!" the umpire shook his head and grunted: "We've come to see Mr Grace bat and don't need you to spoil the show!"'

Alan gave a husky chuckle and from then on we got along famously, finding that we had several interests in common including the vexed subject of votes for women. This reared its head at the dinner table after Sir Brindsleigh had roundly condemned the organisers of a Women's Social and Political Union meeting that he had seen advertised in the local newspaper.

As a guest, I felt (as I am sure did Charles) that it would be impolite to argue strongly with the views of our host about female emancipation even though I was forced to bite my lip when Sir Brindsleigh said to his daughter, who had heatedly defended the suffragettes: 'Oh come now, Alex, one must face facts here. Surely you must admit that even if it were possible for men's minds to remain stationary whilst the woman of the future takes a more active role in society, it will be many centuries before heredity is able to produce the missing five ounces of the female brain.'

Nevertheless, although I said nothing, I silently cheered Alan who burst out: 'With respect, sir, I absolutely disagree with you. The conspicuous absence of women in the field of intellectual work is due solely to the artificial restraints put upon them by their limited education. If we allowed women to complete on fair and equal terms, women would swiftly prove themselves equal to us in terms of achievement.'

The discussion raged on and until Lady Henderson decided to pour oil on troubled waters and said as she rose to her feet: 'Now I think we have exhausted this subject and I don't want to hear another word about it. Alex and Sophie, let us leave the gentlemen to their port.'

'Really, mother, I fail to see why we should be banished

from the table just because the men want to smoke cigars and tell *risqué* stories.'

'This sensible custom allows us to retire gracefully to the powder room,' retorted Lady Henderson but Alex stood her ground and said: 'True, but the need would not arise if we were allowed to excuse ourselves between courses like the men. I think it most unfair, don't you, Sophie?'

Well, the idea of being cast aside like a second-class citizen to leave the men to their own devices has always irritated me and I said: 'Yes, but if the men feel they want us to leave . . .'

'Oh no, Sophie,' said Alan quickly and he turned to Charles and said: 'You would have no objection to Alex and Sophie joining us in a glass of port, would you?'

'None at all,' answered Charles as he looked at Sir Brindsleigh and added: 'But of course the decision must be yours, sir.'

Our host heaved himself out of his chair and said: 'I'll abide by a majority vote. No, we don't need a show of hands, it's quite clear that you and Alan would prefer the girls to stay here. Maria, why don't we take our coffee in the lounge and leave these young people to their own devices? We mustn't stand in the way of progress.'

'Very well, dear, even though I'm sure that it's progress in the wrong direction,' sighed Lady Henderson. She took his arm and the rest of us rose to our feet as she and her husband made their way to the door.

As the door closed behind them, Alex said to the servant who was engaged in placing two silver cafetieres on the table: 'Windrow, you may leave us. I'll call you if we need any more coffee.'

'Thank you, Miss Alex,' murmured the footman. After he had left the room she burst out laughing and said: 'My word, I never thought it would be so easy to drag my parents into the twentieth century! Charles, would you be a sweetie and bring us the decanters of port and brandy on the sideboard.'

Then she turned to the boys and said: 'Now then, gentlemen, Sophie and I would like to listen to all the rude gossip that takes place whilst the port is being passed around the table.'

The boys looked sheepish and each waited for the other to speak. Finally Alan said: 'Sorry, Alex, I'm afraid we don't have any stories to tell you.'

By now I entered the spirit of the game and giggled: 'What can we do to loosen their tongues? H'm, I know! Let's tell *them* a naughty story. Men love hearing girls speak frankly about who has been poking them.'

'Good idea, Sophie,' she exclaimed with glee and she said to the boys: 'Tell me, have either of you two been to the Rawalpindi Club in London?'

[*The Rawalpindi Club was a raffish establishment situated in Albemarle Street, Mayfair. It was managed by the mysterious Colonel Arthur Amos and frequented by the more daring young men about town around the turn of the century. An explicit and uncensored account of a typical evening's entertainment at the Rawalpindi can be found in the previous book in this series,* Cremorne Scandals, Headline Paperbacks, 1995 – Editor]

'Good heavens, no!' cried Charles who, like myself, knew of the Rawalpindi's reputation for wild behaviour. 'Don't tell me that you've ever been there.'

'Oh, but I have, though just the once. Mama and I went down to London just before Christmas to be fitted for new outfits at her dressmakers. As luck would have it, one morning Mama recognised an old friend who was also staying at our hotel and made an arrangement to take tea with her that afternoon. I said to Mama how boring this would be for me and somehow I persuaded her to let me visit the Tate Gallery instead.

'She thought hard for a moment and then said: "Very well, but you cannot go alone, you must have a chaperone."

'Now as luck would have it, who should I see in our hotel but Mr Roger Bacon, the famous playwright to whom Mama and I had been introduced only the previous week at one of Lady Jordache's artistic *conversaziones*.'

'Isn't he the author of that new comedy, *Millie's Midnight Madness?*' asked Alan and when his pretty cousin nodded her head, he chuckled mysteriously.

'Anyway, when I saw Mr Bacon reading a newspaper in the hotel foyer, I went straight up to his chair and after giving a discreet little cough, I said to him: "I doubt if you will remember my name, but we spoke briefly at Lady Jordache's in Oxford last week." He put down his newspaper and looked hard at me for a moment before snapping his fingers and replying: "Oh yes I can, my dear young lady, it's Alex and you are the daughter of Lady Maria Henderson of Sutton Green."

'Whilst this was most flattering, above all I was genuinely surprised and I looked at him in astonishment but he rose to his feet and grinned: "How could I forget such a pretty face? What brings you to town, Alex? Dare I ask if you will be going to see my play at the London Pavilion?"

'"I would love to see *Millie's Midnight Madness*, but I doubt if that will be possible," I answered, telling him how except for that afternoon, every hour of our short visit was occupied. But when I explained how I wanted to go to the National Gallery, Mr Bacon gave a little bow and said: "Well, I wonder whether you might like to come to the Museum Gallery with me to a private view of the new exhibition by Manfred Neumann, this controversial Austrian artist everyone seems to be talking about nowadays."

'"How exciting! I would love to come with you so long as my mother will let me," I said as I waved to Mama who was walking across the foyer to the porter's desk. As I had hoped, she gave her permission for Mr Bacon to escort me to the exhibition of Manfred Neumann's work which was only a few minutes' walk away in Zwaig's, a smart Bond Street gallery.'

She stopped to refresh herself with a sip of hot coffee and Charles asked if Manfred Neumann was as daring an artist as he had heard. A friend of his, who had seen his work, had waxed lyrical about the audacious voluptuousness of the canvasses!

'Oh yes, I would agree that Manfred's pictures are on the very threshold of acceptability. I had to pretend not to be shocked when Roger Bacon and I walked around the exhibition,' she confirmed brightly. 'I can remember how I blushed when we stopped in front of a particularly sensuous picture of a nubile raven-haired girl standing naked in a sedutive pose against the trunk of a large tree.

'Roger studied this painting closely and remarked: "A superb outdoor scene, would you not agree? Note how the rough massive vertical tree imparts a sense of delicacy to the girl's stance and heightens the smoothness of her body's flowing curves."

'Then we moved to another admirably indecent portrait of the same girl, again shown in the nude but this time stretched out lasciviously across a double bed with her legs slightly raised to display the rounded fullness of her bottom. "Pure pornography!" spluttered a middle-aged gentleman behind us, although I noticed that he was still peering at the picture when the three of us left the gallery twenty minutes later!'

This last remark caused a *frisson* around the room. 'The *three* of you left the gallery,' I repeated in a puzzled voice. Alex gave a throaty chuckle as she explained: 'With a clutch of other guests, Roger and I were then invited upstairs to meet Manfred Neumann himself. He was a tall, nicely built man in his mid-thirties with a mop of riotously curling brown hair which he wore long, just touching his collar. His friendly warm eyes swept over my face before he lifted my proferred hand to his lips.

'"A great pleasure to meet you, Miss Henderson," he said softly in an attractive Central European accent. "I hope you found my pictures to your taste or are you amongst those critics who would have me thrown into jail for artistic immorality?

'I laughed and shook my head whilst he continued: "People become angry at what they call my impudent daubs because they challenge not only their ideas of painting but about how life should be lived."

'We become involved in an animated discussion which continued until the other guests had all left. Roger suggested that Manfred and I accompany him to the Rawalpindi Club where he was due to take afternoon tea with an important theatrical impresario. So we piled into a cab for the short journey to Albemarle Street but when we arrived there, a porter gave Roger a written apology from the impresario to state that unfortunately he would be unable to keep their appointment.

'As he read the note, Manfred was then button-holed by Sir Louis Baum, the noted collector of *avant-garde* art and Roger sighed: "Alex, I've booked a private room for tea. I won't pull Manfred away in case Sir Louis is offering him a commission to work in England but I'll just inform him where we will be."

'There was a wide selection of sandwiches laid out in the suite Roger had booked, and there was also a well-stocked cabinet of drinks from which he insisted on pouring out two glasses of brandy. He brought over the crystal glass to where I was sitting on a low *chaise longue* and said: "This is one of the last bottles of a superb cognac presented to the club six years ago by Count Gewirtz of Galicia. I think you'll like it."

'He sat down and I took a sip of what was an exceptionally fine liqueur. I won't beat about the bush, one glass led to a second and a second to a third . . . To be honest, when Roger squeezed himself up next to me and took my hand between his own and began stroking my fingers, I knew that I would soon be travelling down a forbidden road. But a distinct tremor of lust ran through my body when he leaned over and bestowed a firm kiss on my lips. I returned his kiss with ardour, clasping him to me as our bodies pressed together in a passionate embrace.

'I squealed with delight as I felt the palm of his hand caressing my bosoms. Our tongues worked lasciviously together whilst he swiftly pulled off my blouse and slid down the straps of my chemise to expose my luscious creamy breasts. Roger's lips roamed over my titties, licking them up to erection whilst my hand stole down to stroke the huge bulge which had formed in his lap. He gave a hoarse groan when I unbuttoned his flies and let his imprisoned prick out of its uncomfortable confinement.

'His thick tool sprang out into my hand. I wrapped my fingers around his hot stiff shaft and fisted the hot shaft which leaped and bounded in one hand whilst with the other I reached below and ran my fingertips over his ballsack, letting my nails scratch tantalisingly along the wrinkled skin.

'Roger lifted my skirt and I squirmed as he placed his hand firmly upon my pussey. I lifted my bottom from the seat and he tugged down my knickers until they were around my ankles. Gently he separated my thighs and let his fingers play around the moist blonde hairs of my bush.

'We quickly divested ourselves of our remaining clothes. I lay on my back as Roger continued to tease my pussey with his fingers whilst he kissed my titties. He looked up at me with the lust shining from his dark liquid eyes as he declaimed like an actor in one of his plays: "Ah, my darling, you have the sweetest little quim I have seen for a long time. Lie back and allow me to pay homage to your feminine charms."

'I lay back to enjoy the feel of Roger's tongue wending its way down over my belly. He dallied for a while as he licked my fluffy thatch, performing an *entr'acte* so to speak for the exquisite scene to follow. Then his mouth descended onto my cunney and I writhed with abandon when his tongue slithered into my cunt.

'"Oooh! Oooh! Oooh!" I yelped with joy, flooding his face with love juice as I spent in a series of lovely tumbling spasms but my blood was up and I cried: "Fuck me, Roger, fuck me!"

'Roger heaved himself up and smiled broadly as I grabbed hold of his hot pulsing prick and swirled my tongue over his knob. "May I have the pleasure of poking you doggie-style?" he asked politely and I replied: "Certainly you may, but please don't go up my bottom."

'"The thought never entered my head," he assured me. I raised myself on my knees and turned to face the wall, parting my thighs and pushing out my bum cheeks as far as possible. Roger leaned over me and I felt the crown of his cock nudge teasingly against my pussey lips. Then with a single thrust he entered me, filling my cunney with his iron-hard boner. His strokes were long and deep, coming faster and faster. He slipped his arms around me to cup my breasts in his hands, tweaking and pinching the pointy red nipples. I felt him expand inside me and it flashed through my mind how my clever little love channel managed to accommodate Roger's thick rammer. My juices eased its passage as he fucked me in a slow, sensuous rhythm whilst I closed my eyes and let the waves of sheer ecstasy flow through me.

'Not for the first time I wondered if there could be any experience in the world that even approached the heights of bliss one feels as a stiff shaft slides into one's juicy quim.

Roger fucked me in style. He used his thick todger like a maestro conducting an orchestra, varying his angle and speed as he filled my cunney with his beefy love truncheon.

'Well, we must have fucked for at least ten minutes until Roger ended his wonderful performance by shooting wads of creamy spunk into my cunt. I achieved a glorious spend when the frothy warm jism drenched the walls of my cunney. He stayed hard inside me for a while and then slowly withdrew, his shaft still semi-erect and glistening with our mingled juices.

'We then retired to a small bedroom and snuggled up together under the sheets. I was about to lick his cock clean when we were interrupted by a knock at the door. Roger muttered: "Blast it! That will probably be Manfred coming to rejoin us. Wait here a moment and I'll see if I can get rid of him."

'Alas, he did not succeed and he came back into the bedroom followed by the Austrian artist who bowed gravely to me and said: "Ah, Alex *meine leibchen*, you must forgive me for disturbing you."

'But then he growled at Roger: "What kind of friend are you, though? Before we left the gallery I informed you that I planned to ask Alex to sit for me whilst she is in London. However, I can only paint girls I have fucked and I don't know whether this will now be possible."

'I was flattered to hear how Manfred wanted to paint me so I interrupted: "Please don't let me be the cause of any quarrel between you. Manfred, why don't you take off your clothes and join us? This is a nice big bed, quite large enough for three. Roger, you don't mind moving up for your friend, do you?"

'He gave a low chuckle and said: "Oh, very well, I suppose we can find room for him. I've heard all sorts of rumours about Manfred but thank goodness, nothing about his having the slightest inclination towards the life-style favoured by the late Duke of Clarence."

[*This reference is to King Edward VII's dissolute eldest son whose visits to the infamous male brothel in Cleveland Street were hastily covered up by the Palace authorities – Editor*]

'Manfred muttered a riposte in German but quickly undressed and so there I was, neatly sandwiched between two handsome gentlemen, a situation which I did not find displeasing.

'Tactfully, Roger turned his back and dozed off but Manfred was lying on his back with his hands behind his head and a soulful expression on his face. I let my hand steal between his legs and he gasped as I gripped his burgeoning boner in my hand, feeling it swell between my fingers. I gently frigged it until his shaft stood rampantly erect and so not to disturb Roger, who appeared to be fast asleep, I whispered to Manfred that he should remain silent as I pulled back the bedclothes and lifted myself over him.

'Then with one hand I spread open my cunney lips and with the other I took hold of Manfred's cock and directed the tip of his knob into my squelchy cunt, slowly pressing myself down upon the glowing purple helmet, savouring the sensation of his fleshy chopper embedding itself inside my clingy crack.

'"*Wunderbar! Wunderbar!*" he panted as his hands slid around my bum cheeks. I wriggled around to work his cock as far up my love funnel as possible. I began to bounce merrily on his palpitating prick as he released my buttocks to reach up and tweak my titties.

'Now I'm not sure whether Roger was ever really asleep, but when the bed started to rock he awoke from his slumber and turned round to face us. "My God, you two didn't waste any time," he commented drily as he watched this delicious fuck.

'Well, I certainly didn't want poor Roger to feel left out of things so I told him to get up and kneel beside me. I think he knew what I had in mind for he immediately scrambled to his knees and presented me with a mouth-watering stiffie!

'Without missing a beat of my rhythmic fucking of Manfred's cock, I lowered my head and swirled my tongue all around the ruby knob of Roger's majestic member which seemed to grow even harder in my mouth. I sucked his shaft, varying the intensity and timing of the fuck with my delicious ride on Manfred's quivering cock. He suddenly jerked his hips upwards and, letting out a hoarse groan, jetted spurts of spunk into my tingling snatch. Seconds later Roger's prick began to throb and his milky jism rushed up his trembling shaft and spilled out into my mouth. I tried my best to gulp down his copious spend but I was unable to prevent some of his sticky seed dripping down from my lips onto the baby-blue eiderdown. Roger noticed my concern at this unfortunate occurrence and murmured: "Don't fret, my dear, I'll dab a little white wine on the stain and it will vanish before your eyes."'

She let out a sultry little giggle and tipped her coffee cup towards Charles who filled it from the cafetière as he said: 'By Gad, Alex! What a topping tale! Did the wine do the trick?'

'Not really,' said Alex cheerfully. 'But this hardly mattered because Roger fucked me again after Manfred had been called down for a further talk with Sir Louis Baum. It was now already past the time I should have returned to Mama at the hotel, but we quickly dressed ourselves and he apologised profusely to her for keeping me out so late. And this lovely day was capped when Roger insisted on taking us both to the evening performance of *Millie's Midnight Madness* and afterwards we dined with him at Romano's. I would have loved another fuck with Roger

Bacon as I climbed into bed at midnight, but that would have been asking too much!'

I could tell from Alan and Charles's flushed faces how moved they had been by Alex's stirring story and I guessed that both the boys were sporting gigantic erections. To be frank, her saucy anecdote had made me feel randy myself and I said to my dining companion: 'Alan, I know you're a keen sportsman. How would like a game of snooker? I'd be happy to give you a game although I think you'll have to play with one hand behind your back to give me a chance of winning.'

'It's taking part not winning that matters, Sophie,' he replied seriously as he rose from his chair. He looked across at Alex, who had already perched herself upon Charles's lap, and added: 'You won't mind if we take our leave, will you?'

'What do you think?' said Charles indistinctly as he buried his face between the tops of Alex's bosoms which swelled over the edge of her low-cut gown. She winked at me and said: 'Darling, could you do us a favour and tell my parents that Charles and I have gone for a stroll round the garden. We'll meet them back in the drawing room in about twenty-five minutes' time.'

'Of course I will,' I said and so I arranged to pass on the message whilst Alan visited the men's room. 'I'll meet you in the billiards room,' I called after him as I walked towards the lounge where I presumed Sir Brindsleigh and Lady Henderson would be. I threw open the door, but to my surprise, the room was empty. Perhaps Sir Brindsleigh would be in his study, I thought to myself and sure enough I heard a sound coming from behind the dark oak door.

Naturally, I did not think there could be anything untoward happening in Sir Brindsleigh's private den, so I gave a short knock on the door and pushed it open to see the frisky red-headed chambermaid Belinda standing with her back against the wall opposite me, her skirt and knickers in a heap around her feet, whilst facing her was the young footman Windrow whose trousers and pants were also around his ankles. It was obvious that the raunchy couple were in the last stages of a torrid knee-trembler and whilst Windrow was fondling Belinda's breasts, the pretty girl cooed: 'Oh Martin, what a grand fuck! Wasn't it lucky that Sir Brindsleigh went rushing down the road to Lord Nettleton's after dinner.'

As Belinda spoke her hand sidled down to clasp his cock and she giggled: 'Goodness me, your shaft's still stiff. Doesn't your prick ever go down?'

'It takes more than one spend to satisfy my todger,' replied Windrow with a short laugh. 'I might not have the biggest cock in Oxfordshire but I've never had any complaints – not even from Lady Maria!'

I gulped hard on hearing this revelation and it flashed through my mind that Windrow might merely be indulging in a fantasy about poking his mistress. I could hardly imagine that Lady Maria would emulate her husband and engage in sexual relations with the household staff of Henderson Hall.

However, Belinda clearly believed him because she tossed her head and said: 'It's as well that I'm not the jealous sort, Martin Windrow. There aren't many girls who would stand for their boyfriends fucking another woman!'

'Don't be like that, Belinda!' the footman remonstrated as he kissed her cheek and went on: 'I far prefer fucking you than Lady Maria – but remember she gives me five shillings [*twenty-five pence – Editor*] after every poke and that's a lot of money to turn down!'

Then as if to prove to the chambermaid how much he enjoyed making love with her, he spun the girl round so that she was facing the wall and threw up her skirt to bare her pert bum cheeks.

'How do you fancy a doggie-style fuck?' he asked and without a pause Belinda answered with a giggle: 'Yes, please! But you had better not be too long about it. Miss Alex and her guests could be coming out of the dining room at any time now.'

She stepped back a pace and stretched out her arms in front of her with her palms flat against the wall. Then, audaciously wiggling her tight little bum cheeks, she turned her head and smiled to see Windrow take hold of his pulsating prick and position it neatly in the cleft of her delectable arse.

Despite the fact that he had climaxed only moments before, Windrow went to work with a will. Belinda's backside responded to every shove. He slid his arms around her and squeezed her breasts. I could hear his balls slapping against the backs of her thighs as he worked his sturdy shaft in and out of her sticky honeypot in great style.

My hand stole between my legs and I began to rub my pussey as Belinda cried out: 'Fuck me, Martin! Fuck me with your thick prick, you randy bugger! Ooooh, I'm going to spend!'

Belinda's cries of passion echoed round the room as her body was racked by the force of her orgasm. My fingers mirrored the pistoning action of Windrow's cock as I rubbed harder and harder on my moistening pussey. Seconds later he shot off inside her and with a low growl he jerked up and down in frantic movement before withdrawing his glistening shaft for one final plunge as he spurted his jets of frothy jism inside her clinging love channel.

'Oh, that was wonderful, you must have pumped a gallon of love juice into my cunt,' squealed Belinda as she flopped down onto the carpet. Windrow gasped: 'Well it's your naughty pussey that's milked my prick of every drop of spunk, my girl!'

The first wave of a small but pleasant little spend now radiated out from my groin as Belinda said: 'Help me up, Windrow, we had better get dressed before someone comes looking for us.'

She took hold of his hand and clambered to her feet whilst Windrow gave a low chuckle and said: 'Quite right, darling, can you imagine the hullaballoo if Miss Alex saw us like this?'

'You're right, we would be instantly dismissed if Lady Maria or Miss Alex knew what was going on in here whilst they were entertaining their guests!'

Now my closest friends all tell me that I have always possessed a sense of the dramatic and I simply could not resist taking advantage of Windrow's words. So none of them would be surprised at the fact that I said in a loud voice: 'Well, I can't speak for Lady Maria, but in my opinion Miss Alex would probably want to join in!'

The astounded couple almost jumped out of their skins. Belinda let out a frightened little scream and buried her face in Windrow's shoulder as, with a commendable speed of recovery from the shock, the footman swiftly pulled up his underpants and gasped: 'Miss Sophie, I'm so sorry, we didn't hear you come in.'

Naturally they assumed that I would report their lascivious behaviour and Belinda actually fell on her knees and implored me not to tell anyone what I had seen. 'Please don't say anything, Miss Sophie,' she begged. 'Windrow might keep his position because Lady Maria loves to suck his cock, but I'll be dismissed without a reference.'

'Is there anything we can do to make you forget what you've seen?' pleaded her crestfallen partner. I pretended to give some considerable thought to this question although of course I never had any intention of getting the lusty pair into trouble.

They waited on tenterhooks as I affected to weigh up my answer. Lines of tension were etched on their faces until I finally said: 'Very well, I won't say a word about this to anyone. However, there is something you can do for me in return.'

'We'll do anything you want,' said Belinda immediately. No longer able to keep my face set in a severe expression, I broke into a smile and said: 'Just promise me that next time you suddenly fancy a quick fuck, you'll remember to lock the door first!'

Windrow mopped his brow in relief and said with great fervour: 'I swear we will, Miss Sophie! We'll never forget your kindness.'

Now whilst I am usually more than happy to help people without thought of any reward, I subscribe to the view that it does no harm to remind the person for whom one is performing a kindness that one day you might ask them to repay the favour. So I said: 'I hope you really mean that, Windrow. There may come a time when I will ask you and Belinda to put yourselves out on my account.'

And on this note I left them hastily pulling on their clothes, little realising that under two hours later the opportunity would arise for the grateful young footman to repay the favour!

Chapter Four

I hurried back to the vestibule where Lady Henderson was standing at the foot of the stairs. She said to me: 'Ah Sophie, I was just speaking to Alan and he tells me that you are going to play snooker with him. Presumably Alex and Charles will be joining you in the games room after they come back from their walk. Please tell them that I hope they will not think me an impolite hostess, but I have a most tiresome headache and am going straight to bed.'

'Oh dear, I am sorry, Lady Henderson,' I said sympathetically, offering her my arm as we walked up the stairs together. Although I had indirectly heard from the randy servants that Sir Brindsleigh had gone out to visit a neighbour, I asked her if her husband had also retired for the night.

She pursed her lips and replied: 'No, Brindsleigh asked me to pass on his apologies. After we left the dining room, he received a telephone call from Lord Nettleton who asked if he would care to go round to his house and make up a four at the bridge table. Apparently Doctor Johnson had to leave suddenly after being summoned to the bedside of a wealthy patient who apparently had suffered a broken leg in a fall at his home.

'Naturally I expected Brindsleigh to refuse, but when Lord Nettleton told him that Reverend Prosser and Colonel Topping were to be the other guests, he immediately said he would come over straightaway. I was extremely annoyed and remonstrated with him but Brindsleigh muttered something about how vital it was for him to go. He asked me to pass on his apologies to you and our other guests. Now I'm fully aware how much Brindsleigh enjoys his bridge, but I cannot understand the reason for such inexcusable behaviour.'

Of course, I could hardly tell Lady Henderson that I knew exactly why Sir Brindsleigh had dashed out of the house in the middle of his own dinner party! 'I'm sure there must have been a good reason for his decision,' I said soothingly.

'Maybe so, although none springs readily to mind,' Lady Henderson replied acidly as we reached the first floor. She kissed me on the cheek and wished me good-night as she walked across to her bedroom. I sprinted up the next flight of stairs to the games room where not only Alan but Alex and Charles were also waiting for me.

'Hello, Sophie, we were about to send out a search party for you,' cried Charles. I kept my word not to mention anything about how I had caught Windrow fucking Belinda in Sir Brindsleigh's study, so I quelled any enquiries by kissing Alan on the cheek and then passed on to Alex the information about the absence of both her parents.

A servant had carried a silver tray with glasses and a decanter of cognac up to the games room. Alex poured out a generous measure into the crystal goblets as she enthused: 'How wonderful! That means we can enjoy ourselves without any fear of being disturbed.'

'Nevertheless, let's drink a toast to our host and hostess,' said Alan with a broad grin. 'May Aunt Maria's headache vanish by the morning and let's hope that Uncle Brindsleigh has a good excuse for slipping out this evening. Has he really gone to play bridge or is this what the Americans call a cover story for a more nefarious activity?'

'No, I'm sure he really is playing bridge,' I said and

explained why Sir Brindsleigh desperately wanted to make the acquaintance of Colonel Topping.

Alan roared with laughter and commented: 'My God, I hope Uncle Brindsleigh is extremely subtle about any suggestion he makes to Colonel Topping! He came to speak at our college last term about his work as a magistrate and the old boy came over as a very strait-laced chap who does everything strictly by the book. If Uncle Brindsleigh isn't careful, he'll find himself doing six months for trying to pervert the course of justice!'

'Well, here's to Daddy! If that does come to pass, let's all vow to visit him in the clink!' cried Alex. Her face appeared slightly flushed from the effects not only of the cognac but (as she confirmed afterwards) from the excitement of some passionate spooning with Charles whilst they stepped outside for a short walk after Alan and I had left the dining-room.

She winked at me and went on: 'Goodness, it's very warm in here, isn't it? Charles, be a dear and lock the door so that I can cool myself off.'

He obeyed her with alacrity and I realised straightaway that my best friend's blood was up. Unlike the foolish Belinda, Alex had the *nous* to take a simple but necessary precaution before letting herself go! At her request Charles now hoisted her up so that she was sitting on the side of the billiards table, but as she began to unbutton her blouse, Alan warned her to be careful not to mark the green baize cloth.

'You know how proud your father is of that table,' he reminded her. 'Remember, it was hand-built for him by Mr Harper out at Botley.'

'Yes, there would be a fearful row if I damaged it,' agreed Alex as she kicked off her shoes and said to me: 'Sophie, aren't you also too hot? Why don't you come up here and we'll help each other take off some clothes.'

Alan lifted me up onto the handsome mahogany table. He and Charles looked on closely as Alex and I unbuttoned and unhooked each other's dresses which we carefully folded and placed down carefully on the smooth baize. Then we peeled off our stockings and I noticed a bulge form at the front of Alan's trousers whilst we pulled of the rest of each other's clothes until we were naked except for almost identical pairs of lace-trimmed silk knickers.

'Snap! You must also buy your underwear at Madame Monique's boutique in Bond Street,' giggled Alex as she stroked her large creamy breasts which were tipped by stalky red nipples that jutted out proudly and looked ripe for a good sucking.

I wagged my finger at her in mock reproof. 'You silly girl, these are your knickers I'm wearing! You insisted that I borrow them when I told you my parents could never afford to buy me silk underwear.'

Alex smacked herself lightly on the cheek and said: 'Oh, of course, how silly of me to forget! If you like them I will buy you a set for Christmas. But we don't really need our knickers, do we? Boys, why don't you take them off for us?'

Charles and Alan rushed forward and we raised our bottoms invitingly so that they could tug the garments down to our ankles. As we gaily kicked them off, I could see from the protuberances between their legs that both their cocks were at action stations and raring to sink into our eager pussies. Indeed, Charles was already pulling off his shirt, but they had to be patient because Alex suddenly put her arms around me and we rolled backwards onto the table.

In all honesty, what I had in mind was to be threaded by a thick throbbing cock but the sensuous way Alex caressed my bare breasts and tweaked my titties made me light-headed with desire. She smoothed her fingers through the fluffy curls which covered my delicate little notch and began to whisper what she was going to do to me – like how she would stick her tongue up my juicy quim, rubbing her face against my fast-moistening pussey and sucking on my clitty until I spent in her mouth.

This fired me up so much that I murmured: 'Action, not words, if you please!' Alex started to take all the liberties she desired, kissing and sucking my stalky titties whilst she lasciviously squeezed my bum cheeks. Next she eased her index finger into my sopping slit and I sighed and wiggled my bottom as this digit was joined by a second and then a third as she finger-fucked me quite deliciously.

Alex now moved over me and, still keeping her fingers embedded in my juicy cunt, she kissed me vehemently on the mouth. Her velvet tongue skimmed between my teeth to make contact with my own as her fingers plunged relentlessly in and out of my throbbing cunney which was dripping with sticky honey.

'Ooooooh!' I howled when Alex pulled out her fingers from my pussey. Tossing back her blonde tresses from her face, she grasped my bum cheeks, one in each hand, and leaned forward to lick and nibble on my warm, muskily pungent pussey. Then the naughty girl pressed her mouth firmly against the folds of my cunney whilst she probed my quim gently with the tip of her tongue. Her hand slid under me to pry open the soft spheres of my buttocks and tickled the puckered little aperture of my anus.

I bucked up and down in a frenzy of excitement as Alex slithered herself round and over me until we had assumed the classic *soixante neuf* position with myself underneath and Alex pressing her bouncy buttocks against my face as she leaned forward to continue tonguing my tingling pussey.

'Bring me off, Sophie!' she panted as I parted her tight little bum cheeks and kissed her wet slit, inhaling the fragrant odour of her cunt as I licked and lapped her sweet quim. Alex squealed with joy when I found her erect fleshy clitty and she covered my own muff with her lips, running her fluttering tongue along the full length of my hairy crack. My pouting pussey lips unfolded like the petals of an exotic flower and my moans of delight were stifled only by my own sucking of Alex's cunt. I lashed her clitty faster and faster and convulsions of lust sped through our trembling bodies as we moved inexorably together to a shattering spend.

'Feel me coming!' I cried out, raising my head for an instant from her soaking snatch before diving back into her throbbing love funnel. Then, clinging to each other as if our lives depended on it, we climaxed together, shrieking out our happiness before collapsing in a tangle of arms and legs, our mouths drenched with the copious streams of love juice which had poured out from our pussies. Then we disentangled ourselves and sat up, exchanging the tenderest of embraces, pressing our lips together to taste the flavour of our own piquant cuntal jism.

As we expected, this sensual tribadic play had greatly excited our two male spectators. They had torn off their clothes and Alan was the first to climb up onto the table and ask if he could have the honour of fucking me.

'Certainly you may,' I answered as he wrapped his arms around me and laid me down on my back. First we kissed and then his tongue moved downwards, circling my nipples in turn, teasing them up to a fine stiffness. I purred with pleasure as he hauled himself over me and I felt his knob slide between the yielding cunney lips. He eased his shaft in gently until he had penetrated me to the hilt and began to fuck me at a steady rhythmic pace. His hand tweaked one erect tittie and his mouth nuzzled against the other, sucking the little red rosebud until it was as hard as his cock which was dipping so deliciously in and out of my squelchy cunt.

I revelled in sheer ecstasy as Alan Greene fucked me so beautifully that all too soon I could feel the waves of an approaching spend ripple through my body. Indeed, I let out such a long sigh of delight that Alan looked up and anxiously asked if he was pushing too much of his twitching tool into my cunney.

'No, no, no!' I panted and I clasped my legs together to pin every inch of his thick tool inside me. 'Keep going, darling, keep going! I love a good hard fuck!'

Closing my eyes and moving my head from side to side, I thrust my hips upwards to meet his strong pistoning strokes which were driving harder and harder inside me. Alan let out a series of throaty gasps as my cunney muscles nipped his huge quivering cock. My senses reeled as I reached my climax which coursed through my veins in a prolonged series of exquisite electric thrills. Alan's orgasm followed almost immediately – suddenly becoming still, his body tensed and then he shot pulsing jets of creamy jism into my juicy cunt.

He collapsed down on top of me, his chest heaving as he fought to regain his breath. When he had recovered, we looked up to see that Charles had now also climbed up onto the table and was sitting back on his haunches whilst Alex was lying on her tummy in front of him, happily playing with his colossal cock which was standing up majestically against his belly.

For a while she toyed with Charles's tool whilst she kissed his big balls and then she sucked his uncapped bell-end into her mouth, sensuously massaging his prick with her lips and tongue as she held the base of his shaft in her hand. Then she eased her lips back and ran her talented tongue over his helmet before her lips closed over his knob and she swallowed the full length of his blue-veined truncheon.

Alex raised and lowered her head with her lips clasped firmly around his todger, engulfing and releasing him with such consummate skill, rolling her wet tongue around his hot pulsating cock that she brought Charles to the brink of orgasm. He cried out to her to stop in case he lost control and ejaculated too soon inside her mouth.

He bent his head down and whispered some words into her ear. Seconds later she released his cock and changed position so that Alex was kneeling on all fours, her long golden hair and full rounded breasts hanging and with her delectable gleaming backside lifted high in the air. Her thighs parted so that both the red chink of her cunt and her tiny wrinkled bum-hole were delightfully displayed to her almost unbearably excited lover.

As Charles grabbed hold of his shaft and prepared to slide his throbbing tool into the cleft between Alex's saucy buttons, Alan called out to him: 'Steady on, old boy. Especially if you're going to shag her on a billiard-table, wouldn't it be best to ask Alex if she wants you to aim for the pink or the brown?'

'Quite right, old boy,' replied Charles, acknowledging the friendly rebuke with a nod. 'Forgive me, Alex, I should indeed have asked you how you prefer to be poked.'

'In my cunney, please, I adore being fucked doggie-style,' Alex replied instantly. Charles wasted no further time. He whipped his glistening stiffstander into her dripping sheath and set up a pacily rhythmed fuck, his balls slapping her bum cheeks as he jerked his hips to and fro.

A wide smile lit up Charles's face as he happily pistoned his prick in and out of Alex's squishy slit. He held her around the waist as he slewed his thick chopper into the deepest recesses of her cunt and she tensed her trembling legs and raised her bottom higher to meet his powerful lunges.

Her whole body shuddered uncontrollably as the clingy muscles of her cunney contracted in a rapid, shivering motion around Charles's cock and she turned her head and cried out: 'Yes, yes, yes! Fuck the arse off me, Charles!'

But instead of increasing the speed of this glorious fuck, Charles teased the poor girl by slowing down the pace, drawing his shaft out to the very tip of the knob and then with a deliberate lack of speed, sliding it all the way back in again.

'H-a-r-g-h! H-a-r-g-h! Don't tease me like that, you rascal!' Alex pleaded. Not wishing to be unkind, he went back to fucking her at the previous speed, thrusting deep into the very depths of her sodden love channel, heightening the delicious sensations which were clearly running riot throughout her body.

Charles grunted with delight as he gloried in the joys of this magnificent doggie-style fuck. He shifted his hands upwards to fondle her breasts, rubbing her raspberry titties until they were as erect as his stiffie which was nestling inside her juicy cunt. He took a deep breath and his superb masculine torso glistened as he began to fuck Alex at an even faster rate of knots, sheathing his shaft so fully at each stroke that his ballsack fairly cracked against her jiggling bottom.

'I'm coming! I'm coming!' yelled Alex, panting with lust as she shuddered to her climax. As her love channel flooded with cuntal juice, Charles's sticky spunk spilled pulsing jets into her receptive cunney and they sank slowly down on the table, completely exhausted by their passionate love-making.

However, as I watched the sated couple relax in each other's arms, a nasty thought suddenly crossed my mind and I said in a horrified voice: 'My God! Just look how our fucking has stained the baize! Sir Brindsleigh will be furious when he sees what we've done.'

'Don't worry, darling,' said Alex cheerfully. 'I was dying for a fuck but I would have suggested we went elsewhere if I hadn't remembered that Mr Harper of Botley is coming round in the morning to replace this cloth with an even better quality baize.'

'Thank goodness for that,' I said. Perhaps it was because I was so relieved to hear that we had escaped the consequences of our impulsive actions that I clasped hold of Alan's dangling shaft and vigorously frigged it up to attention.

I leaned down to swirl my tongue over the dome of his uncapped helmet which caused dear Alan to let out a throaty gurgle of delight and Alex to smack her lips and ask if she could please share in the sucking-off of her cousin's cock.

'Of course you may, my dear,' I answered sweetly. 'I wouldn't dream of not letting you keep it in the family.'

We giggled and when I motioned to Alex that she should have the first suck of the succulent fleshy lollipop, her eyes lit up. She slid her lips over Alan's smooth, velvety bell-end. She sucked deeply, letting the top of his knob slide against her cheeks whilst she lubricated his swollen shaft. Then she began licking the sensitive underside of his palpitating prick whilst I opened my mouth and popped in the wet crown on which I bestowed a series of feathery kisses which sent Alan wild with lustful excitement. But having his shaft sucked by two pretty girls was simply too arousing and less than a minute later Alan's spunk came hurtling into my willing mouth and my head bobbed up and down as I milked his cock of every last tasty drop of milky jism.

With some success, Charles was attempting to make his recalcitrant tool stiffen up again by frigging his beefy semi-erect truncheon, but when Alex glanced up at the clock, she suggested that we did not tempt fate any longer but that we should all get dressed and retire to our beds.

'After all, it's possible that my father might come back early from his bridge game,' she reasoned. 'And I don't know who would be more embarrassed if he came in here and found us fucking on his billiards table.'

Even Charles had to agree with Alex on this point, even though he was now forced to pull up his pants and thrust his now erect cock through the slit in his drawers. Then as he drew up his trousers, he said: 'Alex, Sir Brindsleigh kindly instructed your chauffeur to take me back to Oxford. He could take Alan back to college after he has dropped me at my hotel.'

A furrow appeared on Alex's brow and she said: 'Oh dear, I'm afraid that Daddy has clearly forgotten all about you because I understand from Windrow that he made Mutkin drive him to Lord Nettleton's and even if he comes back in the next few minutes, it would be dangerous for Mutkin to try and drive you to town. He'll be far too tired and might fall asleep at the wheel. I'm afraid that you'll have to stay the night here. Sorry, I don't have any pyjamas but I happen to know that there are two single beds already made up in the bedroom opposite Sophie's room.'

The boys thanked her and Charles winked at her as he chuckled: 'You don't worry about the pyjamas as far as I'm concerned for, except on exceptionally cold winter nights, I always sleep in the nude.'

'Well, I can't say that I don't prefer a nightshirt, but I can think of other ways of keeping warm in bed,' said Alan meaningfully as he took the opportunity of caressing my bare breasts just before I covered them with my chemise. I playfully slapped his hand and said: 'So can I, but let me tell you now that I'm feeling very sleepy and won't want any more rumpy pumpy till the morning.'

'That's all right,' he said brightly as he bent down to tie up his shoelaces. 'I could also do with some shut-eye and my cock needs time to recover from that splendid sucking-off. I want to be at my best when I make love to you tomorrow because it will be the fourth anniversary of my very first fuck.'

I smiled at him and said: 'My goodness, what a memory you have, Alan. Allow me to offer you my congratulations.'

'Thank you, Sophie,' he replied and then gave a husky little laugh and went on: 'Actually, it is also the fourth anniversary of my second, third and fourth fucks as well.'

'Gracious, that must have been quite a hectic evening,'

observed Charles. Alex said: 'Yes indeed, and I vote that we go back downstairs and get Alan to tell us about it before we go to bed.'

Her handsome cousin demurred at first but then I said: 'Oh Alan, please do as Alex asks. You must know that we find it as fascinating to hear how you passed into manhood just as much as you would like listening to Alex or myself confess how we lost our virginity.'

He put up his hands in surrender and sighed: '*Touché*, Sophie! And I promise that I won't hold back on any of the intimate details!'

When we were all once again fully clothed, we walked downstairs and settled ourselves down in the comfortable armchairs in the lounge. Alex rang the bell for Windrow and told the footman that he need not wait up any longer because Mutkin always kept a set of house-keys and would open the door for Sir Brindsleigh when they returned home from Lord Nettleton's. Then she perched herself on Charles's knees and waited for her cousin to relate the story of his rite of passage to us.

Alan cleared his throat and began: 'Shortly after my sixteenth birthday, my parents decided that the family would accept an invitation to spend a week in Edinburgh with the Lord Provost, General Gibson. My father had secured three compartments in a first-class sleeping carriage for the overnight train journey with my parents in one, my two sisters in another and myself in the third. However, much to his annoyance, it was not possible to obtain accommodation in the second-class sleepers for our servants so he arranged for Blodgett, my father's valet and Glenda, my mother's personal maid, to have the exclusive use of a sitting-up compartment at the end of our carriage.

'My father is a considerate gentleman and he told Blodgett: "There won't be any other passengers around to disturb you and as I don't see why we should make any call on your services during the journey, you should be able to stretch yourselves out on the seats and have a good night's sleep."

'Well, we arrived at King's Cross station promptly at ten o'clock and after my father had supervised the loading of our luggage we boarded the train and inspected our carriage. I had never slept on a train before and was pleasantly surprised by the spotlessly clean compartment with its marble washstand and comfortable bed. After partaking of a cup of cocoa in the refreshment car, I went back to my compartment where I undressed and opened my travelling case for my nightshirt.'

He turned to Charles and remarked: 'Now this wouldn't have bothered you because you prefer to sleep in the nude, but I was annoyed that the servants had packed all my nightshirts in my trunk. But it was a warm summer night and when I drew the curtain, I left the window slightly open to allow in some fresh air before jumping in between the crisp white sheets.

'Lulled by the clickety-clack, clickety-clack of the wheels, I felt my eyelids begin to droop and I was soon in the Land of Nod. But I am a rather light sleeper and I woke up with a start when the sound of the closing of a door-latch interrupted my slumber. My first reaction was that the person I could see in the dim light from the tiny electric bulb in the ceiling gliding towards the window was one of those sneak thieves who have plagued the railways in recent years. Instinctively I threw back my bedclothes, jumped to my feet and, grabbing hold of the burglar's shoulder, I spun him round to face me. I raised my hand to strike the intruder when with a tiny scream, a familiar female voice called out softly: "No, no, please don't hit me, Master Alan! I'm sorry to have disturbed you but I couldn't think of anywhere else to go."

'I peered at my unexpected visitor who I could now see

was none other than my mother's personal maid. "Glenda, what's the idea of barging in here like this?" I exclaimed, forgetting my own nakedness as I stared at the pretty girl.

'She hung her head and repeated her apology for waking me up. I suddenly realised that her downcast eyes were gazing at my cock and I jumped back into bed and waved her towards a chair as I said with some irritation: "Yes, yes, I heard you the first time. However, I'll only accept your apology if you'll just tell me what the blazes you're up to."

'Glenda slumped into the chair and sighed: "Well, I'll tell you, Master Alan, but I'd rather you didn't tell your parents. The truth is that Mr Blodgett brought a hip-flask of whiskey in his case and he was more than a bit worse for wear by the time I lay down across the seats to go to sleep."

'She paused and I looked sharply at her and said: "Carry on, Glenda. What happened next?"

'"I soon fell asleep but was woken up by someone gently pulling my shoulder," she said in a low voice. "I turned round and there was Blodgett standing there with his flies undone, holding his prick in his hand. He leered at me and said: 'How about giving my tool the same treatment you gave Colonel Brooke last week?'"

'"And what was that?" I enquired with interest and Glenda mumbled that I wasn't old enough yet to know about such things. "I was sixteen last week, Glenda, so I'm only two years younger than you," I said pointedly. "Anyhow, even this time last year I would have known that Blodgett wanted you to suck his cock."

'This riposte amused her and she smiled: "Oh, Master Alan, you obviously know more about the birds and the bees than I gave you credit for. Yes, I enjoy giving Colonel Brooke a gobble whenever he stays overnight, but that's because he's a real gentleman. We have some great fun whenever I get the chance to slip into his room. But like he does with all the maids, Blodgett is always pestering me for a poke, and it's not right, is it, Master Alan? I mean to say, surely even a servant girl like me has the right to decide who she wants to shag?"

'"Of course you do, Glenda," I said warmly. "And you can tell Blodgett from me that if he continues to trouble you or any other girl in our service, then I will report him to my father who is certain to dismiss him on the spot."'

'Well said, Alan, I detest all kinds of bullying and this fellow deserved a strong reprimand,' I remarked. Then I noticed that Belinda, the petite chambermaid who I had caught being fucked by Windrow the footman, had quietly entered the room whilst Alan had been holding the floor. She had been listening intently to this spicy narrative. Being in service herself, I was sure she would agree and I said to her: 'I'm sure you would applaud Mr Greene's action.'

'Belinda! I didn't see you standing there,' exclaimed Alex in surprise and the perky girl explained: 'I came in a couple of minutes ago to see if there was anything I could do for you before I went upstairs, Miss Alex. To be honest, I was so interested in what Mr Greene was saying that I didn't want to interrupt him.'

'I see,' said Alex dryly. 'Well, we don't need anything so you can go to bed. As I told Windrow, there's no need to wait up for my father.'

Belinda gave her a little bob-curtsy and said: 'Thank you, Miss Alex, but may I hear the end of Mr Greene's story first?'

Alex looked questioningly at Alan who shrugged his shoulders and said: 'I don't mind letting her stay,' and Charles and I also said that we had no objection to Belinda joining our little gathering. So the chambermaid sat down on the carpet and leaned forward with her elbows on her knees and her head cradled in her hands to hear Alan take up his tale.

He said: 'Glenda thanked me profusely and then she smiled and said: "There is one more favour I would like to ask of you, Master Alan. Blodgett became very abusive when I refused to kiss his cock and ran out of the compartment. He's probably consoled himself by finishing off his whiskey, but I'd rather not go back to my seat for a while. Please may I stay here for a little while till the booze sends him to sleep?"

'Believe it or not, I had no ulterior motive in mind when I replied: "Be my guest, Glenda. This bed is big enough for two. Now don't misunderstand me, what I suggest is that you take this pillow and we can sleep head-to-tail, with our heads next to each other's feet. I promise you that I always wash my toes thoroughly!"

'She eagerly accepted this offer and I must admit that I peeped out from between the sheets to watch Glenda undress herself. My cock started to thicken whilst she peeled off her clothes. When she removed her chemise I caught sight of her firm, jutting breasts and when she wriggled out of her knickers and stood naked in front of me, I gazed in awe at her thick bush of dark pussey hair and my hand automatically shot down to clasp hold of my swollen shaft.

'"Goodnight, Alan," Glenda said softly as she slid into bed. I laid back with my aching stiffstander throbbing away in my hand. But I couldn't very well relieve myself in front of her so I closed my eyes and tried with all my might to push all the sensual images of the delectable girl from my mind. However, I found it simply impossible to do so, and the only way I could keep back the tide of jism which was already pushing up the stem of my shaft was to tell myself that Glenda would quickly fall asleep and I would then be free to bring myself off.

'I let go my cock and relaxed but then I felt a movement at the foot of the bed. I opened my eyes to see her throw off the bedclothes and forcing my legs apart, she climbed up onto her knees between them.

' "Glenda, what the deuce—" I said in a choking voice and she blew me a kiss and whispered: "Relax, Master Alan. I've just realised that it was your birthday last week and I never gave you a present. I'm now going to put that right."

'To my amazement, she slid her hand around my rock-hard chopper and slowly rubbed her fist up and down it as she went on: "My word, I had no idea how well-developed you were for your age. Well, a birthday boy with such a big stiffie deserves a nice treat."

'My cock was close to bursting point as she looked up at me. With a twinkle in her eye she asked: "Doesn't that feel good, Master Alan?" I wanted to answer her but all I could do was to nod my head. I was now far too excited to reply with any degree of coherence. Glenda stifled a giggle and said: "But if you like that, young man, let's see what you make of this."

'She licked her lips as she grasped hold of my twitching tool and popped my knob into her hot, wet mouth. She twirled her tongue over my knob but I came almost immediately and before she had a chance to really suck my cock, a huge flow of spunk gushed out of my prick. Glenda swallowed as much as she could but she could not contend with such a great gush and a rivulet of creamy jism dribbled down onto her chin.

'Nevertheless, I was so excited by what was my first gobble, that my cock was still stiff when she gently pulled it from between her lips. She wiped her mouth with the back of her hand and said: "M'mm, your spunk has a lovely flavour – and what a wonderful long spurt! Now be truthful, has any hussey sucked you off before?"

'Glenda was delighted when I admitted how I was totally inexperienced and that no girl had even tossed me off. She cupped my balls in her hand and murmured: "Master Alan, let me tell you that with a fine cock like that you'll never be short of willing young ladies, especially if you can keep your shaft on jack after spunking. Well, it seems a pity to let your stiffie go to waste. I can hardly wait to have that thick prick of yours inside my quim so let's not waste any more time."

'I scrambled up and pinched my arm to make sure that I wasn't having one of those sweet "wet" dreams which stain the sheets with spunk but end so cruelly just at the climax of an erotic encounter. I smiled as I felt the pain which told me that I really was about to fuck my first girl.

'Glenda lay back with her legs parted and I could see the red chink of her cunney beckoning my pulsating prick to slide inside it. But for some weird reason, the thought that I wouldn't be able to perform suddenly floated into my brain. I looked worriedly down at the pretty minx who was lasciviously stroking her stalky nut-brown nipples.

'Of course, now I know that many young chaps at that age think of little else other than how they might cross the Rubicon. When at last the opportunity does present itself, they often find themselves paralysed by a fear of failure which prevents them doing justice to their undoubted potential. However, Glenda clearly realised how nervous I was. She reached out for my cock and rubbed the purple helmet between her yielding pussey lips. This worked like magic and without further ado I slid into her sopping sheath, delighting in my first experience of having my shaft embedded inside a juicy wet cunt. I almost swooned with pleasure as I buried my boner into the depths of her love funnel and she wriggled underneath me, hugging me tightly as she breathed: "Go on, darling. Keep pushing your prick inside my cunney. More, more! Don't worry, I'll tell you if you go over the top!"

'I was in my own private heaven as she worked her hips in time with my thrusts, letting my shaft sink all the way inside her dripping slit and holding it there before I eased my twitching todger out to plunge forward yet again. As you would expect, I couldn't wait for Glenda to come and with a choking cry, I made one last lunge into her cunney before sending a stream of sticky jism into her eager snatch before collapsing down on top of her.

'"Oooh, that was a lovely fuck, Master Alan, you can really be proud of yourself," Glenda cooed as she ruffled my hair. "For a first-timer you did awfully well."

'I stammered: "But surely I spent too quickly? According to Dr Elstree's manual *Fucking for Beginners*, which my chum smuggled into school last term, a chap should always wait for his partner to climax before shooting off."

'"Never mind, I thoroughly enjoyed myself and believe me, Master Alan, you're bound to please many girls with that big thick cock," she said roguishly. "Anyhow, perhaps we can try again soon and we'll see if you can hold back long enough for me to spend before you oil my quim with those gorgeous warm squirts of spunk."

'Sure enough, an hour or so later the sweet girl invited me to fuck her and this time I could see Glenda savour to the full the voluptuous sensation of my lusty cock slewing in and out of her voracious cunney. She raked her fingernails down my back and ground her pussey against my groin as with a yelp of delight, she shuddered through a stupendous spend. Then I flooded her love channel with a copious emission of frothy white seed. This lascivious coupling exhausted us both and we lay panting for breath in each other's arms.

'Soon I went to sleep with a blissful smile on my face for my unexpected initiation into manhood had surpassed all my expectations. There I was lying next to a beautiful naked girl having just made passionate love to her and with any luck I could anticipate another joust in the morning. In fact, Glenda had the sense to leave well before the waiter knocked on the door with my early-morning tea and although I fucked her several times during our stay in Scotland, she made it clear that when we returned home, we would have to revert to our previous master/servant relationship.'

For a few moments we sat in silence as Alan finished this sensual memoir and then Charles said: 'Most people would agree that the first time one indulges in sexual intercourse is a traumatic stepping stone on the path to adult life. One's first fuck can be idyllic or disastrous and you were fortunate enough to be partnered by a sophisticated girl who gave you the confidence to enjoy the experience.'

'Yes, but Mr Greene deserved his good luck,' piped up Belinda as she hauled herself up from the carpet and leaned against the front of my armchair. 'I wish that all young gentlemen would show such consideration to the servants in their employ.'

[*This subject often comes up in The Cremorne novels – see* Cremorne Scandals *for an account of the indignities endured by the girls in service at Mr Trenton Woodstock's rooms in the West End of London – Editor*]

'Oh come now, Belinda,' remonstrated Alex warmly. 'The only young gentleman who has lived here recently was my brother Timothy. Now I seem to remember that you joined the staff only a month or so before he left the country to take up a post in the British Embassy in Washington. Are you saying that during that short time Tim bullied you into—'

'No, no, no, Miss Alex,' interrupted the pert little chambermaid. 'Mr Timothy and I did have a special understanding – but he was a nice, kind young man and he never forced me into anything that I wasn't happy to do.'

Her explanation mollified Alex who had been concerned to hear anything untoward about her older brother, of whom she had always been extremely fond. Nevertheless, she was curious to know more and she urged Belinda to explain herself further. 'What sort of special understanding do you mean?' she asked her. 'Don't be frightened to speak freely. I want you to be as open as Mr Greene was when he told us about an intimate affair.'

'You won't be annoyed with me if I tell you everything?' said Belinda and I reassured the girl that she had nothing to fear. 'Especially if you don't leave out all the juicy bits!' added Charles with a broad smile.

This put Belinda at her ease. She confessed that, like all the other girls in service at Henderson Hall, she was much taken with Timothy, a handsome young man of twenty-five who, after taking a first-class degree at the London School of Economics, had been invited to work for the Foreign Office. Timothy had been given six weeks' leave of absence before he went to America and Alex explained that he had spent much of his vacation visiting friends whom he would not see again for some considerable time.

'That's right,' said Belinda, nodding her head in agreement. 'He used to go out to parties almost every night. I'll never forget the time he came home a little worse for wear after a shindig with his old football club friends and I had to help him climb the stairs to his bedroom. About twenty minutes later, I thought I would look in and make sure that he was all right. So I opened his door slowly and tiptoed into the room, shutting it quietly behind me.

'I looked across to the bed and my heart began to beat faster when I saw Timmy lying stark naked on top of the bedclothes. He was fast asleep and I wondered whether I should simply leave him there, but it was a cool Spring night and I was concerned that he might catch a chill if he lay there totally uncovered – but how could I move him without waking him up?

'My eyes swept across his broad chest which was covered by a fine down of dark hair and then I had an idea. I looked downwards to the thick bush of hair around his groin and especially at his thick prick which lay across his thigh. I took hold of his right hand and moved it down to his todger, placing his fingers around the base of the fleshy tube. Then I leaned across and pulled down his foreskin before swirling my tongue over his uncapped knob. As I had hoped, Timmy didn't wake up but a smile formed on his face and he began to fist his hand up and down his swelling shaft.

'My original idea was for me to slide the eiderdown from underneath Timmy whilst he tossed himself off in his sleep, but frankly, the sight of his lovely cock was so tempting that I tore off my clothes and straddled him, letting my breasts dangle in front of his face. His eyes fluttered open and he let out a funny little gurgle of astonishment at waking up to find a naked girl resting on top of him.

'"It's only me, Belinda," I whispered to put him at his ease. I moved back to sit on his thighs and grabbed hold of his cock which was throbbing so hard that I knew he would soon be shooting his load. I squeezed his shaft between my breasts and he came off almost at once, sending a fountain of sperm up over his belly. His tool twitched so powerfully that a few flying drops landed on my breasts. This made me feel even randier and my pussey was getting wetter and wetter. I let my nipples slide in the sticky pools of spunk on Timmy's tummy and then lifted my titties up to my mouth and licked off the milky jism as best I could.

'Timmy was now fully aroused to the situation and he entered into the spirit of the game by rolling me over and pressing his lips to mine in a gorgeous French kiss. He slipped a finger into my soaking pussey and rubbed harder and harder until my clitty was hard as a little rubber ball. Next he spread my cunney lips apart and slid a second and third finger into my tingling crack which made me writhe and twist from side to side as he brought me up to the brink of a spend.

'I didn't have to be asked twice when he pulled back slightly from our embrace and muttered: "Belinda, you naughty girl, how would you like me to lick out your delicious love box?"

'"Yes please, Timmy," I answered as I pushed his head down between my legs. Soon he was lapping away with all his might. Oh, how beautifully he brought me off with his clever tongue. My cunney was gushing love juice and my clitty pulsated wildly, wanting more and more as I closed my thighs around Timmy's head, urging him on as I felt wonderful waves of pleasure run up and down my spine.

'"H-a-a-r-g-h! H-a-a-r-g-h! I've come! I've come!" I gasped as I spent all over his face, soaking his mouth and chin in cuntal juice which he gulped down with relish.

'"Now I'm going to fuck you, Belinda," he announced as he heaved himself up over me and directed his erect shaft towards my puffy pussey lips. He groaned and thrust his veiny todger straight into my juicy cunt without any difficulty. His heavy ballsack smacked against my wet bum as he slid his thick tool deep, deep inside my eager quim. At first he moved in and out with gentle plunges and listening to the squishy slurps made by the passage of his prick almost brought me to a spend.

'Then Timmy began to work up a faster pace, burying his boner inside me with long, powerful thrusts which mashed my clitty against his cock, sending a series of electric shocks which made me shake all over as they crackled through my love channel. He held us together until these spasms eased and then he started to stroke his cock in and out of my sticky honeypot at lightning speed until I felt his body stiffen. Then, with one huge heave, he creamed my cunney with a fierce gush of jism.

'I screamed out my joy as the senstions of a truly superb spend sped through my body, forcing Timmy to place his hand lightly over my mouth and whisper: "Shush, my sweet, don't make so much noise or you'll wake everybody up!"

'It was time to call a halt to our fun and he pulled his deflated cock out of my saturated cunt and we cuddled up happily together. We were both in need of a rest after our labours but I dared not stay in case someone discovered that I had not slept in my own bed that night. So I wriggled out of Timmy's arms and slipped on my knickers and went back quietly to my own lonely bed.

'After that night, Timmy and I enjoyed some marvellous fucks, but as somebody said earlier, you never forget the first time.'

'Quite right, Belinda, quite right,' came a slightly slurred voice from behind me. I spun round to see that Sir Brindsleigh had returned from his bridge game and was standing against the door.

'Only sometimes you don't want to remember the first time,' he continued as he walked unsteadily towards and slumped down on the sofa. 'My own was pretty calamitous. I sent a bunch of red roses with my card to a showgirl in the chorus at the Empire and the next night after the show I took her out to dinner. We went back to a hotel afterwards but I'd drunk so much to steady my nerves that I couldn't raise a stand even when she rubbed her hand up and down my cock.

'Imagine how awful I felt when the girl flounced out of the room and called back over her shoulder: "You Etonians are all the same. I suppose you need a pretty boy's bum stuck in front of you to get a hard-on!"'

Sir Brindsleigh snorted: 'The bloody cheek of the girl! Still, I dare say she had cause to think that I was one of the shirt-lifting fraternity.'

Thinking that Alex would be embarrassed by any more of her father's alcoholic revelations, I gave a discreet little cough and asked him if he would like some coffee before he retired. Windrow had thoughtfully left a fresh pot bubbling over a small spirit stove.

Sir Brindsleigh shook his head and grunted: 'No thanks, Sophie, but you can pour me out a large whisky and soda instead. After what happened at Lord Nettleton's tonight, I damned well need to drown my sorrows.'

'Oh dear, didn't you hit it off with Colonel Topping?' I asked and he threw up his hands and said bitterly: 'Hit it off? Why, I can't understand how Charlie Nettleton puts up with him. Oh, I grant you he plays a fair hand at bridge but he's a spiteful old bugger who thinks he's the Lord Chief Justice and not just the beak at some piffling little police court!'

'As bad as that?' I said sympathetically. His face creased into an angry scowl as he went on: 'When I happened to say that, to gain their superiors' approval, some police constables were becoming far too zealous in setting speed traps for motorists, the fellow jumped down my throat and began haranguing me about drivers of these infernal contraptions behaving as if they owned the road. The only consolation was that he became so worked up about my remark that he trumped his own ace of hearts and failed to make an easy small slam.

'On the other hand, it's clearly goodbye to my driving licence for at least three months when that speeding charge comes up in his court,' added Sir Brindsleigh gloomily as Alan handed him his drink.

'This Colonel Topping sounds a right old so-and-so,' commented Alex and then to our surprise Belinda said: 'Excuse me, Miss Alex, are you and your Dad talking about Colonel Topping from Deansgate? Well, I could tell you a story or two about him! Didn't you know that I worked for him before coming to Henderson Hall? Oh, he was a real horror and I couldn't wait to give in my notice.'

Sir Brindsleigh looked up sharply and said: 'Is that so?

tell us more about him, Belinda. Why did you leave his service? Did he ever try to force himself onto you?'

'No, he never tried anything like that with me,' answered Belinda, pursing her lips as she recalled the disagreeable months spent in service with Colonel Topping. 'But he was a bad-tempered old grump who never said "thank you" or "please" to a servant. Come to think of it, he was just as rude to everyone he came across. No-one could blame his wife when she left him for weeks at a time to visit her friends and family down in Hampshire.'

'M'mm, that's all very interesting though I'm afraid it won't really help me put some pressure on him,' muttered Sir Brindsleigh. But hearing that his wife was often away made me wonder whether Colonel Topping had a secret *amorata* to take her place. So I asked Belinda if the Colonel 'played around' whilst he was living alone. A saucy dimple appeared on each of her rosy cheeks as she smiled: 'Oh yes, when I was working for him, he was fucking another magistrate, Mrs Sherratt-Hughes. She would often come round to the house supposedly to talk about cases coming up before them, but all the staff knew Colonel Topping was having it away with her.'

'Oh-ho, that's more like it,' chortled Sir Brindsleigh, rubbing his hands in excitement. 'After his outburst against cars, Charlie Nettleton muttered to me that the Colonel is also down on what he calls immoral behaviour and writes letters to the local newspapers that young men caught larking around with girls should be soundly thrashed.'

Belinda wrinkled her nose and declared: 'Huh, he's a fine one to talk, I must say! Why, I've actually seen him poke Mrs Sherratt-Hughes and I've got the evidence to prove it!'

'What do you mean? Don't tell us you have a signed confession from them!' I frowned and the chambermaid giggled: 'Not exactly, Miss Sophie, but I could show you something just as good. Perhaps I had better explain – one afternoon Mrs Sherratt-Hughes came round to see the Colonel and they closeted themselves away in his study.

'Now whenever this happened, the butler always brought them their tea on the dot of half past four. However, we couldn't find Mr Talbot anywhere in the house so Cook asked me to wheel the trolley into the study. "Of course," I said, but when I got there I wasn't sure whether to knock and go straight in or wait till the Colonel bellowed at me to enter. Either way he would grouse about being interrupted, so I bent down and looked through the keyhole to see if they looked busy with anything important.'

'And you saw more than you bargained for,' I observed and she nodded: 'Oh yes, you can say that again! Colonel Topping had cleared all the papers from his wide oak desk and he was lying naked on his back across it. His prick was standing up and Mrs Sherratt-Hughes was standing behind him with her fingers clamped round his cock. She had also taken off her clothes and the Colonel was playing with her big red titties whilst she rubbed her hand up and down his shaft and uncapped his purple helmet to plant a smacking great kiss on his knob.

'Then still holding his cock, she clambered up on the desk and straddled the Colonel, but then she let go his tool and turning herself towards the wall she thrust her sumptuous bum cheeks in his face.

'"Fire at will, Colonel!" she called out and raised her bottom to invite him to stick his cock up her snatch. However, the Colonel seemed to hesitate and I was amazed to see his shaft begin to lose its stiffness. "Come on then, this is one attack which won't be repelled."

'"Sorry, Hetty old girl, my artillery looks to be out of action again," he apologised. "I'll need to call up some reinforcements. Where's that damned butler got to?"

'Then I almost fell backwards from shock when I found out where Mr Talbot had been hiding himself, for he now stepped out stark naked from behind the curtains, jerking his hand up and down his swollen shaft as he walked towards the desk and said: "You called for me, sir?"

'"Ah, there you are, Talbot," Colonel Topping panted as he pulled up his legs and swung himself off the desk. "Go and fuck Mrs Sherratt-Hughes at the double, there's a good chap."

'"With pleasure, sir," replied Mr Talbot. He jumped up and took the Colonel's place behind the lady who at once reached back to grab his stiff chopper and guide it between her wobbly bum cheeks and into her wet pussey.

'"How does that feel, Hetty?" asked the Colonel as he moved round to kneel on a chair in front of her so that his dangling cock was only inches away from her face.

'"Oh yes, very nice indeed, thank you," she gasped as Mr Talbot buried his boner to the hilt inside her sopping slit. His dangling ballsack flopped against the backs of her thighs. He passed his hand around her waist and he slid his forefinger into her cunt to join his cock for her added enjoyment.

'Watching his butler fuck Mrs Sherratt-Hughes obviously excited the Colonel, because his todger started to thicken. She popped it into her mouth, rolling her tongue around it until he pulled out his transformed tool which was now as stiff as a poker. Mr Talbot continued to poke her as she sucked the Colonel's cock, sliding his shaft in and out of her cunney in an easy rhythm as she rotated her bottom in time with his thrusts.

'Then I suddenly realised that Colonel Topping's Kodak Brownie was sitting on a hall table just a few yards away. I rushed to pick up the camera. Gingerly, I slowly opened the door and as I guessed, the lusty trio were too intent on what they were doing to notice me in the doorway. Nor did they hear the click of the shutter as I took six photographs of the sucking and fucking. Then I shut the door behind me and put back the camera before taking another view of the naughty goings-on.

'The Colonel came first whilst Mrs Sherratt-Hughes was licking the underside of his knob. He gave a throaty moan and shuddered all over as the first spunky jet hit her on the side of her nose. But then she opened her mouth and gobbled furiously on his trembling truncheon and as his spend passed its peak, she gulped in his entire shaft into her mouth, sucking for all she was worth to milk the last drops of jism from his softening shaft.

'He pulled out his limp cock and she turned her head and said to Mr Talbot: "Speed things up and finish me off with a nice pressing of love juice up my cunt. I have to leave here by five o'clock to take the chair at a Mother's Union meeting at the vicarage."

'"By Gad! I hadn't noticed the time," exclaimed Colonel Topping. "Yes, you two had best hurry up because someone will be bringing in the tea trolley any minute now. I'll lock the door to make sure none of those stupid servants comes barging in."

'I'll give you stupid servants, I thought to myself. I straightened up and put the camera in my apron pocket as I wheeled the tea trolley behind a corner. Anyhow, I waited for five minutes and then knocked on the door.

'"Who's that?" bellowed the Colonel and I called out: "It's Belinda, sir. I've brought your tea." I heard him stump across to the door which he unlocked and opened it just enough to push his face through the gap. "Just leave the trolley there and go back to your work, you little trollop," he snapped before slamming the door shut.

'"Who are you calling a trollop, you dirty bugger," I muttered as I walked back to the kitchen. I've waited some time but very soon I'm going to have my revenge on the miserable old scrote.'

'Hold on a minute,' said Sir Brindsleigh, who like the rest

of us had listened intently to Belinda's fascinating tale. 'What happened to the photographs you took with the Colonel's camera?'

'Ah, that's another story, sir,' she said, smiling wickedly as she rose to her feet and went on: 'This all happened only days after I had applied for a position at Henderson Hall. Of course I took up the post as soon as I was offered the job. Well, when your footman, Mr Windrow told me that he was a keen amateur photographer, I asked him to develop the film for me.'

Alan gave a husky chuckle. 'Young Windrow must have been a bit taken aback when he saw the prints,' he remarked and we all laughed but Sir Brindsleigh made an impatient gesture with his hand and looked hard at Belinda as he said: 'Yes, yes, all very amusing I'm sure, but the important question is whether you still possess any copies of these photographs?'

'I should say so,' she said smugly. 'I asked Martin, Mr Windrow, that is, to make up two full sets of prints for me and I've still got one of them hidden in my room.'

'And what became of the other set of photographs? I would be most grateful if you would let me borrow them for a day or two,' said Sir Brindsleigh fervently, but she shook her head and giggled: 'I'm sorry, sir, I don't have them any more. You see, I found this rude magazine called *The Oyster* in Colonel Brooke's bedroom which he left behind after he stayed here last weekend. Well, when I was thumbing through it I read how it was running a competition with huge prizes for the best readers' photographs of pricks and pussies. So I've sent in the prints of Colonel Topping and Talbot fucking Mrs Sherratt-Hughes. Even if I don't actually win, wouldn't it be wonderful if the Editor ever used one of my photographs. Can you just imagine the Colonel's face if someone showed it to him?'

I burst out laughing as I looked across at Charles, who readers will remember I first met whilst he was photographing Celia Parker in the nude for this same contest. 'Oh dear, it looks as if you and Belinda will be locked in conflict for that thousand guineas first prize!' I remarked. A rather embarrassed Charles bit his lip and muttered that there would probably be more than a thousand entries so one more here or there wouldn't make much difference to his chances.

But this was of little concern to Sir Brindsleigh who now offered Belinda a gold sovereign [*A tempting amount for a housemaid who was probably earning only £30 a year – Editor*] for the loan of her remaining set of photographs. 'I'll only need them for a few days and you have my word that I'll take great care of them,' he pleaded with her.

There was no reason for Belinda to refuse and she shrugged her shoulders. 'All right, I'll run upstairs and give them to you right now,' she suggested to Sir Brindsleigh's evident relief. However, whilst she was gone, Alex said to him: 'Papa, I hope you know what you're doing. Blackmail is a serious crime, you know.'

'Who said anything about blackmail?' said an offended Sir Brindsleigh. 'I don't plan to tell Topping that I'll show his wife a photograph of Mrs Sherratt-Hughes sucking his cock unless he makes arrangements for that speeding charge against me to be dropped. No, I'll go round to his house and quietly warn the Colonel that his chopper might be featured in a forthcoming issue of *The Oyster*.

'Then I'll sit back and watch him panic!' he added gleefully but Charles chuckled: 'But he might well not be too bothered by the news if he's never seen a copy of the publication.'

'H'm, you may have a point there, my boy,' muttered Sir Brindsleigh. 'Would one of you young sparks have a copy I could borrow?'

Alas, neither of them subscribed to the magazine but Alan recalled that he had seen the special summer edition on a chair in his tutor's rooms. He grinned: 'Dr Macfarlane's a real sport and he won't mind lending it to me.'

'Jolly good show,' said Sir Brindsleigh happily. When Belinda returned we all pored over her naughty photographs which were so rude that I wondered whether she might indeed win one of the large cash prizes being offered in the competition she had entered. It was now well past midnight and Sir Brindsleigh agreed that it would be best if Alan and Charles stayed the night in one of the spare bedrooms and Mutkin drove them back to Oxford after breakfast tomorrow morning.

'Just one more thing, everybody, don't breathe a word about any of this to Lady Henderson,' he added emphatically. 'Or we'll all be in the soup.'

Sir Brindsleigh led the company upstairs and frankly we were so tired from all the excitement that despite the proximity of the boys to our rooms, Alex and I decided not to risk being caught out. All four of us slept the rest of the night away alone in our own beds. However, in the morning, Alan whispered to me how much his cock was aching for my pussey when he had woken up. Then he asked me if we would like to spend the afternoon watching an athletic meeting at the Parks.

'Actually, it's a challenge match between the Oxford Artisans and a scratch University team. During the vacation only a handful of undergraduates are in town so I've been roped in for the high jump and the half-mile race,' he said modestly.

'I would be delighted to come and watch you run,' I replied and Alex and Charles also said they would like to cheer on his team. 'Thank you very much,' said Alan gratefully. 'If the weather holds, you might think about bringing a picnic. Anyhow, the first races will begin at two o'clock.'

'We'll be there,' I said, kissing him on the cheek as Mutkin entered the dining room and announced that he would drive the young gentlemen to Oxford whenever they were ready to leave. Charles suggested that he meet us at the entrance to the Parks at one o'clock and when we agreed, the boys made their farewell to Sir Brindsleigh and went into the drawing room where Lady Henderson was busy with her correspondence, to thank her for her hospitality before they left the house for Oxford.

The weather looked promising and the idea of a picnic had great appeal. However, we were disappointed to find out from Windrow that it was the cook's day off, but Sir Brindsleigh put down the newspaper in which he had been engrossed and said: 'Never mind, Alex, I'll telephone our caterer, Mrs Moser at the Hartfield Emporium. Even at this short notice she should be able to prepare a splendid luncheon hamper for your party which we can collect when we get to town.'

'What do you mean by "we", Papa?' she asked, concerned no doubt that he might be planning to join us. Anxious frowns formed on our faces because neither of us could indulge in any uninhibited horseplay with her father in close attendance.

But our worries were unfounded for Sir Brindsleigh grinned: 'Have no fear, Alex, I know that you and Sophie wouldn't want an old fuddy-duddy like me around spoiling your fun with the boys. But I have an engagement in Oxford early this afternoon and it will pose no problem for me to drive you to the Parks. Lady Caughey has invited your mother to luncheon over in Witney, but Mutkin can take her there in the Wolseley.'

I thought of the buxom Florrie, the girl with whom Sir Brindsleigh enjoyed a standing arrangement (in every sense of the phrase!) in a bedroom at the Randolph Hotel, and rather naughtily I asked him if he had another business meeting to attend. However, Sir Brindsleigh pretended not to have heard my question but simply folded his newspaper and muttered something about going into his study and telephoning Mrs Moser about the picnic arrangements.

He returned five minutes later to inform us that we could pick up the hamper from Mrs Moser at half past twelve so we should leave Henderson Hall at noon. This gave us plenty of time to change into suitable clothes. Alex had a clever idea as she squinted out of the window at the sun which was now shining brilliantly in a cloudless blue sky.

Happily, all went according to plan and on the stroke of noon we roared out of the gates of Henderson Hall. It was soon noticeable that Sir Brindsleigh was driving more prudently than on our previous journey to Oxford. This made me hope that he had learned his lesson and even if – by fair means or foul – he managed to escape disqualification, in future Sir Brindsleigh would not treat other road users with such careless disdain.

We collected Mrs Moser's hamper from Hartfield's and when we reached the entrance to the Parks, Charles was waiting to help Sir Brindsleigh carry it to a secluded spot in the shade on the edge of a clump of trees.

'Phew! Are you sure Mrs Moser didn't pack luncheon for fourteen rather than four,' said Charles as they placed the heavy basket down on the grass.

'Ah well, that's Mrs Moser for you, she always assumes her customers have gargantuan appetites,' smiled Sir Brindsleigh as he straightened up and gave Alex a fatherly kiss. 'Goodbye, my dear, have a lovely afternoon. I don't know what time I shall finish my business in town so will you or Sophie telephone home to tell Mutkin what time and where he should come to take you home? Oh yes, and please don't forget to return the hamper to Hartfield's before half past six tonight.'

We thanked him for his trouble and shortly after he left

us, I spotted Alan limbering up with his group of his team-mates on the far side of the field. I pointed him out to Charles who said: 'I'll ask him if he would like something to eat, although I doubt if he'll want very much before the start of the meeting.'

In the meantime Alex opened the hamper and brought out a pink linen tablecloth which I helped her spread on the ground. Then we unpacked Mrs Moser's lavish luncheon which consisted of roast chicken, veal and ham pie, rolled tongue, salad and dressing, rolls and butter, cheese, cake plus four half bottles of chilled white wine, two bottles of claret, a bottle of whisky and a half dozen small bottles of seltzer water.

I found Mrs Moser's receipt for three pounds ten shillings and sixpence and showed it to Alex. 'I really would like to buy Sir Brindsleigh a little something to show my apprecia-tion for his kindness,' I said earnestly but she chuckled: 'What are you talking about, you silly girl? We're doing my father a favour by coming here as it gives him the op-portunity to visit Florrie at the Randolph Hotel.'

'You know about Florrie,' I gasped and she laughed. 'Of course I do, Sophie. I guessed that you had found out about my father's bit on the side when we went back there after our afternoon on the river. Is that why you were so keen for Charles and I to wait downstairs for him? Did poor Florrie have to make herself scarce all of a sudden?'

'Something like that,' I admitted and then I added: 'But I think you should know how your father became involved with her.' I would have told her what Sir Brindsleigh and Florrie had said to me there and then but Charles and Alan were now approaching us and I decided to wait until Alex and I were alone together before imparting my information about the situation.

Alan was wearing only a vest and a pair of white athletic shorts and Charles opened up a bottle of champagne so that we could toast Alan's forthcoming triumphs on the athletics track. As Charles had forecast, Alan would only have a small plate of chicken salad and a glass of seltzer water and then he looked at his wrist-watch and said: 'Thank you for a lovely lunch. I must be on my way but perhaps I could meet you back here after the half-mile race which is due to start at a quarter-past four.'

I scrambled to my feet to give him a hug and whispered in his ear: 'We'll be here, darling. Best of luck and don't strain yourself too much. I want you to keep some strength back for some indoor athletics tonight.'

'Have no worry on that score,' he smiled as he kissed me and then ran off at a brisk jog to rejoin his team-mates.

Even with the help of Charles, who was a first-class trencherman, we could not finish more than half of Mrs Moser's repast, although we did manage to get through three bottles of champagne and Charles made a sizeable inroad into one of the bottles of Johnnie Walker whisky. So much so, in fact, that by the time Alex and I had put everything back into the hamper, he was stretched out on the grass, quietly singing a song from 'The Sod's Opera' [*supposedly written by Gilbert and Sullivan but in fact composed by Sir Lionel Trapes [1826–1907], a noted Victorian collector of erotic literature and a frequent contributor to the pages of* The Oyster – *Editor*].

We burst out into a fit of giggling as a horrified clergyman walked by whilst Charles warbled:

> *Oh, give me a damsel of sweet seventeen,*
> *With two luscious thighs and a slit in between,*
> *With a fringe on the edge and red lips I would say*
> *In her cunt I'd be diving by night and by day!*
> *For a quim is a treasure which monarchs admire,*
> *Pussey's the thing which my song does inspire;*
> *A cunney might be a temptation to sin,*
> *But cunt is a hole that I'd ever be in!*

'Maybe so, but you won't be fit for fucking until you've slept it off,' commented Alex as she rolled up Charles's jacket into a pillow and placed it under his head.

'Ta very much, Fiona,' he mumbled and promptly fell asleep, leaving us to wonder who the mysterious Fiona might be. There was no point waiting for Charles to wake up and tell us and as the high-jump competition, in which Alan was taking part, was not scheduled until three o'clock, we decided to go for a stroll along the path by the side of the Cherwell. I began to relate to Alex what Florrie and her father had told me in their bedroom at the Randolph Hotel when Alex grasped my arm and stood stock still, staring across to the far bank of the river.

'Look over there, Sophie!' she said breathlessly, pointing to the middle of a group of willow trees. I followed her gaze and saw a man lying there flat on his back on a dark blue towel. We could not make out his identity because he was reading a book which he held close to his face to shield his eyes from the sun. Clearly, he had earlier been in the river for a swim for he was wearing only a pair of striped cotton bathing drawers and what had caught Alex's attention was the tremendous bulge which tented out between his thighs.

'Whatever can he be reading?' I murmured and Alex answered: 'I've no idea but I'd very much like to find out. Come on, we can cross over by that bridge we just passed and see for ourselves what's giving him the horn.'

At first I protested that we would be invading the gentleman's privacy but Alex remonstrated: 'Perhaps we are, but he'll be grateful if we inform him that he can be seen by people walking along this path, especially if he gets even more excited and begins playing with himself.'

'I suppose you're right,' I said as we turned and began to walk smartly back to the bridge. 'Although I'm warning you now that I shall leave it to you to tell him about how we noticed his stiffie.'

'That's all right, I'm not shy,' she shrugged as we crossed over the river and made our way through the copse of bushes until we came to within ten yards of our quarry. He turned out to be a fresh-faced youth who was so engrossed in the pages of a smutty book that he had not heard our footsteps as we walked towards him.

'Ahem, ahem!' called out Alex. She grinned as he dropped the book and whirled round to face us. 'Young man, do you realise that you can be seen from the path on the other side of the river?'

'Oh dear, no, I didn't know,' he stammered in great confusion. His cheeks flamed a bright shade of crimson as, suppressing a smile, Alex continued sternly: 'In that case, I strongly suggest that you move behind this tree without delay, especially if you plan to carry on reading that naughty book. What is it? H'm, *The Intimate Diaries of Rosie D'Argosse*. Well, that explains the swelling between your legs which so shocked us when we saw you lying here as bold as brass in your bathing suit.'

Then she pursed her lips and said to me: 'Sophie, see if you can find a constable so that we can lay charges against this rude boy.'

However I took pity on the lad, who must have been terrified at the thought of finding himself in the hands of the police, and replied soothingly: 'Come now, Alex, I don't think we should take such drastic action. After all, you could only make out the outline of his shaft under his costume. It isn't as if he was waggling his bare cock at us.'

She pretended to weigh up my words and then replied grudgingly: 'Oh very well then, we'll let him off this time.'

Then she looked down again to our victim who was shivering with fright and said: 'However, I don't think you are old enough to read such lewd material unless you are studying English Literature at the University. Are you in fact an undergraduate?'

'Not exactly,' he gulped nervously. 'But I will be in October as I've won a place at Queen's to read history.'

There was something familiar about his face which I studied carefully as I cocked my head and rested my cheek in my hand. I said to him: 'You know, I have this strange feeling that we have met somewhere before. Now where could that have been? We have been introduced to each other, haven't we?'

'I don't think so,' he muttered but I snapped my fingers and said triumphantly: 'Oh yes, we have and I'll tell you where as well! It was last September at Lord Antony Hammond's twenty-first birthday party in Richmond. And I remember your name too – it's Jason Whetstone and you are related to Antony unless I am much mistaken.'

'He's my cousin, Miss Starr,' he confirmed ruefully. 'Yes of course I recognised you straightaway but I was ashamed to say so. Please accept my apologies for upsetting you and this other lady. Honestly, I really just don't know what more to say.'

I put my finger in front of his lips to silence him and smiled: 'Say nothing, Jason, we were only teasing you. Believe me, Alex and I have seen far more outrageous sights.'

'That's true enough,' said Alex, holding out her hand. 'As Sophie hasn't introduced us, I'll do the honours. My name is Alex Henderson.'

'I'm Jason Whetstone,' he said as he scrambled to his feet and took her hand. 'Are you also a student, Miss Henderson?'

'Not exactly, although I am still considering an offer from my parents to attend a finishing school in Switzerland next month.' I could see Alex run her eyes over the boyish physique of our new chum. She winked at me and said: 'Sophie, why don't you stay here and chat to Jason while I go back and wake Charles up. Then we'll come back here and Jason can help us finish off Mrs Moser's picnic.'

Now that might have been the plan but fifteen minutes later she returned alone carrying the hamper. 'Alex! That hamper is far too heavy to drag all the way over here by yourself,' I scolded her but she replied: 'Oh, don't worry, I took out the empty bottles and dirty plates and left them in a bag next to Charles. He's still fast asleep and I didn't have the heart to wake him. I've written him a note to tell him where we are and I've also left a bottle of seltzer water to refresh himself with when he finally does wake up.'

Jason had eaten only a light sandwich lunch and he soon polished off the remaining portion of the veal and ham pie and he helped us finish the last bottle of champagne. By then we had cast aside all formalities and Alex, who was never backward in coming forward, said to Jason: 'So you only left school this summer. I don't suppose you had the chance to meet many girls at St Dominic's.'

'None, worse luck,' he replied gloomily. 'A friend of mind was found kissing a kitchenmaid in his study and the poor chap was given a public flogging by the headmaster.'

She looked at him in horror. 'How disgraceful! Would the headmaster have preferred it if your friend had been kissing another boy?'

'I'm not so sure he would have minded all that much,' reflected Jason with a grin. 'Because old Doctor Darville-Pike was a bachelor and there was talk that he had a peep-hole cut in the changing rooms of the sports pavilion so that he could see his favourite boys strip off to take their showers after a game of footer. There *were* one or two holes in the wall but to be fair to him, I think it was just a rumour someone started to embarrass him as he was a great one for swishing, especially the pretty boys.'

'You must have had a sore bum for much of the time then,' said Alex and Jason blushed as he drank up the rest of his champagne. 'Unless you were lucky enough to find a jolly girl in the holidays, I'll wager a thousand pounds that the only titties you've ever seen are in paintings or sculptures. Don't be bashful, my dear, answer me truthfully for I really would like to know if you are still *in virgo intacto*. You have my word that you can completely trust me and Sophie. We would never breathe a word about what you tell us to a living soul.'

I nodded my agreement when Jason shot a quick look at me before he quietly replied: 'You would win your bet, Alex, though I assure you that it's not from want of trying.'

'I'm sure it's not,' I said as I thought of how exciting it had been for me to take Phil Colnbrook's cherry back in the dormitory at Dame Chasuble's Academy for the Daughters of Gentlefolk. I guessed that Alex had every intention of furthering Jason's education and whilst I was most interested to see what she had in mind, of course, I stepped back and let her take charge of the lesson.

I didn't have long to wait for Alex was already unbuttoning her blouse and thirty seconds later young Jason Whetstone was looking spellbound at Alex's proudly up-tilted bare breasts. He stumbled towards her when she beckoned him and on her instruction placed his trembling hands on the soft fleshy globes. Then she swept her arm around his neck and pressed his face closer and their lips met in a hard questing kiss.

They slid down onto the blue towel with their mouths still pressed tightly together. Alex helped Jason pull off his bathing costume. I daresay I might have been better employed in trotting back to Charles and keeping him company whilst Alex completed Jason's course in *l'arte de faire l'amour* but instead I walked forward and sat down on a bank of earth to get a grandstand view of my randy friend and her virgin playmate.

Alas, Jason was suffering from an overdose of nervous excitement and his cock stubbornly refused to lift itself up from over his scrotum. Luckily, Alex was wise enough to say nothing but she motioned for me to come over and help and then whispered to Jason to close his eyes and relax. He obeyed without question and I felt him shiver when I slid one hand palm upwards under his pink, wrinkled ballsack and with the other clutched his soft shaft which immediately began to thicken under my touch.

Alex now entered the fray by drawing back his foreskin to reveal a wide bulbous bell-end. 'Ah, that's *much* better,' she said happily. 'Thank you for your assistance, Sophie.'

'My pleasure, darling. I'm always willing to give a nice young man a helping hand,' I answered gaily and she giggled: 'Now I wonder if this pretty cock tastes as good as it looks.'

'Well, there's only one way to find out, Alex,' I told her. 'As the confectioners say when they ask us to try a new sweetie – suck it and see!'

She smiled and bent her head down to kiss the tip of his uncapped helmet. Then she licked all round the ridge of his knob. Jason let out a choking cry of delight when Alex's lips parted and she took inch after inch of his throbbing prick into her mouth.

As her lips slipped further down Jason's shaft she sucked and pulled at his hot, hard length. The ecstatic lad's eyes fluttered open to see Alex's mop of silky blonde hair moving to and fro as she bobbed her head up and down his straining shaft. An euphoric smile spread over his face and he sensibly laid back to enjoy for the very first time the exquisite sensation of soft lips running over his twitching tool. Feeling those moist lips caressing his cock made Jason's back arch in ecstasy and he panted: 'Oh God! That's wonderful, wonderful! Please don't stop!'

He had no cause to be worried on that score, for Alex needed no further urging to continue sucking his virgin cock. However, Jason could not fight against the climax which was already building up in his tightening scrotum and, with a hoarse cry, he shot his spunk deep into her throat, gagging Alex. She could not cope with the rush of creamy jism as she pulled his prick out of her mouth so that the final spermy spasms ran over her cheeks and chin.

Alex smiled nevertheless as she rubbed her wet face in Jason's crisp bush of public hair and then swirled the tip of her tongue around his knob to capture the remaining drops of semen which had oozed out whilst his beefy prick shrank down to a state of half-limber. I thought it would take a little time for him to recover from his first-ever sucking off, but Jason was a healthy young man in his prime. Even though she had just sucked him dry, when Alex began to slick her hand up and down his shaft, it soon swelled up again to stand sky-high as stiff as a soldier on parade.

This sensuous exhibition had stimulated my appetite. I must confess that I was on the verge of whipping off my clothes and climbing on top of him and bouncing up and down on top of his youthful thick tool. However, Alex was in no mood to relinquish her fleshy lollipop and as she deftly unbuttoned her skirt, she called out to me to pull down her knickers, a chore which I could hardly refuse to perform. Then she rolled over onto her back, parted her legs and pulled Jason across to her.

I stayed next to the raunchy pair as Alex whispered: 'Fuck me, dear boy!' Jason raised himself up slightly on his hands and plunged his cock towards the open red chink between her puffy pussey lips. Now maybe it was just beginner's luck, but his thrust was perfectly placed. Alex purred with pleasure as his shaft slid into her juicy cunney and without further ado he began to pump his prick in and out of her soaking slit. This may have been Jason's first poke, but he fucked Alex in great style. She grasped his tight little bum cheeks as his hips jerked to and fro and his shaft slid back and forth inside her squelchy cunt.

'Ahhh! That's the way, you big-cocked boy! Keep driving home, Jason! Fuck me hard, fuck me fast!' she gasped and he increased the tempo until she was frantic with lust.

Nothing loath, he fucked her with added vigour until they wailed in unison as they climaxed together, writhing in delight as Jason's blissful groans mingled with Alex's high-pitched squeals of ecstasy.

It was plain that there was no way that Jason would be able to satisfy the craving for sensual satisfaction which now possessed me. So when he rolled off Alex's soft curves, I took his place and laid my head down upon her beautiful bosoms. She sighed contentedly as I moved my lips first to one breast and then to the other, twirling the tip of my tongue around her erect tawny nipples.

At first she lay passively but then she gave me a wide smile and murmured: 'Oh Sophie, how nicely you suck my titties! Please carry on, I adore it!'

Alex put her arms around me as I continued to nibble the rubbery red stalks. Then I let my tongue travel slowly down across her heaving belly and into her moist mound. She whimpered as I pulled her thighs apart and nuzzled my lips inside her fluffy blonde bush whilst my hands slid underneath the sweet girl's trembling body and clamped themselves around the soft jiggly cheeks of her bottom as my tongue flashed unerringly along her juicy crack.

Her cunney lips opened out like the petals of a flower as I slipped my tongue through the pink folds, licking her out in long slow strokes between the grooves of her finely developed quim. I found her clitty which, swollen with desire, had popped out of its hood to seek further attention. With a groan of sheer sensuous joy, I lost myself in Alex's seductively delicious love channel, relishing to the full the tangy, aromatic cuntal juice which was filling my mouth as she gasped: 'Oooh! Oooh! Oooh! Keep sucking my pussey,

Sophie, it's simply divine! Oh my darling, how I adore the way you tongue-fuck me!'

I was now so aroused that whilst my tongue revelled in her sopping muff, I began to diddle my own pussey, finger-fucking my cunney whilst I sucked Alex's clitty into my mouth, rolling my tongue all around it.

This soon sent Alex over the top and she screamed out: 'I'm coming!' as she exploded into a tremendous climax. I now slid a second and third finger inside my own juicy love funnel, frigging myself up to a delicious spend as my tongue whipped wildly over her clitty. I lapped up the spray of love juice which poured from Alex's cunney whilst she threshed from side to side in lascivious excitement.

Jason watched goggle-eyed as Alex and I hugged and kissed each other. Despite the boy's previous exertions, his shaft was already stiffening up in preparation for a third sensual encounter. I looked hungrily at his meaty tool but then I realised that the odds were that Charles would soon be waking up. If he read the scribbled note which Alex had left for him, he might very well wander over this way to meet up with us.

I said as much to Alex and, with no little reluctance, we dressed and said goodbye to Jason Whetstone, leaving that puzzled young man to wonder if he had indeed lost his virginity to a beautiful blonde girl and her friend or whether he had dozed off into a highly charged erotic dream!

We didn't hurry back but as we crossed the bridge to the footpath leading to the Parks, I saw Charles dashing to-wards us. 'He seems to be in a great hurry,' I observed and then I chuckled: 'So it's just as well we left Jason when we did or Charles would have seen our goings-on which might have upset him.'

'Yes, you're right, Sophie,' she sighed. 'Men are such strange creatures and can get terribly jealous. Charles had no compunction in making up a whoresome foursome with

you, me and Alan Greene – however, watching me being
fucked by an eighteen-year-old youth is an entirely different
matter!'

'Well, what the heart doesn't know, the mind doesn't
grieve,' I commented as I waved to Alex's lover who, when
he saw us, broke into a trot. When he reached us he puffed:
'Ah, there you are, I was just coming to fetch you. I'm
afraid that Alan has injured himself whilst practising the
high jump.'

My hand flew to my mouth as he hastily continued:
'Don't worry, he isn't badly hurt, the poor chap's only
pulled a thigh muscle. He's had to retire from the match,
though, and one of his team-mates is arranging for him to be
taken back to his college. Sophie, I thought you might like
to go with him so I said I would run over to the woods and
bring you back.'

'Thank you, Charles, that's very thoughtful of you,' I
said gratefully. 'Yes, so long as you and Alex don't mind,
I'll stay with Alan for the rest of the afternoon.'

'Of course we don't mind,' said Charles as we walked
briskly back into the Parks. Charles said: 'Look, there's
bound to be a telephone at Worcester College. Why don't
we meet up in Alan's quarters at six o'clock and we can call
Mutkin to meet us there instead. Don't worry about the
hamper, I'll arrange to get it sent back to Hartfield's.'

I thanked him again for his trouble and when we reached
Alan, I was glad to see for myself that he was not in any
great pain although he could only hobble slowly towards the
little Austin Endcliffe tourer which his friend had driven up
to the edge of the grass ready to transport him to his rooms.
'Thanks a million, Nick, you're a real pal,' said Alan as he
heaved himself into the car. 'Sophie, this is my chum Nick
Wright of New York City who lives one floor above me at
the college. Nick, meet Sophie Starr, another good friend
who is kindly going to nurse me this afternoon.'

'How do you do, Miss Starr,' smiled the handsome American as I squashed myself in the seat between Alan and the door. 'If I had known such an attractive girl was going to keep Alan company, I would have thought about pulling a muscle myself.'

'Take no notice of him, Sophie, Nick is already spoken for,' said Alan as his friend engaged first gear and turned the car round into Keble Road. 'He has to pay a fortune in bribes to the porters to turn a blind eye to all the girls who visit him in his rooms.'

Nick Wright laughed and wagged an admonishing finger at Alan although I noticed he did not actually deny the veracity of the remark. Anyhow, he dropped us off at the college gates and I wished him luck in all the events in which he was going to participate on behalf of the University team.

'Oh, I'm only down for the three-mile race and frankly I'll do well not to be lapped by the other runners,' he replied in his pleasant Yankee accent. 'I'm coming straight back here after the race so I hope to see you later.'

He drove off and Alan suggested that we go up to his rooms. We walked slowly through the gardens which are the pride not only of the college but of the University. It is a nice question whether the first impression they make is more taking than the first glimpse of the large quadrangle. The set of quaint old-world buildings on one side is in striking contrast to the stately proportions of the eighteenth-century buildings on the opposite side and of the long front block which includes the Chapel and Hall and the cloister which connects them.

'I'll show you round properly when I can walk more easily,' promised Alan as he acknowledged the greeting of a porter passing by. 'Hold on a moment, Sophie,' he said quickly and then he limped over to talk to him quietly for a few moments before pulling out a coin from his pocket. He dropped it into the outstretched hand of the man who knuckled his forehead and muttered his thanks as he walked off.

'Now I wonder why you've tipped that porter,' I said with an amused chuckle. Alan did not answer but gave me an awkward smile and said: 'I don't think I've mentioned to you anything about an interesting old tradition at the College which goes back to its monastic origins but which is still carried on today. Every morning a porter wakes the undergraduates up by hammering with a wooden mallet on the floor of every staircase.'

'How fascinating,' I murmured drily as we moved off again and he leaned heavily on me as we climbed the stairs to his room.

'And quite unnecessary at the start of the twentieth century,' I added mischievously, but Alan was so intent on us reaching his room without being seen that he ignored my playful teasing.

Fortunately we managed to reach our destination without being seen and once we were safely inside he wisely locked the door and held me in his arms. 'Sophie,' he began, but I put my finger to his lips for no further words were necessary. An onlooker would have felt the sexual heat that emanated from our bodies as we held each other tightly, kissing and cuddling with great fervour as Alan held on to me for dear life. The pair of us staggered as if intoxicated towards his bed upon which we fell in an untidy heap of tangled limbs.

Our passion intensified as our lips locked together and our tongues made darting journeys of exploration inside each other's wet mouths. I shivered with excitement as I felt Alan's fingers skilfully undoing the buttons of my blouse. After I shrugged off the garment I pulled off my chemise and my swelling breasts stood out proudly in all their glorious nudity.

Now it was my turn to help Alan tear off his vest. The bare-chested lad moved his mouth from mine and kissed me all over my neck and throat before his lips reached my erect strawberry titties. He took each stalky nipple in turn between his lips whilst I struggled out of my skirt and then I raised my bottom to let him pull down my knickers.

Alan squeezed my breasts and then dropped one hand down to insert the tip of his finger in my moistening cunt. I closed my eyes and let the erotic electricity of his frigging send sparks of fire throughout every nerve and fibre of my entire body. I laid myself down on the soft eiderdown and Alan gently parted my thighs as he moved himself downwards and dipped his head between my legs. The clever boy began to bring me off the moment that his wicked tongue started to slither up and down my hairy crack. When he darted the tip into my love funnel, the engorged clitty popped out of its hood to greet him.

'Ooooh! Ooooh!' I gasped joyously when Alan playfully nipped on my fleshy love button whilst he shucked off the rest of his clothes. He continued his delicious oral homage to my cunney until I raised his face from my drenched pussey and begged him to fuck me.

'Fill my love hole with your big fat cock!' I cried out shamelessly and, ignoring the discomfort caused by any movement of his thigh, Alan hauled himself over me. My arms clasped his shoulders and I parted my legs wide to wrap them around his waist. Alan cupped my soft buttocks in his hands to raise my pussey nearer the smooth purple dome of his majestic shaft which was nudging its way towards my puffy love lips. He hovered for an instant and then I let out a long, contented sigh as he slid his thick tool into my tingling cunt. He paused for a moment to allow my cunney muscles to accommodate his width before pushing further into my clingy cunt until his balls were nestling against my bum cheeks. Then he began to fuck me.

I was quite delirious with pleasure and my juices flowed like water from a breached dam, keeping my sheath well lubricated for Alan's rock-hard rammer which was now rhythmically pounding in and out of my sticky honeypot.

'Oh Alan, what a marvellous fuck!' I gasped as the walls of my love channel pulsated deliciously around his juice-coated cock. I felt the first stirrings of an approaching orgasm spreading throughout my body.

Alan sensed that my spend was near for he quickened the pace, slamming his shaft in and out of my quim. I quickly reached a tremendous crescendo of excitement. I sucked in my breath as the delicious thrills of a glorious shuddering spend fanned out from my pussey. Alan bucked and heaved to join me on the unique journey to sensual paradise.

'Yes! Yes! Shoot off, Alan, I'm coming!' I screamed, forgetting the fact that Alan was forbidden to entertain females in his room, but I doubt if he was thinking of anything but the exquisite sensation in his cock as he creamed my cunney with a stream of warm frothy spunk. How we revelled in our mutual climax! I lay back and relaxed with a blissful smile on my face as Alan's strong young prick pumped merrily away until I had coaxed every last drain of spermy essence from his balls.

He withdrew his deflated tool and rolled off me to lie in my arms, gasping with exhaustion as he recovered from his exertions. I was ready to carry on, however, and I slid my fingers around his shaft, which was still wet from our spendings, and fisted the soft tube of flesh up and down until it swelled up again in my hand.

I placed my head on his broad chest and whispered: 'Just lie there and relax,' for, unlike some of my friends who are less experienced in love-making, I am fully aware just how much energy a man uses up in fucking. I waited patiently for Alan to regain his composure.

When I sensed that Alan was ready for a further fray, I squeezed his balls and he responded by reaching out to caress the back of my head. Then he gently though insistently lowered my mop of dark silky hair until his throbbing tool was only inches from my face. Naturally I knew what was in his mind. I licked my lips in preparation before planting a wet kiss on the smooth uncapped dome and lapping up the little pool of pre-come around the 'eye' of his helmet.

The highly erotic thought that only minutes ago this thick love truncheon was embedded in my cunt made me tingle all over. I opened my mouth and started to gobble on the ruby knob with relish, sucking on it with loud slurps as my hand jerked up and down his twitching tool. Alan pushed his hips up and down to try and cram every inch of his cock down my throat, but I simply could not take it all in. When I began to choke, the dear lad hastily withdrew until I recovered my breath and clamped my lips back over his juicy todger.

'Woooeee, that's absolutely gorgeous,' he grunted and then an aching cry of release escaped from his throat as he panted: 'Oh God, I'm going to come, I can't stop it! Start swallowing, Sophie, here it comes!'

It was as well that he warned me for Alan sent a huge fountain of sticky spunk spurting into my mouth. I gulped down as much of the tangy essence as I was able, but my mouth was already filled with his quivering cock so some of the tasty jism spilled out between my lips and ran down my chin. I wiped off the creamy moisture and licked it off the back of my hand. I so enjoyed swallowing his copious emission that I was really disappointed when his velvety wet shaft began to lose its stiffness.

Alan fell back on the bed, completely *hors de combat*, and I could see that he was suffering some discomfort from his thigh. I said to him: 'You should lie still and rest if you want to be fit enough to walk without a stick tomorrow morning. Why don't you close your eyes and have a nice snooze?'

Ever the gentleman, he protested: 'That's all very well, but what will you do with yourself in the meantime?'

'Oh, don't worry about me, I'll find something to do,' I said. My eye fell upon the gramophone which Alan had placed on top of his chest of drawers. 'Would it disturb you if I played some records?'

'Not at all, my sweet,' he answered as he pointed to a stack of records underneath a chair. 'You should find something to your taste in my collection – I've everything from arias sung by Melba and Caruso to music hall songs from Marie Lloyd, Dan Leno and Albert Whelan.'

I swung myself off the bed and made Alan cover himself with the eiderdown as I squatted down on my haunches to select the records which I wanted to play. Then I sat on the floor entranced at the superb rendition of a Chopin *étude* by Wesolowski, the brilliant Polish pianist who won such enormous critical acclaim at last year's Promenade Concerts.

The spell was broken by Alan who asked me if I would be good enough to change the gramophone needle. 'Thanks, Sophie,' he said in a drowsy voice. 'Worn needles ruin the records. There should be one or two in the mauve tin next to the machine.'

Unfortunately Alan had no needles left in stock and he frowned: 'Sorry about that, Sophie. I should have bought some when I collected the last batch of records I ordered from Hartfield's last week. However, you could always ask Nick Wright to give you one of the new compressed steel needles his brother sends over to him from America. His room is only on the next floor directly above us.'

'All right, I'll just slip on some clothes and see if he's in,' I agreed, but Alan yawned: 'Oh, you don't have to bother getting dressed. Just slip on my dressing gown, no-one will see you.'

Well, although I thought this might be a rather risky course of action, it would be a bother putting on all my clothes and then having to take them off again when I returned, so I decided to take a chance and slipped on Alan's fawn Vicuna robe.

'I shan't be long, darling,' I promised as I knotted the sash around my waist and kissed him whilst I slipped on my shoes.

'That's all right, Sophie, by all means stay for a chat to Nick whilst I have a little rest,' said Alan sleepily. I think his eyes were already closed by the time I shut the door.

I climbed the flight of stairs to Nick Wright's rooms and knocked on the door. I recognised his Yankee drawl when he called out in a somewhat sharp voice: 'Who's that?'

'Hello there, Nick, it's me, Sophie Starr,' I replied. There was a moment's silence before he answered with a note of distinct relief in his voice: 'Hang on Sophie, I'll be with you in just a moment.'

The broad-shouldered American opened the door. I raised my eyebrows when I saw that Nick was wearing exactly the same fawn Vicuna robe as me.

'Snap!' I laughed and he grinned: 'It looks better on you than either of us. Now what brings you to my humble abode, Sophie Starr? My baser instinct wants you to say that you and Alan have had a terrible argument and you came up here to be comforted.'

'Sorry, Nick, but you're well wide of the mark,' I said lightly. 'I'm here to scrounge a gramophone needle. Alan's thigh is troubling him and I wanted to play some records whilst he has a lie-down on the bed.'

His eyes narrowed as, like the dastardly villain in an old Drury Lane melodrama, he hissed through clenched teeth: 'Foiled again! But I'll have my wicked way with you yet, my ravishing beauty.'

Then, fearing that he may have overstepped the mark, he

hastily continued in his normal voice: 'Forgive me, Sophie, the fact is that I've been cast as the wicked landlord in the OUDS [*Oxford University Dramatic Society – Editor*] production of *Maria Marten, or Murder in the Red Barn* and I can't seem to stop myself breaking out into my lines at every opportunity. Do come in and wait whilst I find a needle for you.'

'Thank you, kind sir,' I said and Nick ushered me inside and waved me to a chair as he opened a drawer in his writing desk and muttered: 'Now where did I put that blessed box?'

He rummaged around in his desk for a while and then, as he triumphantly brought out a small metal box, a girl's voice floated out from the inner room: 'Come on back to bed, Nick, it's getting very lonely in here.'

'Be with you in a minute,' he called out and as I rose to my feet he pressed the box into the pocket of my robe.

'Oh dear, I didn't realise you had company,' I said apologetically and he grinned: 'That's all right, Sophie. Do go through and let me introduce you to Karen, a very special friend of mine.'

'Don't be silly, Nick, she'll be embarrassed to meet someone she's never met before whilst lying in your bed,' I retorted but Nick grinned: 'I assure you that Karen Randall is totally uninhibited. She would love to meet you as she likes pretty girls almost as much as I do.'

'Well, if you're sure,' I said doubtfully as he took my hand and guided me into the bedroom where a pretty blonde girl was sitting up in bed without a stitch of clothing on her body. She made no attempt to cover herself when she saw me enter the room.

Karen Randall was a ravishingly attractive girl in her early twenties, a sprightly beauty with large blue eyes and sensual pouting lips. However, what made my pussey begin to tingle was the sight of her large bare breasts which jutted out so lasciviously towards us and were capped with nut-brown nipples set in circled pink areolae.

Nick smiled at her and said: 'My dearest, this is Sophie Starr, a new friend of Alan Greene's who I hope will soon be equally close to us. Sophie, meet Karen Randall who you never saw here this afternoon. Karen happens to be the daughter of the head gardener and if some toffee-nosed porter found out she had spent any time in my room, her father would be instantly dismissed.'

'I quite understand, and I would ask you to return the favour as far as my presence here is concerned,' I smiled. Nick quickly explained the purpose of my visit, after which Karen insisted that I sit down on the bed. She suggestively ran her hands over her superb bosoms as she said to Nick: 'Well, you're a fine host I must say, Mr Wright. Where's that bottle of chilled white wine that you said was in the icebox?'

'I'm well rebuked,' sighed Nick as he made his way to the door. 'My butler is still on his summer vacation, so will you ladies kindly excuse my absence whilst I prepare some refreshment for us?'

'Off you go, Nick, we can amuse ourselves well enough without you,' said Karen and she made my pussey tingle when she lifted her arms to sweep back the strands of her honey-blonde hair from her face. This action lifted her superb breasts even higher and I recalled Nick's comment that, like myself, this delicious girl enjoyed an occasional tribadic encounter.

Karen must have read my mind for she said: 'A big stiff cock takes some beating, but I sense that you also enjoy serving yourself a light *hors d'oeuvre* before the main course.'

And without further ado she threw off the bedclothes and began to play with herself, spreading her legs wide to allow the fingers of her right hand to slip in and out of her pretty flaxen-haired pussey whilst her left hand busied itself rubbing her hardening tawney titties.

'M'mm, that's better,' she sighed. Then she left off her frigging and, looking straight into my eyes, she said: 'Sophie, please feel free to join me, many hands make light work!'

What happened next was like a dream – I shucked off Alan's dressing gown and slid naked into bed next to Karen whose soft lips rested upon my own as she cuddled up beside me. Then we kissed and as her tongue slithered between my teeth her hand slid in between my thighs.

'You naughty girl,' I murmured although I made no attempt to remove her hand when her fingertips began rubbing against my puffy love lips. I heard myself sighing with pleasure as she continued to play with my pussey. After a while, instead of lying there passively, I put my arms around Karen, holding her soft body to mine. I let out a happy little squeal as her forefinger dipped into my fast-moistening cunney, making me shiver all over with excitement.

Our breasts crushed together as we held each other close. It was now time to decide who should be brought off first. As she had taken the initiative, I thought it only fair to let Karen choose which role she preferred and she elected to take the 'masculine' role. So I lay back and she clambered on top of me and gazed lovingly at my titties before pressing her face between my breasts and sinking her finger inside my wet cunt. Her thumb prodded my aroused clitty and I squirmed with delight at the thrill of it all as her lips closed around my raised nipple and her finger slid deeper into my slit.

Karen was blessed with a most sensitive touch and she added to my pleasure when she moved her face downwards, stopping first to lick out the whorl of my navel before sliding her mouth into the bushy mound between my thighs.

'Ooooh!' I gasped as she slid out her tongue and immediately found my clitty. Licking and sucking at it in an exquisitely delicate way, she swiftly brought me to the very edge of a spend. Then the frisky vixen pulled her mouth away and giggled as she ran one finger down the length of my cunney lips.

'See, the parting of the ways,' she said wickedly.

However, she did not leave me in limbo for very long and soon pressed her lips back against my sopping cunney as she slid her hands under my legs and grasped hold of my taut bum cheeks.

Dear Lord, how well could Karen Randall suck pussey! I almost screamed with pleasure when her clever tongue found the mark. I pushed my curly bush up against the wanton girl's face whilst her clever tongue probed my utmost parameters of sensual desire. Lovingly she began to devour my cunney, lapping harder and harder on my clitty as her fingers prised open my love channel and eased one and then two fingers slowly into my sopping slit.

Then she twisted the digits round as she thrust them inside me. I tried to keep still so that Karen could suck my clitty but I was writhing so furiously that it was impossible for her to stay with me although I managed to rub myself off to a glorious spend against her mouth.

I was so aroused that I would have been more than willing to repay the compliment but, out of the corner of my eye, I saw that Nick had returned whilst Karen was bringing me off. He was now standing naked at the foot of the bed holding his throbbing todger in his hand.

'Nick has come back and I'm going to retire from the field to let him join in the game,' I whispered. Karen gave my pussey a final farewell kiss and said gratefully: 'What a kind girl you are, Sophie. I must say that I'm in the mood to have my cunney filled with his thick love truncheon.'

'Stay where you are, Sophie,' Nick growled as he climbed

onto the bed. 'I'm sure we can think up some wonderful games for three players.'

'I'll say,' agreed Karen, wriggling her head into the centre of the pillow, her fair tresses of hair falling suggestively over her shoulders and onto her heaving breasts. She stretched herself and arched her back as she sensuously caressed her erect tawney titties. She trapped Nick's hand between her thighs as he moved his fingers through the silky blonde bush. He moved himself over her and kissed her creamy thighs and Karen opened her legs for Nick to bend his head and tease his tongue around her damp hairy thatch whilst running one of his long fingers down the length of her crack.

This drove Karen absolutely wild with unslaked desire and she grabbed his head, pulling it down into the folds of her pussey as she panted: 'Oh Nick! Lick out my cunney, you devil!'

'Your wish is my command,' murmured her solicitous lover as he licked his lips and kissed Karen's flat white belly before running his tongue into the tickly cunney hair. His hands slid under her trembling body to encircle her rounded bum cheeks.

'Oooh! Oooh! More, Nick, more!' she cried out as the tip of his tongue forced itself into the red chink between her pussey lips and he began to lick and lap inside her juicy cunt.

If his academic studies were on a par with his skill at sucking pussey, there can be no doubt that Nick Wright would obtain a first-class honours degree. Through his skilful tonguing, Karen soon achieved her spend and lay back with a beatific smile on her face whilst the astute American sucked and swallowed her pungent cuntal juice which was pouring out of her pussey.

Then he lifted his head up and scrambled to his knees as he said to me: 'Sophie, feel my balls. Aren't they heavy? They're overflowing with all the spunk I'm going to shoot inside Karen's sweet love sheath.'

He purred with pleasure as I weighed his hairy scrotum in my hands. Then he swung himself over on his back to lie between us with his thick stiff cock waving high in the air.

'May I give him a nice little gobble before he fucks you?' I asked Karen politely, and when she nodded her assent I hauled myself up and knelt between Nick's muscular legs to take his finely formed helmet between my lips. I clamped my mouth firmly around the mushroom knob and my glossy dark tresses spread out over his thighs. He jerked his hips upwards to stuff as much of his sizeable chopper as possible down my throat. I opened my mouth wider and engulfed his entire prick. He moaned in delight as I bobbed my head up and down, sliding my lips over his hot throbbing tool whilst my fingers toyed with his balls.

I thoroughly enjoyed sucking Nick's delectable boner but when I sensed he was close to a come, I reluctantly pulled my head away from his glistening cock and said to Karen: 'There, he's good and ready to spunk off inside your quim whenever you want.'

'Thank you, Sophie,' she smiled as she straddled his brawny frame. As the nubile minx slowly lowered her puffy cunney lips against the tip of Nick's knob, she added: 'Now brace yourself, Yankee Doodle, I'm going to ride your cock like a cowboy on his mount at one of your rodeo shows.'

Karen pushed herself down upon his sturdy shaft, squeezing her knees against his thighs. Inch by inch, Nick Wright's cock disappeared into her juicy snatch. She settled herself down and then sitting bolt upright, she tossed back her mane of flaxen hair before bending down and kissing him on the mouth with her cunney lips sliding up against the very tip of his straining shaft.

Then she lowered herself down again, enveloping the full length of his prick inside her luscious love funnel. Nick shunted his shaft up and down in time with every bounce of Karen's body upon the tops of his thighs.

My hand had wandered into my pussey whilst I watched this torrid fuck. I had just started to slide my fingertip into my moist notch when there was a sharp knock on the door and Alan Greene limped into the room. His presence did not appear to upset Karen and Nick who merely gasped out a greeting whilst they carried on with their prurient coupling.

Nevertheless, I felt extremely embarrassed at being found naked on his chum's bed and gulped: 'Oh Alan, what must you think of me? I'm afraid I was carried away by Nick and his pretty girlfriend.'

To my great relief, Alan was anything but annoyed and said cheerfully: 'That's quite okay, Sophie, I knew that Karen might be spending the afternoon with Nick when I suggested that you stay up here and chat to him whilst I had a snooze. Nick and I have found that most of our girlfriends take up the offer when we ask them if they would like to share their favours.'

'Is that so?' I smiled and he replied: 'Oh yes, I really cannot remember the last time a girl refused to take part in our rude romps. I must ask you to forgive the impertinence, but it was my guess that you would not be offended by any such proposition.'

'Well, you were absolutely right because I'm not offended at all,' I answered gaily and, looking across at Karen's gleaming body bouncing happily away on Nick's twitching todger, I added: 'At least, so long as you aren't planning simply to stand there like a spare prick at a wedding!'

Alan threw back his head and laughed whilst he slipped off the athletics vest and shorts he had pulled on to come up to Nick's rooms. He clambered up beside me and after we exchanged a wet open-mouthed kiss, he flipped me over onto my front and I turned my head to see him pick up a tube of pomade [*perfumed hair ointment – Editor*] from the bedside table.

'Do you want to go up my bum?' I asked and he blushed slightly at my directness as he answered: 'Yes please, Sophie. I was about to ask if I could fuck your lovely bottom.'

Now I am not over-keen on this particular mode of poking, as I hold the view that it is better to go in through the front door rather than the tradesmen's entrance. However, variety is the spice of life and I am not totally averse to the occasional bottom fuck.

So I nodded my agreement to Alan's lascivious request and I watched him anoint his pulsating prick with the oily liquid. Then he moistened my bum hole and angled my legs a little further apart to afford a better view of the puckered little orifice. He grasped hold of his greasy prick and slid his knob between my bum cheeks, pressing it firmly against the tiny starfish-shaped hole of my rear dimple.

I turned my head round and urged him to slide it gently into my bum-hole. 'You have such a big cock, Mr Greene, that I don't know whether you'll be able to get it all in.'

Fortunately the pomade eased Alan's bulbous knob into the wrinkled little orifice without too much difficulty. My sphincter muscle gradually relaxed and he managed to embed two or three inches of his chunky cock whilst one of his hands came snaking round my side to tweak my titties and the other moved down into my bush to massage my clitty. I reached back and spread my cheeks as the excited young rascal worked his sturdy shaft into my backside until I was plugged to the limit.

The groans of passion from our bed-mates were now reaching a crescendo. Alan stayed still with his cock sheathed in my bum as we watched Karen flinging herself up and down on Nick's twitching tool. With one enormous upwards thrust of his hips, Nick rammed his todger one final time and Karen shrieked with delight as he pumped out his sticky jism into her honeypot. This rousing finale to their fuck aroused Alan even more and he began to plunge his prick backwards and forwards, screaming out: 'Oh, Sophie, that feels so good! I can feel your bum sucking in my cock and choking out all the come from my balls!'

'Yes! Yes! Yes! Spunk into my arse, big boy!' I panted and with a hoarse cry Alan immediately obliged by shooting warm jets of creamy jism which further lubricated the tight sheath. As he spurted into me, he continued to work his shaft back and forth until, with an audible 'pop', he uncorked it from between my wiggling bum cheeks.

Now, as I have mentioned before, Alan Greene's love truncheon has afforded me many hours of great pleasure over the years, but even in his prime his prick has invariably needed as long as half an hour to thicken up again after a good poke. But on this occasion his cock remained as stiff as a board. With a twinkle in his eyes, he gasped: 'Don't let's waste this hard-on, Sophie. But it's your turn now to do the work. Will you go on top and ride me like Karen rode Nick?'

'By all means,' I answered and I climbed over him, holding open my cunney lips as I slid slowly down over his quivering cock.

'Woooh!' he cried out happily as I slithered eagerly up and down his shaft. Alan matched my thrusts with his own, jamming his chopper upwards into my clinging cunney.

This was a short but sweet fuck and I soon felt Alan's cock throbbing wildly as I ground down upon him one last time with the muscles of my love channel gripping his tool in a tender vice. He shuddered all over and squirted a torrent of hot jism into my cunt. I bucked and twisted around with uninhibited abandon until I climaxed just before his shaft began to shrink down after its Herculean labours.

Karen raised herself up on her elbow and sighed: 'Look at these two limp cocks, Sophie! And yet these strapping young fellows have the effrontery to call themselves the stronger sex!'

'True enough, but what can we do to stiffen their shafts?' I asked and she answered with a coy smile: 'Well, we could give them a little exhibition which would show them that we girls can enjoy ourselves even when there are no thick pricks for us to play with.'

I sensed what Karen had in mind and said severely: 'You naughty girl, fancy making such a shameless suggestion. I've a good mind to punish you for being so rude.'

'Yes, Sophie,' she meekly agreed, rolling her beautiful naked body over towards me and exposing her delicious backside to us all. 'I suppose I really deserve a smack bottom, don't I?'

'Indeed you do,' I replied as I scrambled up on my knees beside her and placed my left hand on the small of her back. Then I raised my right hand and with light, quick slaps I playfully paddled Karen's quivering bum cheeks which wiggled so seductively as I spanked them. I watched the colour of her skin change from milky white to a rosy pink. She cried out: 'Oooh! Oooh! Mercy, Sophie, mercy! No more, I beg you, enough now!'

'All in good time,' I said whilst I continued my chastisement of her delectable bottom. 'You richly deserve this for being so saucy. Besides, I just adore the way your bum cheeks jiggle when I smack them and the boys and I enjoy seeing your lovely botty change colour.'

'Quite right,' said Nick hoarsely as he squeezed one soft fleshy sphere. 'Karen, your luscious arse should always be this fine shade of pink.'

However, this comment did not mollify her and she yelped: 'Ow! Ow! Ow! Why should I be the only one to be whopped? If I've been a bad girl, Nick Wright is just as much to blame for making me suck his cock. You should tan his hide too.'

'M'mm, there's something in what you say,' I said and gave her bum one final slap before passing her a pillow on which she could rest her tingling bottom. Then I turned to Nick and sternly commanded him to assume the position for punishment. He did not protest but struggled to sit on his haunches and then bent himself forward so that his tight dimpled bum cheeks were raised high in the air. Karen reached out and passed her hand lightly across his bare bottom and the pair of us began to spank him in rhythm. Karen smacked his right cheek and I smacked the left one as I exclaimed: 'Take that, that and that, you impudent boy! How dare you present yourself to us with such a limp prick!'

'Ouch! Go easy, you two!' he gasped and then, to the accompaniment of the crack of our hands against the rosy cheeks of his arse, Nick took a deep breath. Slowly expelling the air from his lungs, he slicked his hand up and down his thickening tool, drawing back the foreskin to make his wide purple knob bound and swell in his hand. Once his shaft had swelled up to its former majestic height and girth, Karen left me to continue spanking Nick's bottom and hauled herself on her hands and knees in front of him.

The adorable blonde beauty grabbed hold of his stiff todger in her hands and began to rub his pulsing prick whilst she swirled her wet tongue all around the ridge of his uncapped knob. Then she flicked her tongue under the mushroom helmet. Her head bobbed to and fro in a sensuous tempo as she fucked Nick's cock with her sweet suctioning lips.

How she revelled in sucking his trembling love truncheon! I stopped smacking Nick's bum so that he could concentrate solely on this delectable sucking-off. Karen had gobbled the full length of his nine-inch chopper into her mouth and she grasped the chubby cheeks of his backside to move him backwards and forwards whilst he held her head firmly in his hands. She was clearly enjoying herself as she sucked away lustily, now teasing his tightening ballsack with her fingernails whilst she moved her tongue around his fleshy column, licking and lapping around his quivering cock.

Nick let out an ecstatic sigh and then he called out more urgently: 'I'm coming, Karen, I can't stop it! Suck me! Fuck me! Suck! Fuck! Ohhhh . . .'

His hips jerked faster and faster as he pistoned his prick in and out of her mouth until he could contain himself no longer. With one final forward thrust he spurted a stream of frothy hot jism into Karen's throat.

To my delight I looked across at Alan and saw that this erotic exhibition had aroused him so much that his colossal cock was standing up as hard as an iron bar against his tummy. He moved up to face me and ran his hands gently over my heaving bosoms, tracing circles with his fingertips around my stiffening nipples. I ran my fingers through his hair and then pulled his head down to my breasts. He pressed them together and moved his face from side to side to lick each tawney stalk in turn as he murmured softly: 'Sophie, you have the most delicious titties in the world.'

'M'mm, thank you for the compliment,' I breathed as I drew his hand down to my moist muff where my pussey was already tingling with anticipation. 'But how about my pussey, Alan? Doesn't that also deserve your attention?'

'Of course it does,' he mumbled thickly. His hand moved around my damp curly bush until his long fingers slithered into my dripping snatch, skilfully finger-fucking me by pressing and releasing the pulsating clitty. This caused blissful waves of sheer delight to spread out from between my legs through my entire body.

I slid my own hand down to seize hold of his throbbing todger. Alan quickly twisted his muscular body round so that his face was buried between my legs and the tip of his boner was level with my mouth. Well, as my intimate acquaintances are aware, I rarely say no to a *soixante neuf*

and without hesitation I swirled my tongue over the gleaming ruby knob before closing my wet lips around this
succulent cock and moved my mouth up and down his hot,
satin-smooth shaft.

Meanwhile, Alan's mouth had already clamped down on
my cunt. I purred with pleasure as his soft tongue ran along
my crack and impudently flicked my clitty. I squirmed with
delight for, although his tongue could not probe my love
channel as deeply as his fingers, having his cock in my
mouth at the same time made it all more exciting. I knew I
just had to have his thick shaft inside my pulsing cunney.

So I wrenched my lips away from his smooth helmet and
pushed him across my body until he was on top of me and
his cock was safely ensconced inside my sopping slit. Our
glistening nude bodies thrashed around in sheer ecstasy
when Alan started to pump into me with great swinging
plunges. I squealed with delight as he clutched my soft
bottom cheeks and we enjoyed a savagely passionate fuck.

'Keep going, you rascal, keep going!' I panted when Alan
showed signs of flagging. Beads of perspiration appeared on
his forehead as he gritted his teeth and thrust his rampant
rod into the deepest recesses of my love funnel. If anything,
his cock seemed to grow even larger inside me. He sighed
blissfully as he felt the walls of my clinging cunney open and
close around his twitching tool as it slewed in and out of my
juicy quim.

I gently squeezed Alan's hairy balls as they slapped
against my thighs. From his sharp intake of breath, I knew
that he was near his climax. His body stiffened and his shaft
began to tremble as I felt the first tiny drips of pre-come
leaking from his knob. Then, seconds later, Alan drenched
my cunt with a fountain of sticky spunk. I let out a joyous
yelp as I shook like a leaf as the force of my own shuddering
orgasm swept me up to the highest peaks of excitement.

I must record that it was whilst Alan and I were lying in

each other's arms, gasping for breath after this thrilling joust, that the idea of writing an intimate diary was conceived. As we recovered our composure, we browsed through Nick's copy of the Canadian author Mr Horace Bent's new book, *An Advanced Course in Fucking*, in which I noticed a paragraph decrying the ever popular 'missionary' position. I decided that this view demanded a riposte – for, in my opinion, it is no mere accident that most couples prefer to poke in this manner. Therefore I decided to contact the editor of *The Cremorne* and ask if he thought his readers would be interested in an unexpurgated account of my somewhat hectic love life and the rest, as they say, is history.

Be that as it may, the four of us were now quite exhausted. After we dressed ourselves, Nick made us tea and, despite having earlier enjoyed Mrs Moser's superb picnic luncheon, I helped the others wolf down the plates of sandwiches which he produced from his larder. I have always held that fucking is the most natural stimulant for the most sluggish appetite. These carnal exercises also seemed to have done little harm to my partner's pulled thigh muscle for he managed to walk unaided down the stairs after we took our leave of Karen and Nick and returned to Alan's rooms.

However, my blood was still up and thankfully there was still the time and opportunity for one further bout of fucking before Alex and Charles came round as arranged promptly at six o'clock. They were extremely aroused by my account of what had happened with our new friends upstairs and in no time at all the four of us were squashed up on Alan's bed, caressing each other's naked bodies. Although Charles's thick love truncheon was more than ready to fuck either of us immediately, Alan's cock naturally needed more time to recover, so Alex opened the proceedings by asking me if I would be kind enough to kiss her pussey.

'What a silly question,' I smiled as, without further ado, Alex lay back and spread her legs while I caressed her smooth thighs. She trembled all over when I knelt down in front of her and ducked my head into her sweet-smelling cunt. I parted the silky strands of her fluffy blonde pussey hair with my fingertips to reveal her swollen clitty. As I worked my face into the enchanting cleft, I inhaled the appealing pungent aroma of her arousal whilst I spread her cunney lips with my thumb and middle finger. I placed my lips over her clitty and sucked it into my mouth where the tip of my tongue began to explore it. As I lapped away, I could feel her clitty expanding as her legs drummed up and down on the mattress.

The more I vibrated my tongue, the more reaction I achieved from dearest Alex who was now moaning loudly. I savoured the cuntal juices which were flowing freely out of her pussey. I sucked even harder, moving my tongue quickly along the grooves of her cunt. With each stroke she arched her beautiful body upwards, pressing her clitty even harder against my fluttering tongue.

'Yesssss!' she yelled out and I felt her explode into a delicious spend as her clitty moved violently up and down inside my mouth.

Alan was so excited at the way I brought off Alex that he managed to rub his shaft up to a stand. This was just as well for I do not think that Charles could have waited any longer to join in the fun and games. We immediately formed a superb shagging chain with Alan positioning himself to have his cock sucked by Alex whilst Charles fucked me from behind doggie-style whilst I continued to lick and lap on Alex's delicious pussey.

Unfortunately, poor Alan could not continue after he spent. We could see that he was a mite annoyed when Nick came in to borrow a book and stayed for some while. I gobbled Charles whilst Nick smeared some butter on his cock and fucked my bottom. However, Alan nodded his head and gave a wry smile when Alex chided him: 'Never stand on your dignity, Mr Greene, there is nothing in the world so slippery.'

Envoi

There may be some people who have been shocked by my explicit memoirs although if they have reached this concluding page, they must have *sub rosa* enjoyed reading the book!

To them, I say that all animals copulate and we would be foolish to listen to those killjoys who wish to deprive us of the delights of this natural physical need and thus defy nature.

And to those foolish folk (and alas there are members of my own sex amongst them) who believe that ladies should think of intimacy as a duty rather than a pleasure, I can do no better than to refer them to the little verses supposedly composed by the famous Lillie Langtry:

> *Let those who never tried believe*
> *   In women's chastity!*
> *Let Her who ne'er was asked receive*
> *   The praise of modesty.*
>
> *Though woman's virtue's true as steel*
> *   Before you touch her soul;*
> *Still let it once the magnet feel*
> *   'Twill flutter to the Pole!*

A Message from the Publisher

Headline Delta is a unique list of erotic fiction, covering many different styles and periods and appealing to a broad readership. As such, we would be most interested to hear from you.

Did you enjoy this book? Did it turn you on – or off? Did you like the story, the characters, the setting? What did you think of the cover presentation? How did this novel compare with others you have read? In short, what's your opinion? If you care to offer it, please write to:

The Editor
Headline Delta
338 Euston Road
London NW1 3BH

Or maybe you think you could write a better erotic novel yourself. We are always looking for new authors. If you'd like to try your hand at writing a book for possible inclusion in the Delta list, here are our basic guidelines: we are looking for novels of approximately 75,000 words whose purpose is to inspire the sexual imagination of the reader. The erotic content should not describe illegal sexual activity (pedophilia, for example). The novel should contain sympathetic and interesting characters, pace, atmosphere and an intriguing storyline.

If you would like to have a go, please submit to the Editor a sample of at least 10,000 words, clearly typed in double-lined spacing on one side of the paper only, together with a short outline of the plot. Should you wish your material returned to you, please include a stamped addressed envelope. If we like it sufficiently, we will offer you a contract for publication.

EMPIRE OF LUST

VAMPIRE LUST IN THE CORRIDORS OF POWER!

Valentina Cilescu

Elected to lust!

The malevolent sex vampire, the Master, and his insatiable entourage are extending the boundaries of his hideous but seductive power. While the spirit of journalist Andreas Hunt lies imprisoned in a crystal tomb, his body is inhabited by the Master and used as a tool to forge a seemingly respectable career as a Member of Parliament.

White witch Mara Fleming must also bend to the Master's evil plan. Trapped in the curvaceous frame of flame-haired acolyte Anastasia Dubois, Mara is forced to play the part of a vampire sex-slut. Meanwhile the Master's Queen, the evil dominatrix Sedet, inhabits Mara's luscious body, subjecting it to a series of intoxicating depravities.

As his creatures subvert politicians and media moguls, the Master plans his final assault on government. Is there no power on earth that can prevent him bringing the British Establishment crashing to the ground like a house of cards?

FICTION / EROTICA 0 7472 4191 0

More Erotic Fiction from Headline Delta

EROS IN SUMMER

Anonymous

In summer, so they say, as the temperature rises so does one's ardour. This couldn't be more true of the virile Sir Andrew Nelham and his nubile cousin Sophia. Andy tastes the pleasures of the Sussex seaside towns while on business – and pleasure *is* his business – as Sophia relaxes in Brighton after an arduous winter.

Sophia, open and amorous as ever, finds no shortage of holiday companions to play with, while Andy discovers that the tourist attractions are by no means limited to the sights. From the intriguing and tantalising temptations of Parson Darby's Cave to the sumptuous titbits offered at Arundel Castle by a delectable proprietress – served under rather than over the table – Andy's experiences satisfy all appetites. Their seaside jaunt climaxes in a party at the select and somewhat outré Fitz Club, where they celebrate their new summer friendships in the most delightful way.

FICTION / EROTICA 0 7472 4463 4

A selection of Erotica from Headline

BLUE HEAVENS	Nick Bancroft	£4.99 ☐
MAID	Dagmar Brand	£4.99 ☐
EROS IN AUTUMN	Anonymous	£4.99 ☐
EROTICON THRILLS	Anonymous	£4.99 ☐
IN THE GROOVE	Lesley Asquith	£4.99 ☐
THE CALL OF THE FLESH	Faye Rossignol	£4.99 ☐
SWEET VIBRATIONS	Jeff Charles	£4.99 ☐
UNDER THE WHIP	Nick Aymes	£4.99 ☐
RETURN TO THE CASTING COUCH	Becky Bell	£4.99 ☐
MAIDS IN HEAVEN	Samantha Austen	£4.99 ☐
CLOSE UP	Felice Ash	£4.99 ☐
TOUCH ME, FEEL ME	Rosanna Challis	£4.99 ☐

All Headline books are available at your local bookshop or newsagent, or can be ordered direct from the publisher. Just tick the titles you want and fill in the form below. Prices and availability subject to change without notice.

Headline Book Publishing, Cash Sales Department, Bookpoint, 39 Milton Park, Abingdon, OXON, OX14 4TD, UK. If you have a credit card you may order by telephone – 01235 400400.

Please enclose a cheque or postal order made payable to Bookpoint Ltd to the value of the cover price and allow the following for postage and packing:

UK & BFPO: £1.00 for the first book, 50p for the second book and 30p for each additional book ordered up to a maximum charge of £3.00.

OVERSEAS & EIRE: £2.00 for the first book, £1.00 for the second book and 50p for each additional book.

Name ....

Address ....

....

....

If you would prefer to pay by credit card, please complete:
Please debit my Visa/Access/Diner's Card/American Express (delete as applicable) card no:

Signature .... Expiry Date ....